WAGES OF SIN

ALSO BY MARK WHEATON

Luis Chavez Mysteries

Fields of Wrath

City of Strangers

WAGES OF SIN

A Luis Chavez Mystery

MARK WHEATON

THOMAS & MERCER

Text copyright © 2017 by Mark Wheaton
All rights reserved.

Published by Thomas & Mercer, Seattle

www.apub.com

Amazon, the Amazon logo, and Thomas & Mercer are trademarks of Amazon.com, Inc., or its affiliates.

ISBN-13: 9781477819449
ISBN-10: 1477819444

Cover design by Damonza

Printed in the United States of America

To Hershy

PART I

PART I

I

Had it already been a year?

Mrs. Contreras looked out her front window, careful not to trouble the blinds. The man in black was there, just on the other side of her gate, as if deciding whether to enter. He never did and she imagined he never would.

She'd first seen him on that night—that horrible night—fourteen years ago. It had been unseasonably hot all that week. The window unit in her bedroom barely worked, so she'd taken to sleeping in the living room under the ceiling fan. That was when it had happened, right out in front of her home.

The house at 6780 Diaz Boulevard was nothing special, built in the late fifties after the original, almost entirely Latino citizenry of Chavez Ravine had been relocated with false promises by the City of Los Angeles to make way for Dodger Stadium. To Mrs. Contreras, now pushing eighty, this wasn't ancient history. Whenever she saw young Latino men in their Dodger gear or heard sports broadcasters refer to the stadium as "Chavez Ravine," she wondered if they didn't know what had happened there.

Or maybe they knew full well and didn't care. It was the twenty-first century.

Why you got to live in the past, abuela?

Maybe that was why she'd come to sympathize with the man in black. He couldn't escape the past either.

She would never be able to accurately remember how many shots there had been. One day she'd remember seven, another eight, another four, another nine. She imagined that she'd been awoken by the first, but what if it had been the second or third?

Whatever the case, she'd thrown herself off the sofa and onto the floor. Only one bullet struck her house, entering the front window and embedding itself in the ceiling. As plaster drifted down into her hair, she'd realized that if her instinct had been to stand rather than fall, the bullet might've ended up in her head.

The shots ended and she waited for more. More never came. She waited for screams, for footsteps, for anything but heard only silence. After a few minutes distant sirens drew close, and she crawled to the window. There was a car parked in front of her house with two men slumped in the front seat. One was rotating his head, as if unable to control his neck. The other looked dead.

Then she saw the one on the sidewalk. He was a teenager but well dressed. She would later remember thinking he looked as if he'd returned from church. This turned out to be the case.

When the police arrived, they knocked on her door immediately, having seen the bullet hole. Once they'd confirmed she was uninjured, a barrage of questions ensued. For the next several hours she told everyone the same thing.

"No vi nada."

I saw nothing.

A crowd gathered soon thereafter, the usual gawkers and rubberneckers. But Mrs. Contreras wasn't interested. She wanted to close her front door, put something between herself and the *pinches estúpidos* gangbangers destroying her life, her street, her feelings of security, and now the life of some innocent teenager caught in a cross fire.

She'd seen the two men pulled from the car, clocked their tattoos, saw the weapons removed from their pockets and drugs taken from within the vehicle. The teenager had only a small catechism in his hand. His body remained on the sidewalk for some time before a hearse finally made its way up the street to claim it.

That was when she was introduced to the man in black.

"*¡Ya valió madre!*" a teenager clad in a white sleeveless shirt screamed at her from across the street. "You know you saw something! Bet all you do all day is sit at that window sticking your nose in your neighbor's business. So who pulled that trigger? What'd you see, *puta*?"

He was beaten and bruised, as if he'd been in a fight. His eyes were filled with tears, and two of his friends held him back from the police line. Otherwise, she knew he would have been over her fence in a flash, his hands at her neck as he asked the same questions. She'd never seen anyone filled with such fury.

He'd left when the hearse left but came back the next day and the day after that. He'd come back for several weeks thereafter. At first, she'd thought he was affiliated with the gang members who had been shot. She soon learned, however, that the teenager caught in the cross fire was his older brother. The dead boy's name was Nicolas Chavez. His brother was Luis.

She didn't see him for a while after that, but on the one-year anniversary he was back, this time wearing clothes similar to that of his brother. His hair was cut short and he didn't look like a criminal anymore. He came back for the next three years but then vanished. Until last year.

When he showed up one year earlier, he wore the vestments of a priest. Mrs. Contreras almost went outside to greet him but decided against it. Tonight she considered it again. His face was filled with such sorrow. As he gazed down at the spot where his brother had left this world, he looked lost. At one point he knelt in prayer, and Mrs. Contreras looked away, feeling as though she was invading his privacy.

She went to the kitchen to make herself a cup of tea but ended up saying her own prayer for the fallen young man and his troubled younger brother. She asked the Lord to grant her visitor the peace he sought and to bless all those who still felt the loss of the dead teenager.

When she came back to the window a few minutes later, the man in black, Luis Chavez, was gone.

Chief Deputy District Attorney Michael Story was running late. His girlfriend had selected a restaurant conveniently located five minutes from the courthouse, but somehow, being Michael, he'd turned that into twenty even with downtown practically empty on a Saturday night.

Thank God for valet parking.

"I'll keep it close for you, boss," said the valet outside the skyrise as he handed Michael his ticket.

"Thanks," Michael said, hurrying to the door of the building but seeing no restaurant in sight. "Where am I—?"

"Take the first elevator all the way to the top," the valet said, indicating the building's well-lit but otherwise nondescript lobby. "You'll get off and there'll be a second elevator bank, but the girl'll need the password."

Lord.

"Which is?" Michael asked, hoping he didn't sound annoyed.

"Um . . . *pescador.*"

"Thanks."

He hurried inside, mashed on the elevator button, and waited for an interminable amount of time for the car. When the brass deco-style doors slid open to reveal a rickety freight elevator prettied up with sheets of velvet attached to the walls, he sighed. This was exactly the kind of place Naomi went for and why he found himself yet again somewhere in his city he'd never have thought to go on his own.

Love'll do that, he thought.

Naomi Okpewho had started out as a temp sent up to help with the Marshak case when it was blowing up almost a year ago now. She'd worked out so well that she'd stayed on as his assistant through the Jiankang Pharmaceuticals case, during which the probe into the murder of a priest had led to the exposure of a triad-backed unlicensed drug manufacturing ring. The case had become global news. It took Michael and, well, his silent partner Father Luis Chavez to finally put a stop to it.

But things had settled down after that. The frenzied media had found another tragedy to feast on and the spotlight on Michael had gone dark. Michael and Naomi had been dating for three months now, even before his divorce from Helen was finalized. Their age difference— Naomi was a full ten years younger—hadn't been the stumbling block Michael had assumed it would be. A native of Abuja, Nigeria, Naomi hadn't dated much as an undergrad at Stanford or during her time studying law at Pepperdine. Though drop-dead gorgeous, with a beautiful smile and long braids that descended all the way to the small of her back, she had an intense focus and energy that most boys—always "boys," not "men" in her retelling—found off-putting.

They all wanted tall, blue-eyed blonds with honey-colored tans, she'd say, describing Michael's soon-to-be-ex-wife to a T. Future power wives. Or, well, first wives.

He was thankful for the callow nature of these *boys* for overlooking someone so wonderful as Naomi. Sure, she was a brilliant lawyer and a deep thinker, but she was also adventurous and fun. She'd authored Michael's move to Silver Lake—an area of the city he'd never considered before—emphasizing her hatred of suburbia ("White people in Priuses as far as the eye can see," she'd say caustically, a Prius driver herself). He'd taken the plunge and purchased a four-bedroom place on Ivanhoe two blocks from the Silver Lake Reservoir, where they'd often walk on weekends to discuss cases.

On top of that, his kids had been quick to love the carefree Naomi. When they visited, she always had some new adventure in store for them.

Though they hadn't officially-officially moved in together to the point they would need to alert human resources, she stayed over more nights and weekends than not. While his house wasn't the sprawling estate Helen's father had bought for his daughter and son-in-law in Bel Air, Michael and Naomi had made it a home. They cooked together in the kitchen, ate on their deck looking out over the tops of palm trees and the roofs of similarly ramshackle Silver Lake bungalows, and were friendly with their neighbors. But unlike those other couples, who might unwind in front of the television, they were more likely to be up reading in bed, surrounded by half-filled file boxes, legal pads, and laptops until they collapsed from exhaustion well past midnight.

Thinking about the life they'd cobbled together so quickly made Michael feel satisfied—perhaps for the first time. He was determined to enjoy it. He hoped it wouldn't be another late night for Naomi. It was Friday and they both could use a break. When dinner was over, all he wanted was for her to follow him home, off-load all her weekend work to the living room, then fall into bed and call it a night. They had no weekend plans—no charity functions, no parties, no dinners with friends—giving them two whole days to get work done.

The universe wouldn't blink out if they managed to get a full six hours of sleep for a change, would it?

When the elevator doors opened, Michael found himself in front of a young woman in sailor shorts and a vest that revealed sleeves of vibrantly colored tattoos. She was perched on a stool in front of a second elevator bank. She didn't so much as look at him.

"Hi, my party is already up there . . ." he began.

Still nothing. He sighed and leaned past her, touching the elevator's call button. The button lit up when he pressed it, only to dim when he removed his finger. He glanced down the hall to look for stairs but saw none.

Then he saw the large koi fish tattooed on her thigh.

"Sorry. *Pescador*," he said.

"Welcome," the woman said, the word animating her like a clay golem. She waved a key card in front of a nearby reader and the elevator opened right up.

"Thanks," Michael said.

Three more stories up and Michael stepped out into a fairly large restaurant perched on the side of the building. While there were a few tables inside, most were out on a deck that overlooked the city. A short flight of stairs led to a smaller rooftop bar above, the partial ceiling revealing a DJ up there as well. But Michael was escorted to a small corner table with no view whatsoever, where Naomi pored over an open file folder by candlelight. He knew there was no spot he'd rather be.

"Sorry I'm late," he said, kissing her cheek before he sat.

"I'd be alarmed if you weren't," she admitted. "How was the call with the US attorney? Can they help any more with the Chinese?"

"Not really, though I can't tell if it's because they don't want to or because they can't," Michael replied. "It's a customs case with immigration issues, so they keep looking for ways to make the whole thing federal with national security overtones to freeze me out. How's Sittenfeld?"

Naomi darkened. "Getting worse. This guy must know where some serious bodies are buried, given all the political weight being thrown around."

Michael saw Charles Sittenfeld as a typical entitled scumbag out of Beverly Hills. A banking executive, he'd become very wealthy over the past few years, less due to his own skills and more because of family connections, shrewd investment advice from some of his politically connected friends, and dumb luck due to the rising LA housing market. He'd taken this as proof that he'd been anointed by the universe in some way and responded by creating a constellation of mistresses, whom he'd put up in apartments selected for their geographical proximity to his office, gym, golf course, and elderly parents' Palisades estate. When he concluded his wife of twenty-five years had become a needless drain on his expenses, rather than go through a potentially costly divorce, he decided she needed to go.

Instead of doing the deed himself, however, he listened to his own most oft-repeated business maxim and sought out the right man for the job. Through a lawyer friend, he contacted a hired killer and negotiated a $100,000 fee. The lawyer friend, whom Michael strongly suspected was having an affair with Sittenfeld's wife, had put Sittenfeld in touch not with a hired killer but an LAPD reservist, who happened to look like the Mongols biker gang member he claimed to be. Everything was recorded, the paper trail was so clearly laid out a child could trace the steps taken, and the eyewitnesses were unimpeachable.

But somehow cases that looked like slam dunks from the outside always seemed to spell trouble for the LA district attorney's office.

"Part of why I wanted to talk to you about it outside the office is that I may have inadvertently found something that could lead to additional charges beyond the scope of this investigation during discovery," Naomi admitted. "Problem is the warrant—"

Michael interrupted, raising a hand. "Should I hear this? If this is you admitting to exceeding the bounds of a warrant, we may need to tread lightly."

"That's a good question," Naomi said. "I'm genuinely unsure. I thought about contacting my old constitutional law prof at Pepperdine about it. Even thought about hitting someone up anonymously at Michigan State Law or Texas."

"Do you have the warrant here?" Michael asked.

Naomi passed it over. Michael read it. It was a fairly standard property search warrant that included Sittenfeld's hard drives, online storage, and e-mail accounts. There were limitations, however, restricting it to only matters relating to the hired killer case.

"This is pretty explicit," Michael said. "You're saying there's evidence of another crime?"

Naomi hedged. "It's on the threshold."

"Capital crime? Federal crime?" Michael asked.

"It depends on how far down it goes. The indications—"

"I don't want to hear about indications," Michael said. "I'll need hard evidence in what you've already gotten access to."

"Can I plead the 'where there's smoke there's fire' defense?" Naomi asked.

Michael scoffed, then shook his head. "We couldn't prosecute, and it might even pollute a future investigation. It's fruit from a poisoned tree. Can't go there."

"What about an expanded warrant? One with fewer restrictions?"

"Any judge worth his salt would see that coming from a mile away," Michael said. "And he's all lawyered up now. It's asking for trouble."

Naomi frowned and took a sip from her cocktail. She turned her eyes back to Michael. In them he could read how troubling whatever she'd found had been. It wasn't good. He didn't think she'd do anything rash, but then again she was young.

"How about if I talk to Deb about it?" Michael asked. "Obliquely of course, but enough to see if she knows a judge who owes us a favor. If you believe there's something there that outstrips the original warrant, of course we can't let it slide."

Naomi's smile returned. The restaurant was so dark Michael hadn't been able to read the cocktail menu without the help of the table's candle, but her smile made it seem like high noon at midsummer.

"Thanks, Michael," she said.

They put the work talk aside and ordered dinner. At one point Michael had put his hand on the table and Naomi had put her hand on his. He hadn't moved it since. He resisted an urge to rise from his chair, cup her face in his hands, and kiss her right there in the restaurant. Then he did it anyway. Her smile got even broader. When dinner was over, they wandered upstairs to see the view. The cool of the evening and a misty breeze kept most patrons downstairs. They ordered drinks from the bar and listened to the DJ. Michael slipped his arm around Naomi's waist and they kissed, not caring who saw them.

As Naomi's arms pulled Michael into her, he felt his ambitions shrink. He'd so long dreamt of power, of the DA's office, of the governor's mansion, even the White House. But right now this was all he wanted in the world.

They kissed some more on the elevator ride down and finally broke apart at the valet station.

"Follow me home?" he whispered.

She slipped her ticket to the valet first and grinned at Michael. "Follow *me* home?"

"Ladies first . . ." he answered, making a sweeping gesture with his arm and giving her a low bow.

Her Prius arrived at the curb a moment later, and she placed the leather satchel containing her files—a gift from Michael—into the passenger seat. "See you in a minute," she said as she got behind the wheel, and then she drove off.

An eerie feeling gripped Michael. Naomi had once used a peculiar turn of phrase to describe sudden apprehension. *The mouth of my grave has opened.*

He looked up and down the block and found himself completely alone on a deserted downtown street. Was he just feeling Naomi's absence? Or was this fear justified? Conventional wisdom had it that Downtown Los Angeles cleared out at night, as if those who worked there in the daylight hours were unwelcome among the dark souls that populated the area after nightfall. Naomi had convinced him this was nonsense, but right now Michael couldn't hide his fear. There were no cops, only streetlights casting the first few floors of each neighboring skyscraper in shades of yellow and orange.

Then darkness all the way to the sky.

How many people could see him right now? How many people had been waiting for the right moment to catch him alone, a couple of drinks to the wind? The shadows across the street seemed to grow and move. A car screeched around a corner a couple of blocks away. He wished he had his gun, the one he'd bought when he moved to Silver Lake, being mindful of the high crime pockets along Sunset Boulevard.

And then he saw him. Halfway up the block came a hulking figure, his body half-obscured by either the blanket or sleeping bag he was wrapped in despite it being an unseasonably warm March evening. The man moved with purpose, taking long deliberate strides directly toward Michael. Michael could see the man's eyes as they locked in on him.

It's a homeless guy, Michael thought. *He'll ask for change. Give him the money you were going to give the valet so you don't have to show him your wallet.*

But the man showed no signs of slowing. It looked as if his plan was to bowl Michael over rather than hit him up for change. The guy had a full head of steam and was moving like a bulldozer. Michael took a few steps back to the building's doorway, but the sleeping bag–wearing man immediately altered his trajectory. He looked like some kind of mountain dweller clothed in piles of buffalo skins to ward off subzero temperatures.

Why couldn't he play it cool? They breathed the same air, trod the same streets. They were Los Angelenos, right? Michael fought for people like this.

He was about to nod in greeting when the headlights of his Range Rover swept across the sidewalk as it pulled up to the valet station. The valet hopped out, holding the driver's-side door open. Michael glanced to the homeless person one more time, dropped all pretense of greeting, and hurried to the other side of the car.

"Shelter's two blocks that way, friend," the valet said without malice, pointing down the side street. "You're almost there."

The man said nothing but turned quickly at the corner and stormed down the block in the direction the valet pointed. The valet turned to Michael and shrugged. "He gets lost."

"You know him?"

"Nah, but I see him. He's tried to stash his stuff behind the building here and there. Crazy as hell."

Michael nodded and handed over a five. The valet thanked him and closed the door.

Once he was underway, Michael saw that Naomi had called his phone. He hit her number to call her back, but it went to voice mail. He tried again and gave up. He knew she'd laugh at him for being frightened of a homeless guy. She'd list all the horrible things it said about him, and he'd know they were true.

He made his way up Grand Avenue to the 101 freeway. The highway was empty. As he neared the Silver Lake off-ramp, he saw the flashing lights of emergency vehicles on the street ahead.

The fear returned.

As traffic slowed, he tried to see what was happening. It wasn't on the street—that much he could tell. He thought it might be a struck pedestrian or bicyclist. Maybe a homeless person. How awful was it to feel oneself praying for that?

But as he neared, his face began to burn. He felt guilt like he hadn't his whole life. He knew what was up there, knew it as plainly as he knew his own name. And it was his fault. His fault for pulling her into his world and for daring the universe not to punish him for feeling a little happiness.

As his pulse quickened, he forced the thoughts away. He conjured the image of Naomi sitting on their couch, bundled up in her robe, shaking her head as she chastised him for being late, not just to dinner but coming home. He'd shrug and sigh, then wrap his arms around her and not let go. Not ever. He'd say they should throw everything in the car and go overnight to Lake Arrowhead or Montecito the next morning. Sure, they'd be working the whole time, but how nice would it be to have a change of scenery?

Of course, it wasn't to be. He didn't recognize Naomi's Prius at first, as he was looking at the undercarriage, which faced the street at an odd angle. The car had rolled. The front tires were bent inward, giving the whole car the look of a turtle trying to withdraw into its shell. As he was waved through the intersection, the wheels of the Range Rover crunched over broken plastic, safety glass, and other debris.

He looked at the wrecked Prius, its broken headlights casting light on the grassy curb where it had finally come to rest, and the dark realization that it could only be Naomi's came over him. The entire passenger compartment had been flattened, the roof had collapsed, shattering the windows, and it now rested flush with the doors. It was only then that Michael realized it hadn't been hit in the intersection but must have tumbled down from the overpass above. He glanced back and saw the highway guardrails torn away.

Michael marveled at the speed Naomi must have been going to impact the rails so violently.

Was she drunk? Michael thought. *Or . . . was she trying to get away from someone?*

Even as he fought to remain rational, to look for the solution to the situation no matter how elusive, he could hear himself screaming. Seeing nowhere to pull over, he slammed the SUV into park and left it in the street, engine running. His heart pounded as he turned toward the crash site. The smell of gasoline hung heavy in the air, and the sky was alive with blue and red flashing light.

He forced his body forward, but there was a telling lack of urgency to the paramedics already at the scene. His hope faded with every step.

The mouth of my grave has opened.

||

Like many recently arrived immigrants, St. Petersburg–born Gennady Archipenko worked more than one job to support his family. Unlike many of his contemporaries, however, this quickly resulted in his purchase of a multimillion-dollar custom-built modern steel-and-glass home along the Venice Canals, private preschool for his four-year-old daughter, Nina, and a nanny and night nurse for his three-month-old son, Aleksey, as well as a hefty investment in his young wife Yelena's budding catering enterprise. But those who only knew him through his day job likely assumed from his youth, his lack of ostentation, and the hard-charging way he worked that he still inhabited some squalid apartment in West Hollywood off Plummer Park.

Which was the way he wanted it.

Gennady had one driving force in life—to make people rich. This included himself, though not at the expense of others. He had a fervent belief that if his clients prospered he would, too.

By day he worked as a financial adviser at a local branch of one of the nation's largest banks. His branch offered all sorts of commission-based financial plans and investment portfolios that Gennady compared to the fully loaded SUVs and bloated laptop computers sold by big-box retailers. The impressive-sounding list of options inflated the sales price, even if the unknowing customer might never use them. These kinds of accounts preyed on those who didn't know better. Gennady thought this true of several of his bank's products.

So instead he made it his business to find out exactly what his customers wanted from their money and created portfolios based on that.

Looking to buy a house within the next five years? Go with CDs.

You're in your optimal earning years and hope to retire in twenty years? Try the bond market.

Looking for high-yield investments and can stomach big losses? Try mutual funds.

He believed if he did right by these customers, they'd recommend him to their friends. When he subsequently struck out on his own, which was always the hope, he'd only need 10 to 15 percent of these people to follow him in order to keep going. Not that he'd need them for anything but appearances. It was simply good practice for his night job, which required 100 percent customer loyalty and trust, as it wasn't strictly legal.

"Okay, so how much money do you have in Tallinn?" Gennady asked his latest client, a handsome and always impeccably dressed Ghanaian named Oris Namboh.

Based in Europe for the past ten years, Oris ran a successful commercial production company. He was now relocating to Los Angeles and was looking to bring his acquired wealth with him without having to lose a substantial portion to American taxes. Gennady had been recommended to him by a friend of Oris's wife, a Russian-born heiress who'd had several friends emigrate to Paris, London, New York, and LA in the great current now flowing out of the former Soviet Union.

"I've got about seven million euros in Tallinn, about twice that in Paris, twice that again in Russia—"

"Where in Russia? Moscow or Petersburg?" Gennady said, his finger rising from the tablet he was typing this all into. "Sorry to interrupt."

"Petersburg. Does it matter?"

"Depends on who you are. Proximity to the Kremlin can be impactful."

Oris laughed. Gennady ran the numbers on the tablet, getting more information as he did. "Is Los Angeles a permanent move? Or do you plan on leaving again within the next ten years?"

"It's our dream to move to the South of France at some point," Oris admitted. "Have you ever been? It's incredible."

Gennady had not but nodded anyway. "That's good," he said. "What I'd like to do is use that Paris account as your primary and build everything from that. On paper, your money will be consolidated there even as you do business in America. You will incorporate, probably an S corp, here in California that you'll use to pay employees and expenses. You will pay yourself through this. Your money from Estonia and St. Petersburg will come through there as investment, not income or bonds. You will diversify into international funds, and that will be reciprocal with your bank in Paris. Given regulation on both sides of the Atlantic, it will take some time, but it'll all come through eventually. You will pay taxes, but only on what you earn in America, and only after you've covered your operating expenses, which will be substantial."

"I'm not sure what they'll look like," Oris said. "It could vary."

"Good thing it won't be up to you," Gennady countered.

"What do you mean?"

"*I* decide the number, based on the information you give me," Gennady explained. "Every year we will zero out your profits based on operating expenses—social security, Medicare, overhead, and so on. But it will turn out that your corporation is *very* generous with its employees and will match your retirement contributions each year, which will be international, with a loose reporting structure. You will barely break even while providing jobs for California workers. Not only won't you be investigated, they might give you a prize. As long as your paperwork and fees are paid on time. Which they will be."

Oris eyed Gennady carefully for a moment, as if wondering whether he was being scammed. He leaned forward. "And your cut? For start-up and upkeep?"

"A hundred thousand dollars, but not payable till the end of your first corporate year," Gennady said. "If at any time during that year you wish to transfer your account to someone else, I am owed nothing. No prorated amount. No deposit. No money ever changed hands. Anything you did was on your own with advice from a friend."

"Really?" Oris asked. "That doesn't sound like good business."

"This is for my protection, not yours," Gennady replied. "If you get cold feet, if it turns out there are aspects of your business that you failed to clue me in on, I can walk away free and clear. If you do decide to go with me, on paper I'm little more than an accountant, albeit one who scurrilously overcharges you."

Oris laughed. Gennady let him.

"Does all that make sense?" Gennady asked.

"It does," Oris agreed, extending his hand. "You are straightforward. I am accustomed to people lying to get my business. You do not. In that respect you remind me of my wife, who is from Samara. Is being unimpressed a particularly Russian trait?"

Gennady laughed. "I would say so, yes. But as far as Russian women go, so is incredible beauty."

"Absolutely," Oris agreed. "Thank you."

"Any time."

The two had met at a small Brazilian restaurant Gennady favored in Santa Monica. It catered to locals and had twelve tables all told, with four more they placed out on the sidewalk on warm evenings. If two diners chose to carry on their conversation in Russian, as Gennady and Oris had, no one thought twice. The ocean was only seven blocks to the west, and a breeze carried in the sea air.

Gennady walked Oris to his car, a brand-new Lamborghini Aventador Superveloce, a bonus gifted him after a successful marketing launch by the manufacturer itself. He waved as Oris tore off into the night, then walked the three blocks to where his more discreet Mercedes GLS was parked at a meter. He climbed in and began the short drive down to Venice.

Though there would be more traffic, he took the ocean route down Ocean Avenue and rolled the windows down. He'd loved the sea since he was a child watching ships come in from the storm-riven Baltic. Having an ocean close centered him. As long as he had it in sight, he always knew where he was. It was also the reason he'd wanted to move to Venice, specifically to a house on the canals. The Venice canals were a squared-off grid of four interconnected waterways with large houses along each. Some of these homes had stayed in families for generations. Moving into the canals was near impossible, given the desirability of the location and the competition from the endlessly wealthy of Los Angeles.

But Gennady had lain in wait. He befriended canal homeowners and real estate agents that specialized in the area. When one tipped him off that that a looming divorce could mean a quick motivated sale of the large contemporary, he knocked on the front door and presented an all-cash offer that would've been impossible to refuse in any circumstance. Back home, Petersburgers marked their status by how many windows their home had facing the Neva River. His children would have their version of that facing the Venice canals.

As he wound through Santa Monica, Gennady texted his wife to tell her when he'd be home, then checked the voice mail on his night job phone. There were two dozen messages, most relating to stock trades that clients wanted handled when the Tokyo Stock Exchange opened.

He glanced at his watch. It had been open for half an hour already. It'd be a late night.

He switched to his day job cell, where he found the same number of voice mails, albeit with comically less at stake. A nighttime client might carefully lay out the instructions for a trade they needed perfectly timed in order to profit a couple million dollars off a currency exchange. A daytime client would ring in the same heady fever over something needing to happen at the opening bell in New York, but the result would be only three or four thousand dollars.

Of course, Gennady gave each request equal weight—retention over profits—and made mental notes as to which needed to be done tonight and which could wait until morning.

The last voice mail on the day job number took him by surprise. It was neither client nor colleague but a woman who identified herself as Naomi Okpewho from the LA district attorney's office. Adrenaline surged through his body as he listened.

"I'd like to find a time to sit down with you in person," Okpewho said, her voice coming in and out as if she was speaking while driving. "My office is looking into the financial dealings of Charles Sittenfeld. Your name has come up in our investigation."

Gennady was surprised. When Sittenfeld was arrested a few months back, he'd recognized the name and went through his inbox to see if he'd ever interacted with him. Though Sittenfeld was considerably higher on the bank's food chain than him, they had communicated about certain accounts from time to time. None of it was illegal or even quasi-legal to Gennady's mind. He wondered if the district attorney's office was fishing, or if there really was something in Sittenfeld's files with his name on it.

He pulled over and listened to the voice mail a second time, wrote down the phone number Okpewho had left, and made a mental note to see if there even was a Naomi Okpewho in the DA's office and whether she was on the Sittenfeld case. Even if there was nothing to it, returning the call and making a contact in the DA's office was worth doing, wasn't it?

Pulling back on the road, he tried to remember if he'd had any in-person dealings with Sittenfeld. There'd been a few unexpected phone calls that Gennady had written off as his managerial style—surprise those lowest on the totem pole to let them know the bosses kept an eye on them—but nothing else. He hadn't perceived the man as particularly intelligent or potentially useful, so he'd only answered what was asked and nothing more.

But now that the man had been accused of planning a murder, he wondered what other secrets he could've divined if he'd looked deeper.

He had to rise early—half past four—as Sunday sunrise Mass began at six. But even if he hadn't had to rise early, Luis wouldn't have slept. His visit the night before to 6780 Diaz Boulevard had been particularly difficult this year, given that it was only a couple of months from what would've been Nicolas's thirtieth birthday.

Nothing filled Luis with greater sorrow than how he had treated his brother in the months leading up to that night. Once Nicolas had gravitated toward the church and the priesthood beyond, Luis spent all their time together badgering and insulting him for his choices. He'd repeatedly called him out at school to make sure everyone knew Luis Chavez wasn't following in his brother's pious footsteps.

Yet here he was fourteen years later, the youngest parish pastor in the Los Angeles archdiocese, following the death of St. Augustine's Church pastor Father Gregory Whillans. His service there had started off well enough, the respect of parishioners bought by the whispered retellings of Luis's deeds fighting injustice in the city: first against the murderous abuse of field workers on factory farms, then in stopping a man-made plague involving purposely tainted pharmaceuticals that primarily affected poor immigrant communities.

But then—nothing.

One day the answers stopped coming. Whereas he'd felt such purpose before, now he was at a loss to tell people how to fix their lives, save their marriages, find new jobs, receive financial help, or most importantly, pick out God's from the many voices in their heads.

Worst of all, Luis had lost track of that voice in himself. In his first year as a priest, hearing God's voice was as easy as plucking fruit down from a tree. He'd kneel in prayer, open his mind, and God would walk in, as if picking up a conversation they'd dropped a few hours earlier. Now his mind would be clear, but only the world would walk in—the nonsense thoughts of the day, the pull of secular cares. Sometimes, he believed, he even heard the devil.

But no God. Not for weeks, maybe even months. All his questions, usually so numerous, had become one.

God, why hast thou forsaken me?

That morning, Luis had tried to pinpoint the last time he'd heard the voice of God. As with his previous attempts, he couldn't nail it down. All he knew was that it had now been months rather than weeks. In his private thoughts and prayers, this was an issue to grapple with to be sure. In front of the congregation, where he was meant to be nothing less than a vessel for God himself, however, it was enough to drive him to distraction.

At first, Luis had improvised. Everything that came from his mouth was imitation and approximation. He focused on scripture and saints, timely homilies and sincere prayers. But he knew the parishioners could see right through him. He was false, pure and simple. And as they lost faith in their pastor, they would lose faith in the Almighty by extension.

This was not a test his mentor, the late Father Whillans, had prepared him for. Not only that, he didn't understand its point. For God to try him in this way was understandable. Luis was on earth to be tested.

For God to extend that to the congregants was inexplicable. Why test their faith in this way?

"Are you all right, Father?" Father Serabia, a recent transfer who'd been at St. Augustine's for six months, asked Luis as they prepared breakfast in the rectory kitchen.

"I'm fine, thank you," Luis said, this lie his first sin of the day. "How's the team?"

Though he'd been there less than a season, Father Serabia had already turned around the boys' basketball squad at St. John's, the parochial school attached to St. Augustine's, where Luis taught as well. The team hadn't lost a game yet. Sports reporters had even begun writing about the surprise winning streak.

"Going well. They care about each other. It's not a victory unless everyone was allowed to contribute. Did have a request from one of the boys, though. Do you know Humberto de la Loza?"

Luis did. Humberto, fifteen, was in one of Luis's classes. Smart if not necessarily studious.

"What about him?"

"His brother, Ruben, is due to be sentenced next week. Their mother wanted to know if someone from the parish could attend."

Luis thought about this. "Does Ruben come to Mass?"

"No, he hasn't. But she assures us that he will."

"What are the charges?"

"Possession of narcotics. Intent to distribute."

Luis shook his head. "Let him take the first step to us. Otherwise, we're being used."

Father Serabia nodded and went back to his preparations.

Luis felt guilty over his response. His vanity made him worry that Father Serabia and, by extension, the de la Loza family would find him less than charitable. This hurt his pride, too. He second-guessed himself, wanting to reverse his decision and go to the sentencing himself, then changed his mind again. His head spun. He excused himself and returned to his room.

Once there he tried to imagine what Whillans's counsel would be. He formulated what he'd say to the older priest and waited to hear the old man's voice come back. When there was nothing, Luis sank onto his bed, feeling more and more like he'd been left with an unearned inheritance. Without God guiding his actions, he felt like someone who was all book learning and no real experience in the field. His approach could only be academic.

He was about to leave for the chapel but hesitated. He knelt and prayed, asking for guidance. Then he asked for nothing. Then he listened.

There was nothing.

He rejected the instinct to curse the darkness and recited lines from Saint John of the Cross's immortal *Dark Night of the Soul.*

> *For no one saw me,*
> *Nor did I look at anything,*
> *With no other light or guide*
> *Than the one that burned in my heart.*

Even Mother Teresa, it had been revealed in recent years, had endured long periods where she felt outside the light of God. She'd bemoaned her own personal abandonment by God to a German priest in several letters but continued her good works regardless.

Twenty minutes later, now outfitted in his alb and chasuble, Luis led the procession of St. Augustine's priests up the aisle as the small choir sang. After the opening prayers had been read from the sacramentary, Luis moved to stand in front of the early-morning congregation and raised his hands.

"Good morning," he said to the six hundred or so assembled before him. "Peace be with you."

"And also with you," they responded in an ocean of murmurs.

As per the norm he went on autopilot. The ritualized nature of Mass and the Eucharist made it easy to do so. Opening prayer, prayer over the sacraments, communion, prayer after communion, gospel reading, scripture reading, hymns. Maybe it was the visit to Diaz Avenue, maybe it was Nicolas's birthday approaching, or maybe he was beginning to lose hope that God's absence might be temporary the more days he lived outside of him, but performing the sacraments was particularly difficult today. Looking at the parishioners, he felt as if it were written on his face: *Fraud.*

I'm lying to you. And you know I'm lying to you.

He was lost.

When communion was finished, Luis felt like turning on his heel and walking back to the sacristy. If he locked himself in long enough, everyone in the building would eventually leave and he'd be able to excuse himself without further embarrassment. He could then return to his search for God in private.

As quickly as these thoughts formed, however, he banished them.

More pride, more selfishness, he chided, unable to hide his sins from himself.

He saw a familiar face in one of the front pews, a priest. For a moment he couldn't place the man, remembering only that Pastor Whillans hadn't liked him for whatever reason. Then the name came to him: Father Uli Belbenoit. Whether Whillans's disdain came from something Father Belbenoit had done or if it was because he was the assistant to Bishop Emeritus Eduardo Osorio, Luis didn't know.

Bishop Osorio, then only Father Osorio and still a few years from retirement, had overseen Luis's initial path to the priesthood, a thread Luis had taken up at his mother's insistence after the death of his brother. That Luis was immediately enraptured by it and found a new life there was as much a surprise to him as it was to Osorio.

Osorio couldn't be thinking of Nicolas, too, could he?

Now distracted, Luis sailed through the liturgy and communion feeling barely present. As he consecrated and administered the sacrament for each parishioner, he felt their eyes searching him, needing him to be more than he was, but to no avail.

At the end of Mass he stood by the chapel doors, bidding the congregants a good week, but found fewer returned his greeting. It wasn't only that. Fewer confided in him, fewer asked for blessings, fewer asked to be kept in his prayers. He was sending them away, their spirits still hungry.

"Father Chavez?"

The crowd thinned out. Father Belbenoit now approached, his hands wrapped around a small book. He smiled in greeting to Luis, who shook his hand.

"Thank you for coming, Father," Luis said. "How is the bishop?"

"He sends his regards," Belbenoit said placidly, his English faintly accented by the French inflections of his youth. "He has been ill or would've come himself."

"I'm sorry to hear that," Luis replied. "I'll say a prayer for him."

"No need, no need," Father Belbenoit said. "It's his arthritis. It makes it hard for him to walk. But there's nothing to do for it. His Excellency takes it as a reminder that his earthly form isn't long for this world and he will soon be with God. I haven't seen him this relaxed in some time. He's beginning to let go, and there's some relief in that."

"I'll pray that his pain is lessened," Luis replied, "and nothing more."

Father Belbenoit smiled, then seemed to remember why he was there. "The bishop wanted to reach out to you when Father Whillans passed but wanted to do so in person. He knew what this loss would mean to you. Only, the illness has prevented this from happening. He was hoping, thereby, you might come to him."

Luis studied the priest before him. He was probably ten years older than Luis but still seemed a pup. He was losing his hair. A preemptive comb-over matted what was left to his pate.

"Please thank His Excellency for his kind thoughts," Luis said. "I will make it a priority to see him in the next few weeks."

"You mistake me, Father Chavez," Father Belbenoit said. "He hoped you could see him today."

"On a Sunday?" Luis said, realizing too late how incredulous he sounded. "Please understand I mean no disrespect, but the parish is in a state of upheaval since I've been put in charge. I don't have time for social calls, unfortunately."

Luis hadn't meant for any animosity he felt toward Bishop Osorio to come across so nakedly. To his mind, Osorio had grown into a busybody who used his connections within the archdiocese to stick his nose in the business of others. But did that make him such a bad person, particularly given the debt Luis owed him? Or was this another game in which he wanted to see if Luis would come when called?

"Oh, it's not a social call," Father Belbenoit said. "He was recently reacquainted with someone and was looking to arrange a meeting between the two of you."

Judge not, that ye be not judged, Luis thought, chastising himself for allowing such uncharitable thoughts into his head.

"I'm sorry," Luis said. "It's not my parish. It's me. I haven't been myself lately."

"That's what we've heard," Father Belbenoit said lightly. "The bishop wanted you to know you're not alone. That this is something we all know. But that God always finds a way to let you know he is a constant. To that, the bishop asked that I give you this book. His wish is to see you put together with its owner. I have met him, and his desire to see you is genuine. It is his greatest wish in the world. The bishop feels as if he's been tasked with making it come true."

Luis took the proffered book. Father Belbenoit, his mission completed, put his hands together and bowed before stepping away. The book was an old nondescript Bible. If the bishop had meant it as a riddle, Luis would have to investigate it later. He had to prepare for the eight-o'clock Mass.

As he pocketed the book, however, he realized the texture of its soft, aged cover was familiar to his fingertips. He had held this book before.

He flipped it open to the title page. *The Holy Bible in King James Version, Translated out of the Original Tongues and with Previous Translations Diligently Compared and Revised. Gift and Award Bible. Self-pronouncing Words of Christ in Red.*

Below it all was a small book plate announcing that this Bible was presented on this date, in good faith, to Sebastian Chavez.

His father.

III

Standing behind her desk at the San Gabriel auto dealership that bore her name, Helen Story could barely contain her enthusiasm.

"It worked!" Helen said into the phone. "The paperwork's signed. The first auto hauler will arrive on Tuesday."

Though it was still early on a Sunday morning and he'd gone to bed only hours before, she appreciated that her boyfriend, Oscar de Icaza, tried to match her exhilaration.

"That's amazing," he replied groggily. "He's taking all the inventory?"

"Every last car."

"Wow. I'm proud of you, babe."

Helen beamed. When she'd opened the lot with backing from elements of the Los Angeles triad, an arrangement that had come out of Oscar and his gang's own involvement with the organization, she knew there'd be strings. When unwanted inventory appeared on her lot from triad-affiliated dealerships all over the Southland, she realized there was enough to hang her. The difference between a sale and a used car that never moved could be as little as a few hundred extra miles on the odometer or the wrong color interior. She'd inherited a stockpile of misfit cars. Rather than be cowed, however, she'd gone to work. It had taken months, but she'd finally made inroads with a dealer who had six lots around the Bakersfield–San Bernardino area. He needed inventory at fleet prices. She needed turnover. They'd agreed to terms over the phone, then signed a contract that morning. She could still feel the satisfying bite of the celebratory champagne she'd allowed herself on her tongue.

"Now I can reach out to the manufacturer, start bringing in the cars people actually want," Helen said. "Then we break ground on the next lot and begin scouting locations for a third."

Oscar chuckled. Helen waited for him to say something meant to subtly check her ambition. *Aren't you getting ahead of yourself? Putting the cart before the horse?*

"Do you have any idea how much it turns me on to hear you talk like that?" Oscar replied. "You're going to take over this town, Helen. Top to bottom."

Helen closed her eyes. When Oscar said he was proud of her, he was. This was in stark contrast to her ex, Michael, who regarded her successes as detracting from his own. She conditioned herself to play down her victories in order to keep things on an even keel. To be subservient and the sole provider of emotional support in the marriage no matter the personal cost. Realizing all this didn't make her hate Michael so much as herself for letting it come to that.

With Oscar, she was slowly returning to her true self. And with every step, he loved her, desired her, made her laugh, and even proved to be easy with her kids. While she wasn't so crazy as to believe a career criminal was a sure bet, she loved him and was in love with him.

Her thoughts were interrupted by the fast-walking approach of one of her sales associates, Miles, whom she'd only hired a month earlier. "There's some crazy homeless guy out there punching wind-shields," he said. "We tried to talk to him, but he's belligerent. He might've broken his hand."

"I'm going to have to call you back," Helen whispered into the phone.

"I heard," Oscar replied. "Want me to come over and take care of him?"

Helen laughed. "I'm on a roll this morning. Pretty sure I can handle it."

"Cool. Congratulations again on your deal. You earned it."

Helen hung up and turned to Miles. "Did you call the police?"

"Julie's calling now."

"Where is he?"

Miles pointed out the window. Helen took one look at the disheveled, clearly inebriated man crumpled between two Volkswagen Tiguans, cradling his bloody knuckles, and sobered.

"Hang up the phone," she called across the sales floor to Julie. When the young woman had, Helen sighed, unable to avoid an explanation. "It's my ex-husband."

She was barely out the door when she heard her employees tearing into this new piece of gossip like meat tossed to a pack of jackals. They knew their boss's ex was a chief deputy district attorney. How this would affect her authority was anyone's guess.

Why today, Michael? she wondered. *Couldn't you have waited for a Tuesday, when we're half-staffed?*

Maybe she should've taken Oscar up on his offer.

Helen stepped quickly across the lot, heels clicking imperiously on the asphalt as she walked. She wasn't going to put up with any of Michael's crap today. When she saw him up close, saw how bad off he was, she grew angrier. What if he'd turned up at the house looking like this? How could the kids, who were thankfully up the coast in Morro

Bay with their aunt and uncle for the weekend, have looked at their father the same way again?

"Michael? What are you doing here?" she demanded. "We've called the police. You can't be here. Please leave."

"Where's Oscar?" Michael bellowed, his words slurring. Helen had never seen him so drunk. "I need to see him."

"Are you *crazy?*" she asked. "You didn't drive here like this, did you? You can't go off the deep end whenever you want to, Michael. You have three children."

"They killed Naomi," Michael shot back. "I need to see Oscar."

Helen gasped. *Naomi, Michael's assistant turned girlfriend Naomi? The one who the kids muted their enthusiasm about to avoid hurting her feelings?*

"Oh, Michael, I'm so sorry," Helen said, kneeling beside him. "She was killed?"

"She was driven off the road late last night," Michael said, practically spitting mad. "Cops say it was a single-car accident. That there's nothing on the traffic cameras, no marks on the car from another vehicle, no witnesses. But she went through a highway guardrail. You know how fast you'd have to be going to punch through that? Someone *must've* hit her. Otherwise, she would've had to pull three lanes over, turn, and almost race straight for it, like on purpose. It couldn't have been an accident."

Though she wasn't in love with Michael anymore and hadn't been for some time, Helen hated seeing him like this. He'd suffered an agonizing loss and, being a man who uncovered conspiracies for a living, couldn't help but look for one here.

"What's Oscar got to do with it?" she asked quietly.

"It's his territory. Echo Park. He'll know something."

Helen straightened, perturbed. "If you think Oscar murdered your girlfriend, at least be man enough to knock on his door and tell him that yourself."

When Michael looked up at her, his eyes betrayed pain rather than anger. "Not like he'd talk to me without your say-so. It's why I came here first."

Helen realized this was probably true. That Michael picked up on this, having only met Oscar once, was the surprise.

"I'll call him," she said. "But he's not going to know anything about it. I promise you that."

"Thank you," Michael said, slumping back down.

"And I'll call you a cab. Go to the bathroom and clean yourself up."

Michael seemed ready to reply, but Helen had already turned to stalk back toward the showroom. She was praying Oscar wouldn't make a liar out of her.

As he made the drive from St. Augustine's to Bishop Osorio's apartment in East LA, Luis tried to remember the last time he'd seen his father, but couldn't. It wasn't that the memory was particularly troubling and something he'd repressed. On the contrary, it was probably something so inconsequential, so meaningless, that he hadn't known to mark it at the time. There'd been no final confrontation with thrown dishes and slamming doors. No ultimatums. No unforgivable last act.

The best Luis could piece it together, his father went to work one day, came home that night, went to work the next day, then didn't come home. Rather than call the police or go looking for him, Luis's mother had done nothing. He'd come back a couple of nights later, then vanished again. Same for a weekend. Then nothing. Sure, Luis had seen him a few times after that, a former tenant picking up something he'd left in the garage, but there was no interaction.

It hadn't been some great dramatic withdrawal, a final fight followed by the old man storming out on his wife and children, never to be seen again. Nor was it the proverbial "going out of the house for cigarettes, never to return" mystery either.

Though his absence put the family's financial burden squarely on his mother Sandra's shoulders, it relieved other stresses. The old man had been a drunk and a depressive. Without this in her life, Sandra's physical appearance changed dramatically. She lost weight, her smile came easier, she didn't look as drawn or tired. She also became more outgoing, making friends with neighbors and other parents at Luis's school. Before, these kinds of interactions would inevitably be marred when she'd have to introduce people to her husband. She was free of this now and happy.

That said, she never showed any interest in dating, despite Luis figuring she had her share of would-be suitors. Her independence had been hard-won, and she was going to hold on to it.

When she died, Luis was already well on his way to the priesthood and had accepted being an orphan. He never expected to see his father again and doubted Sebastian even knew he was back in Los Angeles, much less that he'd become a priest.

So as he sat outside Bishop Osorio's modest Silver Lake duplex, having skipped midmorning Mass, he tried to imagine what had brought together the man who'd given him life and the one who'd given him his vocation. Maybe it was simple. His father was dying and looking to make amends. Luis tried to force himself to care but couldn't. The old man had been a ghost to him for so long that his physical death felt like an afterthought.

Resigning himself to whatever lay inside, Luis climbed out of the car and went up to knock on Osorio's front door.

"Welcome," Father Belbenoit said, opening the door wide. "Please come in. The bishop is in his parlor."

"My father?" Luis asked.

"Will be along shortly. The bishop thought he might sit with you first."

Luis hadn't anticipated any alone time with Bishop Osorio but simply nodded. Father Belbenoit led him down a narrow, musty hallway to a small first-floor room off the duplex's staircase. The floor was covered with overlapping Persian rugs, upon which sat an assortment of old hardwood furniture. On the walls were enough crucifixes of various origins and designs to fill a museum, as well as framed photographs of Osorio through the years, including several at the Vatican alongside multiple pontiffs. There were also medallions, the one closest to Luis reading *The American Cardinals Dinner, The Catholic University of America, April 19, 1996, Los Angeles, California,* and featuring the engraved signatures of eight cardinals on the back, led by the former Los Angeles archbishop.

Even cardinals get souvenirs, Luis guessed.

In the midst of all this, shrunken onto the sofa in a long violet cassock and matching three-peaked biretta, with a breviary open on his lap, was the aged form of Bishop Emeritus Osorio. He raised the book and smiled at Luis. "I was told that when you went 'undercover' to those factory farms you took a Bible with you, not a breviary," Osorio said. "Is it not a priest's duty to pray the Divine Office no matter where he is? It then occurred to me you might not have one, so I wished for you to have mine."

Luis took the proffered book and nodded. "As you say, I was undercover. A man with a Bible isn't necessarily a priest. A man with a breviary most certainly is."

To Luis's surprise, his answer seemed to delight the bishop, as if he were a child who'd somehow managed to win a rook off a grandmaster in chess.

"That's what Pastor Whillans liked about you so much," Osorio said, smiling. "Even when your answer goes counter to doctrine, you voice it anyway. It's your church now I suppose, so you can do what you wish. But you'll pardon us dinosaurs if we aren't a bit mystified even on our way out the door."

"I meant no disrespect, Your Excellency," Luis said. "Thank you for the gift."

"You're very welcome," Osorio said.

But Luis realized something about the exchange bothered him. "Who told you I took a Bible?"

"Your driver I think," Osorio replied. "Oscar de Icaza. He is a friend."

Oscar de Icaza? A friend to the Bishop Emeritus?

It beggared belief that Luis's childhood friend and onetime criminal compatriot turned minor gangster palled around with an aged bishop. But how else could he have known?

"But we're here to speak of another of our mutual acquaintances, aren't we?" Osorio said, indicating for Luis to sit in one of the chairs. "Sebastian Chavez has been a recipient of the church's charity for many years. Unfortunately, in recent years I've become increasingly worried that my intervention on his behalf has only enabled him in his negative choices. Did you know that he is a master carpenter? And I mean that in the union's terms, not as a mere adjective."

It rang a distant bell, but Luis shook his head anyway.

"In a perfect world he should have no trouble finding work," Osorio continued. "But his alcoholism prevents it. So instead he sells himself and his labor piecemeal in the parking lots of hardware stores and near job sites. When sober, he can drive any nail in three strikes. *Tap-tap-tap.*" Osorio rapped his knuckles on the sofa's armrest for emphasis. "He sets the rhythm for the entire project, and any contractor thinks it his lucky day. But once he's amassed a day or two's pay in his pocket, Sebastian returns to the bottle, and the contractor wonders what happened. A cliché, no?"

Yes, Luis silently agreed. *But one shared,* he realized, *by any number of my own congregants who bear the pain of years of manual labor throughout their bodies.*

"He gets fired, sometimes he gets blacklisted, and when he hits rock bottom, he comes to Sacré Cœur," Osorio said. "Or at least he did when I was there. The current parish pastor, Father Struxness, had quite enough of him and told Sebastian not to come back unless it was to attend AA meetings. So he washed up on my doorstep. Against my better judgment and out of a sense of loyalty to your family, I wrote him a check. I wouldn't see him for a month, and then he'd return with the same story, often in the middle of the night. This cycle repeated. By the time you arrived in Los Angeles last year, however, I hadn't seen him for months. I saw no reason to bring it up. But then a few weeks ago he returned out of the blue. This time he didn't ask for money. He wanted to thank me. He'd attended the meetings, done the hard work, and was finally determined to turn his life around. Also he'd found God. It was only then that I told him of your presence in the diocese."

It was a lot to take in. The first half firmly squared with Luis's perception of his father. He had no idea what to make of the coda. Was this another trick? A way of eliciting sympathy from an old bishop that made it easier to extract a check?

"What does he want from me?" Luis asked.

"Ask him yourself," Osorio said, indicating the doorway.

Luis turned. Father Belbenoit ushered the gaunt figure of a man who looked like a decades-older version of Sebastian Chavez into the room. He had the appearance of someone who'd recently lost a lot of weight, but in muscle mass as well as fat. His shirt collar was stretched and sunken, as if what once pushed it to its limits had deflated. His face was that of a man who'd spent far more years of his life outdoors than in, for better or ill. His hands were leathered and tough, more like work gloves than appendages. All of this was familiar.

What was different was the light in his eyes. Luis didn't remember seeing that before. His eyes looked hopeful, even optimistic. They seemed to warm as they took him in.

"I am looking for those things that make a positive life, Father," Sebastian said, answering Luis's question. "But if you have nothing to say to me, I will understand absolutely."

Luis stared at this man, his only blood relative, and nodded.

"Good," Luis said, then exited the room.

As he climbed behind the wheel of his parish car a moment later, Luis snuck a glance back to Osorio's front door. No one had followed. Unsure if he'd wanted anyone to, Luis keyed the ignition, reversed down the driveway, and returned to his parish.

IV

It was too beautiful a Sunday morning to give it away to banking, Gennady thought.

Yelena had let him sleep in, given his late night with Oris, and was downstairs playing with the baby. Their daughter amused herself with drawing after drawing of her latest obsession, princesses and unicorns. He had plenty of work to do but nothing that couldn't wait a few hours.

"Nina? Did you hear the whales singing this morning?" he asked his daughter after coming downstairs. "They want you to come play with them."

Nina stared at her daddy with wide eyes. "The whales sang to you?"

"They did. They said your name, mommy's name, even Aleksey's name. They're waiting for us."

They packed plenty of snacks, diapers, wipes, and blankets and made their way to the marina in Yelena's hybrid SUV. Ten minutes later they were on the water headed west toward Catalina in their cabin cruiser, the *Nina*.

Gennady didn't know if they'd see anything but didn't care. Yelena and Nina loved the ocean as much as he did, and the bumpy ride always put Aleksey right to sleep. He hoped a nap meant he'd be awake should they see any whales, though he wasn't sure a baby that young would even know what to make of them.

"If you see anything, what do you say?" Gennady called to Nina, who stood at the prow in a life jacket almost larger than she was.

"Whale ho!"

They'd only been out forty-five minutes when they came across three fin whales. They were quite large, easily sixty feet, and spouted a number of times before going back under to feed in the channel's deep underwater canyons.

"You know how you can tell where a whale is about to surface?" Gennady explained. "You watch the water for signs of turquoise. Means something is coming up from underneath."

Nina watched the waves with twice as much intensity. Gennady angled the *Nina* north. They were soon rewarded with the sighting of a humpback. The ridges and bumps on its fins differentiated it from its larger, smoother cousin.

"Whale ho!" Nina shouted, pointing to a ring of turquoise as the humpback surfaced again. It spouted, then arched its back and raised its tail out of the water.

Yelena took out snacks for Nina and breast-fed the newly awoken Aleksey as Gennady let the current decide the boat's direction. Spinner dolphins cycled out of the water a few dozen yards away, delighting his daughter. He had decided to head back when three more whales appeared alongside them. They were much smaller than the fin whales and their bodies heavily barnacled.

"Barnacles mean gray whales," he told Nina, shutting off the engine and allowing the boat to drift after them. "Probably two males and a female."

They watched them for a few minutes longer, but the grays were quickly out of sight. Gennady turned the engine back on and headed to the marina.

There was no real cell signal on the water, another thing Gennady liked about a morning jog out onto the Pacific. But as they neared the harbor, he felt his two phones buzz and chime in unison.

He took the first from his pocket and saw a text from their next-door neighbor: *You okay? Saw the police.*

A shiver ran through his body as he listened to the accumulated voice mails while guiding the boat into the marina. He didn't want to alarm his family, but he was practically shaking as he tied up at their berth.

"What's going on?" Yelena asked, Aleksey having fallen asleep again on the way back.

Gennady played for her a voice mail left by the police.

"This is Officer Ron Lamott, LAPD, Pacific Division," a male voice said, all business. "We had a report of a break-in to your residence at Grand Canal and Court E. We're here now, and there are signs of forced entry."

Yelena nodded, and they ran their valuables through a mental list. They didn't have any art and Yelena didn't wear much jewelry. Tech-wise, they had Gennady's multiple laptops and iPads, the television, and so on, but there wasn't much. They kept no cash at the house. They'd come from Russia with their entire lives packed into two suitcases, but their families hadn't any antiques or heirlooms regardless.

Everything burned during the Siege, Gennady's grandmother was fond of saying, having endured it as a girl. She wore the experience as a badge of honor, as did many Petersburgers.

"Anything broken in the house is insured anyway," Gennady said as they buckled the kids into the SUV. "We should be fine."

But he knew that wasn't necessarily the case. While it was true that they had no more or less than any of their affluent neighbors—well, likely less—whoever hit their house could have targeted him for things that insurance wouldn't cover, like information. Gennady wasn't careless with his client records, but the thought worried him nonetheless.

"Is Mara home today?" Gennady asked, referring to Yelena's partner in her catering group. "You may need to take the children over."

Gennady waited for Yelena's eyes to tell him that the reality of this was sinking in, that her sense of security had been irreparably damaged. She knew of his parallel careers, naturally, but they never went into great detail about either. When instead of faltering she held up her phone and showed him that she'd already texted her, he was relieved.

They made the short drive home, parked, and were trudging to the house when they saw the gathering of neighbors and uniformed officers milling around on the sidewalk. The neighbor who'd texted Gennady, a deeply tanned former tech specialist named Terry, spotted Gennady and signaled the cops.

"The homeowner," Gennady saw him say. His name in absentia.

"I'm Officer Lamott," one of the officers said, introducing himself. "We entered the premises after receiving the call from your neighbor, Mr. Belknap. Judging from the security footage, we believe it might have been some sort of prank or even gang initiation."

Officer Lamott and his partner, Officer Atterbury, led Gennady into the house as another neighbor Gennady barely knew, an older woman named Mrs. Pamatmat, ushered Yelena and his children to her house to wait.

"Do you know if you set your alarm when you left this morning?"

I did, Gennady thought.

"I doubt it," Gennady said. "We were only going for a little while."

Officer Lamott nodded in commiseration. "Well, the damage seems to have been superficial, however extensive."

Gennady wandered around the downstairs, seeing that the home invaders had slashed all the pillows and seat cushions on all of the chairs and sofas. They slashed at the drapes and smashed all the glass in sight, except for the windows.

Which might've been heard outside.

When he walked into the kitchen, it was more of the same. The glass in the cabinet doors was shattered, as were dishes, vases, measuring cups, and drinking glasses. The knives had been removed from the knife block and were nowhere to be seen. The lower cabinet doors had all been kicked in. Yelena's large mixer had been raised from the counter and thrown down onto the hardwood floor with such force that it had cracked right through. It appeared that someone had tried to pull the refrigerator out of its nook and dash it to the floor as well but hadn't gotten very far.

"We checked the stove," Officer Lamott said. "Gas line's intact."

"That's good," Gennady said absently.

They moved to the bedrooms upstairs. In the baby's room every stuffed animal and blanket had been shredded. In Nina's room it was the same. Her bedclothes were scattered and ripped, her own beloved stuffed animals torn to pieces, and her collection of ceramic horses and cupcakes she'd painted with her mother were in pieces on the floor as well. The master bedroom was tame by comparison—torn sheets and stabbed pillows, the flat-screen TV mounted on the wall dashed to the ground, but that was it.

Fearful of what he might find, Gennady was nervous entering his office, only to see it had been left relatively unscathed. A large glass cabinet in which Gennady kept various family keepsakes and even the framed pictures on the wall were intact, unlike almost every other bit of glass in the house.

"Our theory, based on the security footage we've watched on your neighbor's tablet, is that they hit this room last and were interrupted by our sirens." Officer Lamott paused here, puffing his chest and putting his hands on his hips in a gesture of pride. "Judging by the footage taken by your neighbor's cameras, they were inside for about three minutes total. There were four of them, but their faces were covered."

Technology, Gennady thought, and nodded.

He looked around his office. He checked the closet and found the six laptops he kept there—mostly broken ones that he thought might one day be salvaged—missing. Also gone from his desk and its drawers were his numerous backup drives. His current laptop, which he slid under the desk when he wasn't using it to keep it from Nina, was also gone.

"I know it's a mess right now, but can you tell us offhand if anything's missing?" Officer Lamott asked.

Gennady knew he had to be careful with his answers.

"We had a MacBook we mostly used for photos." Gennady had noted that among the missing. "Other than that we had our phones and our iPad on the boat."

"Lucky break," the officer said. "We have our print guy on the way to take fingerprints, so stick around so we can print you and your family to make exclusions. Anyone else have routine access to your home?"

"Our cleaning lady, but she's only here on Tuesdays."

Officer Lamott nodded.

"Mr. Archipenko, do you know of anyone who would want to harm your family?" Officer Lamott asked.

"Not at all. We don't even know that many people."

The officer told Gennady to take another look around, then headed out. Gennady waited a beat, then returned to the master bedroom. Two of the shredded pillows still on the bed were from Nina's room. He didn't think their placement was by accident. He pulled them aside and found the knives from his knife block arranged underneath them in a fanlike pattern.

It was a good cover, coming in like vandals, then stealing all his computer equipment while threatening the lives of his family. Just the kind of thing the police wouldn't catch if they'd already been handed a motive.

Three minutes.

It suggested they weren't only professionals, they also likely knew the layout of his house ahead of time.

He jogged downstairs and went to Mrs. Pamatmat's house to confer with Yelena. They decided he'd wait with the kids as she packed a couple of bags to take to Mara's house. They spoke little but communicated plenty through eye contact. He didn't want to scare her, but she needed to know how serious it was. Gennady also had a quick chat with Nina, telling her she had to listen to her mother. She didn't say much, confirming she also understood the gravity of what was going on, if not the specifics.

"Will we be coming home?" she asked.

"When the four of us are together, that's our home wherever we are," Gennady said. "You understand?"

Nina nodded, but Gennady could see tears beginning to form. He gave her a hug as Yelena returned. She'd seen the damage, though Gennady had removed the knives.

"Do you know who?" she asked him as they loaded the SUV.

"No," Gennady said. "Not sure it matters."

She nodded, kissed him, then got behind the wheel and drove away. Gennady was happy for once to see his family disappearing into the distance. They wouldn't be safe at the house, he'd decided. Those who took his drives and computers would come to discover they each had a kill program installed that would render them useless. They'd come back.

But they'd made a mistake. They thought he could be scared away by property damage. They had obviously never messed with a Russian.

Though he was meant to celebrate an evening Mass after returning to St. Augustine's from Bishop Osorio's, Luis found himself at Children's

Hospital for the third time that week. Without his having meant it to, a small miracle was being attributed to him that he had to deal with. A baby had been born to the Gualberto family that few thought would make it to term. When Mrs. Gualberto—Amy—went into labor two months early, the doctors told her and her husband that the baby, who suffered from a transposition of arteries within the heart, wasn't likely to live more than a few hours.

In what he thought was among the cruelest things he'd ever witnessed, Luis overheard a doctor telling a nurse, "At least they still have the other two," meaning the Gualbertos' older children.

Luis went in to baptize the child, named Cynthia, before she died. He'd become accustomed to this part of his vocation much faster than he'd believed himself capable when he'd first discovered how often he'd be called to do it. But life was most fragile at its beginning and end points, he had learned, and thereby the closest to God.

He'd blessed baby Cynthia as well and comforted the family. The mother and father, however, were less upset than he thought they'd be. They firmly believed the child would live, and no doctor could dissuade them from this. Mrs. Gualberto's brother, on the other hand, had taken Luis aside in the hallway and asked about funeral arrangements.

Two days later Cynthia was still alive. Luis came back in and blessed her again, as the hospital had decided to operate on her tiny heart. Though very dangerous, they were utilizing a new technological process by which a 3-D model of Cynthia's tiny heart was created from an MRI scan that the surgeon could practice on beforehand. As this removed the exploratory period, it cut the surgery time in half, and lo and behold Cynthia survived, her birth defect repaired.

Luis was immediately hailed by the Gualbertos as a *cura milagroso*. Priest of miracles.

Of course, he believed the real *hombre de los milagros* was whoever came up with the 3-D printer technology but dutifully returned to Children's Hospital to check on the family that Sunday night.

"We will encourage her to a life of service to the church," Mrs. Gualberto said.

"If that is her vocation, the church will be very blessed to have her," Luis replied.

Mrs. Gualberto smiled, and Luis went to the bed where Cynthia lay in a nest of wires and tubes. He stared into her face and waited for this miracle to spark something within him, reopen the connection with the divine. Wasn't this evidence of his good work? Weren't all things?

But as it had been all week, he saw flesh and machines and a soul peering out from behind two dark eyes.

Where is God? he wanted to ask her. *If he is guiding you through this, please lead him back to my heart.*

He turned to the Gualberto family. Cynthia's survival had cemented their faith. There was a nurse who'd be on shift a few times when he'd visited who seemed similarly uplifted.

So why couldn't he be? It made him envious to be forced to look in from outside. Another sin.

Luis did his best to push the feeling aside and prayed with the family for a while longer, then blessed the child a third time. When he stepped out, he was told that someone had been brought in to the emergency room, a derelict who'd been struck by a Metro Rail train and who was likely to die. Luis went to the person, a woman of indeterminate age, and pronounced the last rites. She was still murmuring the names of what he took to be long-absent relations when he exited.

Once out in the parking lot, Luis made it all the way to his car before practically collapsing to his knees in prayer. Anger and resentment came instead of wisdom. He clenched his hands together until his knuckles were white and sweat beaded from his forehead.

"Hey, Padre, sorry to interrupt you, but do you know if you can exorcise a chicken? Mine's got all these crazy demons, and I need the eggs, not the drama. Can it be done?"

Luis shut his eyes again, muttered an amen, then got to his feet. Oscar was leaning against Luis's parish car, taking a drag on a cigarette. He wondered if his old friend had sensed the depths of his suffering. If he had, the expression on his face revealed nothing. Oscar proffered the cigarette to Luis, who shook his head. He produced a half-empty bottle of beer from behind his back and offered this as well. Luis shook his head again but cracked a smile.

Oscar shrugged and shot the rest in one swig before throwing the bottle as far as he could down an alley across the street. When it shattered into hundreds of pieces, Oscar turned a satisfied smile toward Luis.

"Hey, Padre."

"Did you follow me here or something?" Luis asked.

"Called St. Augustine's. Guy who answered said you'd be here. You don't answer your cell anymore?"

"Barely," Luis replied. "Sorry."

"I wouldn't either if I had a choice," Oscar admitted. "Going to buy you a meal now, as you need to listen to what I have to say."

"I'm sorry, Oscar," Luis said. "I'm not in the mood for conversation."

"Not what I said," Oscar retorted sternly.

Luis realized his old friend wasn't going to let him off the hook.

Oscar pointed down the street. "You eaten yet?"

After a short walk down Sunset, they ended up at a chicken and waffle joint. Though there was a waiting list, Oscar nodded to the hostess, who ushered them right in. They sat, and Oscar ordered for the both of them. Once the waitress had gone, Oscar slid a cell phone to Luis.

"Play the first voice mail."

Luis did so. It was Michael Story.

"Saturday night, Sat-ur-day night," Michael said, slurring his words. "Here. Echo Park. Silver Lake exit. Right off the bridge. Cameras got nothing, or they're just telling me that. I don't know. But you're the boss, right? The big boss? If it happens in your neighborhood, you have to sanction it if it's murder, right? If it's murder. It's murder."

Michael continued to ramble. Oscar took the phone back. "It's two more minutes of that."

"What's he talking about?" Luis asked.

"His girlfriend was in a car accident. Went off the 101 freeway. Thing is they'd had a couple of drinks. They're not telling the papers, but when I checked into it, she was just over the legal limit. Sounds like she'd been burning the candle at both ends. That plus alcohol equals a smashup."

"Yet there's a deputy district attorney on your voice mail accusing you of being an accomplice to murder."

"Right?" Oscar said, clapping his hands. "I knew you'd get it. I know he's your friend and all, but if he'd said that to my face, I'd be stomping his ribs in."

"He's not my friend," Luis shot back. He was sorry that he'd lost someone close to him, but found the chief deputy DA opportunistic at best, corrupt as all hell at worst. "Not at all."

"Okay, fine. But you want him to live and me to stay out of jail, right?" Oscar asked. "Don't answer that. I need you to have a word with him."

"With Story? And say what?"

"Come on. How many favors do I ask you versus how many do you ask me?"

Luis seethed but knew Oscar was right. Besides, it wasn't Michael's fault that his girlfriend had died. He should be more charitable in that respect. "Fair enough. Is there any chance in the world he's right?"

Oscar shook his head. "He was right about one thing. If it was a hit, I'd know about it. I don't but am a paranoid person. So I talked to people who worked the crime scene and then the guys who towed the car away. There's nothing. It's completely clean. No marks on it whatsoever. Tire tracks on the highway are consistent with somebody drifting, then losing control when they tried to right themselves. I know Michael thinks it's something else, but it's a car accident. It sucks, but there it is."

"I'll give him a call," Luis said, rising. "Thanks for the food."

"No, no," Oscar said, taking Luis's wrist. "One other thing."

"You're kidding."

"Come on, Father. Don't make me be a jerk to a priest in front of all these people."

Luis sat back down and shrugged. "What?"

"Your dad."

Luis was surprised. He knew he hadn't put his father in the rearview forever when he'd driven away from Bishop Osorio's place. He just hadn't expected it to come back around so quickly. And particularly from Oscar.

"Since when are you the bishop's errand boy?" Luis asked.

"Since he cast around for the one person he thought you might listen to," Oscar said. "He knows you're going through a bunch of stuff right now."

"How does he know that?" Luis interjected.

"Word gets around," Oscar said pointedly. "And you're hardly that difficult to read. Even I know you're not yourself. But as to your father, Bishop Osorio is way too old to be dealing with this. Sebastian coming around, making a fuss, asking questions."

"About what?"

"About your dead brother. He's obsessed with that night. He's like Michael. He's convinced that an accident is really a murder."

The version of his father Bishop Osorio had described had sounded downright normal. Oscar's version of him as something between an annoyance and a lunatic was much more in keeping with the man he remembered.

"It's guilt," Luis said. "He wasn't even in our lives by then. What would you even have me do?"

"I want you to take over. Relieve some of the bishop's burden here. It takes a lot out of him. I can't tell you how to be more present, but you need to be the priest your father comes to instead of Osorio."

"I wouldn't even know where to find him," Luis said lamely.

"Allow me to hook you up. He's off MacArthur Park in a one-bedroom shack. You want the address?"

When Luis left a few minutes later, Oscar remained in his chair. He ordered a beer and then another one. Everything he'd told the priest about Naomi's accident was true. *Almost.*

The call from Michael Story had bothered him, and that much he had told Luis. Something *had* happened on his turf without his knowledge. Oscar was not accustomed to people knowing more about his business than he did and he'd wanted answers. It was true that he'd been out to the scene, both on the side of the highway and then where her car landed. He'd also seen the vehicle itself in the impound yard. Or at least what was left of it.

But two things he hadn't told the priest lingered in his mind.

First, though there were no marks on the car that suggested it had been hit, the engine told a different story. It appeared as if something had been installed, an after-market modification, that was then removed after the fact. It wasn't something someone would notice unless they knew what to look for. But Oscar wasn't your average someone. He could see the tooling done to put various pieces of equipment in place, and the way the metal housing had been bent confirmed they had definitely been removed following the accident.

The only time he'd seen anything that connected to an engine that way—to the car's guidance system, axles, and brakes—had been when he'd first looked over the schematics of one of those retrofitted self-driving cars. The kind the tech gurus and taxicab companies were hoping would be the norm on LA streets within the next decade.

The second thing was in a single frame of security video taken by a camera mounted on a gas station canopy a few exits up the highway. The vehicle in the shot was a nondescript SUV that Oscar later learned had been stolen the day before down in San Diego. What caught his eye, however, was the face of the man behind the wheel. Though he hadn't seen this person in several years, he recognized him all the same. He looked older now but still had the dull-eyed stare of the monster Oscar knew him to be. He was accompanied in the vehicle by four other men, but Oscar couldn't make their faces out.

It didn't matter.

It had confirmed beyond all doubt: Naomi Okpewho's death wasn't an accident. And the devil himself was back in Los Angeles.

Oscar had set the hard drive containing the security footage ablaze. As the flames burned green, twisting the metal and scorching the board, he prayed that if the man in the image ever found out he'd been seen, he would accept Oscar's fiery tribute as reason enough to let him stay alive.

Oscar feared it wouldn't be enough. Not even close.

V

For Michael, Sunday was a blur. He hadn't known if Monday would be any better, but it turned out to be worse. He'd had one job. Pick up Naomi's parents from the airport and drive them to the Los Angeles County medical examiner's office to formally identify their daughter. He'd been sober enough when he picked them up but had no idea what to say. He became so flustered on the drive that he talked about anything that popped into his head to avoid the reality of what they were doing.

He'd seen dead bodies before. Most horribly, he'd had to identify the murdered body of a former whistleblower who'd become his lover the previous year. The image had never left him. He didn't want Naomi's corpse to haunt his memories of her from there on out and refused to see her, leaving the grisly task of identifying her to her parents.

After promising to pick them up the next morning to go to the funeral home and make arrangements, Michael had gone home, emptied a bottle of Maker's Mark, passed out for a couple of hours, then drank a bottle of Shiraz a friend of Naomi's had brought by a few months earlier when she'd come for dinner. When he woke up from that, it was well past noon on Tuesday. He'd missed picking up Naomi's parents, the appointment with the funeral director, and a lunchtime call he was supposed to have with his boss, LA district attorney Deborah Rebenold.

There'd be no talking his way out of this one. Naomi's parents would know what a louse their daughter was dating. He couldn't show his face at the funeral now, could he? In his despair, he considered driving down to San Pedro and throwing himself off the bridge but then dismissed the thought as melodramatic. It would shatter his children's lives and give confirmation to Helen that she'd wasted too much of her life on a loser.

Once a survey of the kitchen cabinets revealed he was completely out of alcohol, Michael decided to wander down the hill to his local liquor store and repair the issue. When he grabbed his cell phone, he found four voice mails. The first was from Naomi's father, though he only hung up. The second was from Deborah, who in syrupy tones let him know she had marked his absence from the phone call and told him "to take all the time he needed." The third was from Father Luis Chavez, who succinctly said that Oscar "had nothing to do with the wreck that killed Naomi Okpewho."

Why the hell is he in my life? Michael wondered as he cut off Luis's cursory condolences.

He didn't recognize the number of the fourth and was about to delete it without listening to it but then heard the opening line.

"My name is Gennady Archipenko, and I was given this number by your office. I had been inquiring after Naomi Okpewho," the young-sounding, Russian-accented man explained. "She left a message asking after my financial dealings with Charles Sittenfeld, who worked at my bank. My house was robbed this past Sunday only hours after Okpewho was killed. The very information she requested was stolen in the form of laptops and discs. What I recovered over the next two days might be of interest to you and your office. Please do call me back. I would like to meet in person."

Killed. The man had said *killed.*

Up until now Michael had felt like a crazy person trying to convince others of something obvious to him but unseen by them. But here was a man who seemed to believe the same as he did, all forensic evidence aside.

Then he hesitated. What if it was a trap? But the idea of a bullet waiting for him somewhere down a dark alley didn't sound so bad right now. At least he'd die a justice-seeking hero in the line of duty.

That isn't such a bad legacy to leave for the kids, is it?

He rang Archipenko back. When it went to voice mail, he texted the number instead.

I'd love to meet. Can you see me today? Maybe even right now?

It took Luis two days to decide to approach his father. He'd prayed on it, sure, but nothing came of that. He'd gone through the motions of teaching class at St. John, celebrating Mass, visiting parishioners, hearing confession, and chairing a parish meeting with the other priests of St. Augustine's. He'd kept a line open to God, as it were, in case the Almighty had something to say to him, but mostly he thought about his dad.

Though it was easy to recall the negative memories, these exhausted themselves soon enough. Positive ones began to trickle in. Ones of Sebastian at Christmas, sitting with his sons in front of the television, even riding around with them in their old car, a '78 Ford Thunderbird, which got incredibly hot in the summertime.

But it was Luis's mind playing tricks on him. He realized he was remembering photographs, not actual memories. They were pictures his mother had kept around. This led to other memories, such as when they'd gone to Dodger Stadium together. The photo his mother took was of her two boys standing close to the field, suggesting they had far better seats than they could've afforded tickets wise. Luis knew his father had been there and began to reconstruct the evening, inserting his dad's face into his already-murky memory. He couldn't recall if Sebastian had shaved off his mustache by then, but as he had it in the Christmas picture Luis remembered the strongest, that was the image transposed onto the baseball memory.

He did this with several others. A walk up the beach in Malibu, a trip to the Santa Monica pier, a childhood excursion across the border into Tijuana, the first time Luis had ever been to Mexico. Each of these memories, which were vague and aided by his mother's photos and later conversations with his brother, helped solidify an image of his father.

It took some doing, but after careful mental editing Luis had put his father back into his childhood one memory at a time, realizing how much he must've excised him.

When Tuesday rolled around and he had an evening off, he dialed up Oscar and asked where he could find Sebastian.

"Did you talk to Michael Story yet?" Oscar asked.

"Left a voice mail," Luis replied. "Where's my father?"

"Your dad's working a site near Melrose and Highland," Oscar said. "Seven hundred block."

Luis was pensive on the drive over. Traffic was bad. Part of him even hoped he'd left late enough in the day that he'd missed his window. *At least I tried.*

He thought of Pastor Whillans and what he might say about that. He realized the old priest would've scowled at him. Echoed Oscar's remark and told him that he wasn't himself. Not only that, he wasn't the man God expected him to be.

Where was it written, after all, that God had to be responsive to his priests?

With this in mind, he took a shortcut through Hancock Park and made it to the construction site with daylight to spare. After parking at a meter, he jogged across the street to the three-story multiunit behemoth that was eating up half a city block. The individual units looked like closets from the street level, but given the location, Luis figured the renters would pay thousands a month.

Though it was late in the day, there were still at least three or four dozen men hard at work framing the structure. Luis slipped through the chain-link fence that surrounded the work site, cupped his hand over his eyes to block the sun, and tried to spy his father up on the higher levels.

"Can I help you?" a gruff, but not accusatory, voice asked.

Luis turned to see a man in a hard hat approach from alongside the structure. He figured he would've gotten it worse if he wasn't wearing the collar.

"I'm looking for Sebastian Chavez," Luis said. "Is he here?"

"All the way up," the man said, worry edging into his voice. "Is everything all right?"

"Yes, family matter," Luis assured him, surprised to hear someone voicing concern over his father.

The workman took a couple of steps back, then returned with a second hard hat.

"Got to wear this on site, Padre."

"Thank you," Luis said, putting it on as he went to the nearest ladder.

"Sebastian's one of the best we've got," the worker enthused. "Works like a man half his age. Brings his own tools. Never misses a nail."

It was a surprisingly impassioned endorsement. Luis wondered if the workman feared he was there to take Sebastian away. He nodded and headed up the steps.

Sure enough, Sebastian was all the way on top, nailing struts to rafters that would support the eventual roof. Though Luis could see and hear nail guns being used, his father was doing delicate angled work. As Osorio had said, Sebastian had a quick hammer and seemed incapable of missing. When he drove a nail, there was no hesitation, only focus. It was hypnotic to watch.

Sebastian finally noticed his son and gave a friendly wave, as if having expected him. He put his hammer and nails back in his tool belt, unclipped his safety line, and headed over to Luis.

"You found me," Sebastian said, cradling his hard hat. "Praise God."

Okay.

"I'm glad to see you," Sebastian said. "We didn't leave things right at the bishop's house."

"We didn't leave things at all."

"No, I suppose not," Sebastian said.

They went down to ground level, Sebastian waving to a few other workers as the crew cleaned up the site and prepared to quit for the day. He led Luis to the mouth of the building's underground garage, the concrete of the ramp and lower levels long poured and dried.

"A man named Oscar de Icaza came to speak to me on the bishop's behalf," Luis said. "He asked that you leave Osorio alone, as it's becoming a bit of a strain on the old man's constitution."

"Ah," Sebastian said. "Who's Oscar?"

Luis gave him the short version.

"I remember now," Sebastian said. "It was probably during one of our conversations about Nicolas. Osorio said that he knew people in the underground. They said the same thing as the police. Nicolas was killed in a cross fire. One gunman emerged from the dark to kill two men waiting in a car. Nicolas walked past on his way home from Sacré Coeur. Nicolas was unlucky."

"Yes," Luis said, not wanting to dwell. "That's what they say."

"Then why," Sebastian asked, "does God say something different?"

"What do you mean?"

"God told me that it was Nicolas who was targeted and the two men were the ones caught in the cross fire."

Luis was stunned. The voice of God, so elusive to him, spoke to his father? What Sebastian was saying sounded downright crazy.

Though the shooter had never been caught, it was known that there were two OGs in the car that night. They were heavy hitters with one of the local gangs. They'd recently been implicated in a murder, so it wasn't a surprise that someone had taken a shot at them as revenge. It had made sense. Someone targeting Nicolas? The idea was ludicrous. But . . . was it any less crazy than the many things that God had revealed to Luis?

This was the second person this week trying to make sense of a grisly death by suggesting it was premeditated murder. This time the accusation was backed by divine authority.

"Are you sure you're hearing God?" Luis asked as gently as possible.

"I am!" Sebastian replied. "As sure as I am of anything in this world. The reason I went to Bishop Osorio was that I believed that if God was telling that to me, he would probably tell Osorio as well. The bishop loved Nicolas like a son. I don't know if he's ever recovered from his death."

Luis was surprised by this. He'd never heard Osorio say such a thing.

"Did God tell you why Nicolas would've been targeted?" Luis asked.

"No," Sebastian admitted. "I tried to speak to the police about it, but they didn't care."

They didn't care then either, Luis thought.

"I had no idea where else to turn," Sebastian said.

Luis regarded his father for a moment. Taken on their own, Sebastian's words weren't that surprising. He was a man who'd lost so much in life. At some point, he'd taken stock and tried to pinpoint where it all went wrong. So much was his own fault that it perhaps became easy to focus on the single event that wasn't.

"Maybe I'll talk to Osorio," Luis said. "And I have a few contacts in the police. I can try that, too."

"That's what the bishop said," Sebastian admitted. "He said you helped people."

Another surprise.

"That's why you wanted to see me then?" Luis asked.

"No, I wanted to see you because I wanted to get to know my son," Sebastian explained. "I'm not asking you to welcome me back into your life with open arms. I'm asking for you to give me a chance to convince you that I'm not the man you remember any longer. That I've changed."

"I barely remember you at all," Luis admitted.

"Maybe that's a good thing," Sebastian said with gravity. "A fresh start then."

"Are you looking for forgiveness?"

"Aren't we all?" Sebastian replied glibly. "But no, that's not it entirely. I can't make you love me as a father, but I do want you to let me love you as a son. I've been without love in my heart for so long that it made me old and embittered. When I began to love the Lord, I realized how much I missed that feeling. I wanted more of it. I wanted to love. And I knew the place to start was right here."

He tapped Luis's chest. Luis wondered where this man was when his mother was dying or when his brother had been savagely torn away and he truly needed a father.

"Could we try?" Sebastian asked.

Luis wondered if this was God in some way coming at him from another angle. He'd long regarded all challenges put in front of him as done so by God. How could this be any different? He had to trust his instincts even if the voice of God had grown silent within his own mind.

"Okay," Luis said quietly.

"All right," Sebastian replied. "That's all I can ask."

Luis rose and indicated the break in the chain-link fence. "Do you need a ride home?"

"Sure, I'd appreciate it," Sebastian said. "But what I'd like first is for my son to pray with me. That all right?"

Luis returned to his father's side and knelt even as other workers passed by, sending them curious glances.

"It'll be fine."

Michael showered, shaved, and sobered up in the hours between when he'd first heard from Gennady Archipenko and when he pulled into the parking lot of the Brazilian restaurant Archipenko had recommended as a meeting spot. He'd thought he recognized the name when the young Russian had mentioned it on the phone. When he saw it in the flesh, he realized he'd taken Helen there to celebrate some long-ago anniversary. He couldn't remember if it had been in the early days, when he'd arranged for the occasion weeks in advance, or later, when everything was a last-minute race thrown together in hopes of feigning preparation.

Things would've been different with Naomi, he told himself, then wondered if this was true.

Though he thought he looked in pretty good shape, the look on Archipenko's face as he rose from the table to shake his hand told him he still appeared fairly rough.

"Are you all right?" Gennady asked after Michael ordered a tea and a caipirinha.

"You don't need me to be all right," Michael replied. "If you've got nothing real, then who cares? You'll never see me again. If you have something actionable, you want me angry, bereft, vengeful. Anything but 'all right.'"

Gennady stared at Michael for a moment, then looked down. "I'm sorry. I didn't realize you and Ms.—"

"Okpewho. Naomi Okpewho."

"I didn't realize the nature of your relationship."

"That's okay. But yes. If you have something for me, I'm a loaded gun. Just point me in the right direction."

It was a melancholy statement, but with enough humor to make Gennady smile. Michael had checked the young man out. Though he hadn't been arrested, indicted, or even implicated in any crimes, his name had elicited a chuckle from a detective in LAPD's Commercial Crimes Division.

"We get that name now and again," the detective had said. "We weren't sure he was a real guy for a time. Somebody who might've taken a meeting with somebody else. We've checked him out down to his socks, and he's clean as a whistle. Not so much as a moving violation or parking ticket."

"Do you remember every name?" Michael had asked.

The detective laughed. "Experience has taught me that you don't get that many calls about someone without a reason."

As Naomi said, where there's smoke, there's fire, Michael thought.

"He'll have to come up for air at some point," the detective continued. "Then we'll open a file on him."

Michael wondered what the detective would say if he knew he was sitting opposite the young Russian right now.

"So, let's hear it," Michael said to Gennady.

Gennady waited so long to reply that Michael pushed himself away from the table to leave. But then the Russian raised a hand.

"Ms. Okpewho called me about Charles Sittenfeld," Gennady explained. "I barely knew the man and had no clue about his murder-for-hire dealings. So I had no idea why she would call."

"All right."

"But then I took a look into Sittenfeld's accounts at the bank myself."

"You can do that?"

"No, not really," Gennady admitted. "But let's say curiosity got the better of me once I found a knife under my wife's pillow."

"Okay."

"I think Ms. Okpewho came across what I did," Gennady explained. "He's a very arrogant man. Someone who did the bare minimum to cover his tracks."

The fruit from a poisoned tree, Michael realized.

"So what's the crime?" Michael asked.

"Difficult to ascertain," Gennady said. He took a small plastic key drive from his pocket and placed it on the table. "Which is why it might be better for you to look through the records than me."

"But there has to be something there you found actionable, right? Otherwise, we wouldn't be here."

"Yes," Gennady said cautiously. "The transactions recorded on that drive are not, on their face, irregular. They are high-dollar financial transfers involving a priority client who moved money from foreign banks into an account here in Los Angeles. The money in that account was then distributed out in ways similarly above suspicion."

"So?"

"Sittenfeld was the man at the switch for all of these transfers," Gennady said. "The *only* man at the switch, and thereby had complete oversight. He signed off on each one over the course of almost thirty years. All for one priority client, all for transfers coming in from a handful of foreign banks. What's suspicious is that all that money together adds up to almost twenty-three billion dollars."

Michael sat up straight. He could be cynical about a lot of things, but $23 billion was a massive amount to pass through the hands of one man, no matter how many years it took.

"Who is the priority client?" Michael demanded.

"That I don't know," Gennady said. "But I can make an educated guess. There is strict regulation in place regarding financial transfers. If it is from a corporation, your government is exceedingly thorough when it comes to making sure no one is trying to evade taxes. Understand?"

"Sure."

"But let's say it comes in from a nonprofit, from a nongovernmental agency, from a charity, or so on, where it's not taxed. Then the government doesn't even glance over to whet its appetite. The only time it goes into those books is if there's a full-fledged investigation."

"Even to the tune of twenty-three billion?" Michael asked.

"Apparently," Gennady said, tapping the drive. "Once to the tune of a hundred million a day, every day, for forty business days in a row."

"Four billion came in through Sittenfeld's account in a couple of months? And no red flags went up?"

"Not one," Gennady said. "I'm still marveling at it. It doesn't even feel like real money at that point. Like Sittenfeld was playing some kind of game and these were the made-up dollar amounts that went with it. But the bank paid out interest on the days it sat in our accounts. *Millions* in interest over time. But did anyone question if this money was real? Absolutely not."

Michael leaned back in his chair. If there was any shred of truth to this, it would imply that Naomi had somehow stumbled upon one of the largest and longest-running money-laundering schemes in US history.

"How do you keep something like that secret?" Michael murmured.

"I have no clue," Gennady said. "The most likely answer, on the bank side of it, is that it was willful. This changed over time. Early on, Sittenfeld was clearing a few million here and there. Still big money, but if he was careful you can understand how it could slip through the right cracks. That changed in the last decade. Do you have any idea how much money his bank lost during the recent financial crises and the meltdown of the housing market? They were in crisis mode. Then one of their officers steps forward and says, 'Well, I have a solution.' When they counter by saying it's illegal, all he has to do is show how he's gotten away with it for years. Someone offers you enough money to keep the lights on, sometimes you look the other way."

"And he must've made those in on the secret wealthy, too," Michael added.

"I'm sure," Gennady agreed. "The media thinks Sittenfeld wanted his wife dead over a few million dollars in a divorce. I think it must've been so much more than that. I doubt ours could have been the only bank involved."

Michael was flabbergasted. The idea that there could be even more money than this laundered through his city seemed impossible, even if it was done over several decades. He went to press Gennady on what he meant by this, but it turned out that Gennady Archipenko had said the last words he would ever speak.

The bullets came into the restaurant from the west, shattering the large bay windows overlooking Tenth and Santa Monica. They splintered the restaurant's wicker blinds, exploded the faux pre-Columbian pottery resting on shelves around the small dining area, and tore through the display case holding the day's assortment of pies and cakes.

They also pierced the heart of a waitress, the upper torsos of two diners out on the sidewalk, and the Adam's apple of the man who seemed to hold the key to Naomi's murder. As the small dark hole in Gennady's throat spit blood, the Russian's gaze met Michael's. A second bullet sliced through the man's shoulder, changed direction as it ricocheted off the bone, burst apart, and sent several shards into Michael's right forearm.

Michael grunted and flinched. As he dove from his chair, he saw the burst of muzzle flash from out in the street less than twenty yards away. Bullets rebounded off every surface, punching through the Formica-topped tables and drilling into the walls. Michael thought he'd been hit again—this time in the leg—only to realize he'd been cut by the razor-sharp edge of a shattered vase.

As he ducked behind the counter, he looked back and saw Gennady leaning against an overturned table. The young man's eyes were wide and his breathing labored as blood continued to trickle from the wounds to his neck and shoulder. He was growing pale and probably wouldn't last another two minutes. He made eye contact with Michael, his mouth open, as if asking, *Is this really happening?*

Gennady blinked as bullets continued to dance around him. Michael looked out to the street as the muzzle flash drew even closer, then back to the Russian, his lackluster eyes and gray face indicating that he was going into shock. Michael closed his own eyes and pictured Naomi. It was a calming thought and one he wanted to hold in his mind if it was to be his last.

He bolted out from behind the counter and ran straight into the cacophony of gunfire.

VI

Then it was over.

Michael anticipated the searing pain of hot lead, praying that if it was truly his time, a bullet would go through his head and spare him lingering agony. Then suddenly the storm started to pass. There was still gunfire, the street was still illuminated by a strobe of muzzle flash, but the hailstorm of bullets striking the restaurant had subsided.

He reached Gennady and pulled him from his seated position to the floor.

"Gotta stop this bleeding," he told the Russian, surprising himself with how calm and even he sounded.

He grabbed a napkin and cupped it around Gennady's throat, applying pressure but trying not to press down so hard he'd strangle him. But as blood soaked the napkin, Gennady's hand took hold of his own and pressed harder. Michael got the message and gripped the young man's neck as if he were trying to squeeze the life out of it. It took so much of his focus that he didn't even notice when the gunfire stopped completely and the three uniformly massive men in black pants, gray T-shirts, and thick, torso-covering body armor entered the restaurant.

"Multiple vics!" one yelled out to another, presumably outside. He looked to Michael, then knelt by the waitress. The first bullet had pierced her heart, killing her instantly. Unlike with Gennady, there was barely any blood, but her expression was frozen in a last pain stricken grimace. "At least one fatality!" he added.

He moved closer and squatted next to Michael, putting his own hand on Gennady's throat. "You kept him alive," he said evenly. "And I know you want to stay with him, but you need to look after your own wounds."

Michael was about to protest when he looked down and saw blood still leaking from both the wound on his forearm and the cut to his leg which was deeper than he'd initially registered. He nodded and moved aside as the armor-wearing man went to work to staunch Gennady's bleeding throat.

"Ambulances are on their way," one of the other men called into the restaurant.

"You SWAT?" Michael asked, barely hearing his own words, his eardrums still ringing from the attack.

"Not even," the man said. "Armored car security. Hoping we don't get in too much trouble. We put the shooter down hard out there but did some property damage along the way."

"I'm the chief deputy district attorney for Los Angeles," Michael said. "You'll be all right."

The security guards opened up after that, retelling their story as paramedics arrived to take charge of the wounded. It turned out they'd been dropping off coins and picking up bills from a large liquor mart a block down. When they'd heard the gunfire, they'd assumed they were the target of some kind of armed robbery. After spying a man in the middle of the street blazing away at a restaurant full of people, they'd decided to get involved.

"The shooter was an amateur," the guard said as he inspected Michael's wounds. "He was wearing some kind of tactical armor, but it was cheap, ill-fitting stuff. He had serious hardware but couldn't aim worth anything. He was like a kid with a water gun, dropping empty magazines and replacing them like he had an endless supply. When we shot back, he didn't know what to do. He didn't have cover, didn't have a fallback position. We're combat vets. Even a Jihadi would've hit the deck. He stood there blindly firing back, wondering why we weren't intimidated by him."

"Any idea who he was?"

"No clue," the guard said as paramedics came to relieve him. "White male, barely into his twenties, wild-eyed crazy. Bet they discover that he was high as a kite, too. Looked like he'd been on the street awhile."

Michael began to feel light-headed, his loss of blood finally getting to him. What had Luis said? Oscar wasn't involved? *Well, I wonder what he has to say about this.*

"Your friend got lucky," the guard said, indicating where Gennady had sat. "Took a million-to-one shot. Went straight through his throat. Should've taken his head off at that range, but the bullet went through clean. From the looks of it, he'll probably never talk again, but I've seen guys survive much worse. He was still awake when we got here, which means the world."

"I thought he was dead," Michael said, feeling increasingly disoriented.

"That's the thing about a war," the guard said, patting his shoulder. "It forces the docs to have to get pretty skillful when it comes to wounds like that. He'll never be the same, but at least he's not in a box."

Michael nodded. *Not like Naomi, you mean.*

When the paramedics reached Michael, he was already trying to leave. The trouble was he'd lost so much blood he was in no position to argue. They told him it was possible there were more shards in his wound and he needed to be X-rayed.

Michael panicked at the idea, not out of fear for his own mortality but because in the confusion after the shooting he'd found Gennady's key drive and tucked it into his pocket. If he went to the hospital and possibly had to go under for surgery, there was a good chance someone would come across it. If that happened, it might wind up in the wrong hands.

So he looked for a hiding spot within arm's reach. The dining room was completely exposed, but he spied a break between the baseboard and electrical box under the restaurant's decimated display case. With no alternatives, he shoved it inside and prayed no one would find it. Then he joined the paramedics for a ride to the hospital.

As they drove, Michael asked if there was any update on the status of the other victims.

"The ones outside are in critical, but they'll probably make it. The man who was shot in the throat is in surgery. That one's iffy. The waitress—well, she's been identified as Carrie Meallaigh. She had three small children."

Michael gritted his teeth, furious all over again.

When they reached the hospital, Michael was hurried in to be X-rayed, only to discover that what splinters were left in his body could be easily extracted with only local anesthetic. He called Helen first, who turned out to have already heard the news about the shooting on television, including reports that the chief deputy DA had been inside, and had been trying to reach him. He told her that he was perfectly all right, that he was in the wrong place at the wrong time, and that it was likely random and drug related.

Of course, he didn't believe this at all, but it seemed to mollify Helen.

Once he was stitched up, he emerged from the observation room, popped a handful of painkillers while pocketing a prescription for several more, and went looking for an update on Gennady. He found DA Rebenold instead.

"He yet lives," she said dryly.

"Indeed. Does this hospital have a secure wing?"

"Thought you got a scratch," she shot back.

"For one of the other victims. He needs police protection."

Deborah cocked her head. "What do you mean?"

"The shooter targeted him and me the same way they went after Naomi," Michael said. "There should be officers here at the hospital."

"Naomi? 'They'? 'The shooter'? All indications point to this being a random shooting," Deborah said evenly. "We don't have an ID on the gunman, but he's covered with needle tracks. He was out of his mind."

"Bet you don't have an ID on the gun, either," Michael replied.

"In point of fact, we don't, but that's becoming a common enough problem. It was another one of those ghost guns somebody made from 3-D printed parts. It had practically fallen apart from one usage."

"Yeah, but it's clean and untraceable. Ask yourself—how'd a junkie get it? Much less the high-powered ammunition he filled it with. I'm telling you, Deb, these are all connected."

Deborah straightened, visibly annoyed. She took a photograph from her pocket and showed it to Michael. It was Gennady Archipenko.

"Mind if I ask what you were doing meeting with this man?" Deborah asked.

"That's the other victim I was saying needed our protection. He was shot first."

"Could you answer the question?"

Michael wasn't happy with the way this was playing out. "Naomi had contacted him regarding the Sittenfeld case. His house was broken into a few hours after she was killed. It was trashed and made to look like the work of vandals, but he said they only stole laptops and hard drives, while leaving jewelry, cash, and electronics behind."

Deborah reacted with surprise.

"Now, are you going to say these three things aren't linked?" he asked.

"All I have to go on is the evidence, and the evidence says that Naomi was driving drunk," Deborah said quietly. "She could've injured or killed someone else. And you had been with her just prior. So I'm cutting you some slack, given the guilt you must feel—"

"Oh come on, Deborah!"

"But these delusions of yours are getting difficult to ignore."

"Archipenko looked into Charles Sittenfeld's financial dealings and saw what Naomi saw," Michael cried. "He'd been involved with all kinds of illegal activity spanning—"

Deborah interrupted, raising a hand. "You need to stop."

"But this is huge!" Michael scoffed. "He was telling me about money laundering on a massive scale. The exact kind you hear about people getting killed over. Sittenfeld or whoever he's in business with found out that Naomi was close and activated some kind of hit squad here in Los Angeles that's been tying up loose ends. You've got to get to Sittenfeld and lay this at his feet. Only then will you find out who's behind all this."

Deborah didn't reply, instead moving to a window at the end of the hall, where she looked out over the dark city. Michael wondered if she could see all the way to the ocean. When he thought she'd been hypnotized by whatever lay outside, she tapped the glass.

"What is it with the women who get close to you?" Deborah asked evenly. "Naomi is dead. Your wife, who I didn't have to make up reasons to dislike, is shacked up with a gangster. Even that whistle-blower from last year—what was her name? The Marshak case. She was killed, too."

Annie Whittaker.

"What did Oscar Wilde say about losing one's parents?" Deborah added glibly. "One is tragic but two is careless? You're getting careless, Michael."

"I fail to see the humor. We're talking about people's lives."

"Oh, me too," she agreed. "On my way here I got a call from Senator Elizabeth Calvin, the chairwoman of the Senate Select Committee on

Intelligence. She told me Charles Sittenfeld has been removed from our custody for his own protection and that the case against him was to be necessarily delayed while he assists the government with another matter. It was a very short call. I rang Men's Central Jail, and sure enough he was gone. Nobody knows where, either."

"Deb, you can't be serious," Michael said, pulse quickening. "If they think he needs protection, I'm right. There's an active threat here."

"She also informed me that Gennady Archipenko is a money launderer in his own right and did not have the authority to hand over sensitive records from within his own bank," Deborah continued. "He is being suspended immediately and investigated on charges of corporate espionage."

Michael couldn't believe what he was hearing. If this had been any other situation, he would have expected her to be frothing at the mouth in anger at having her authority challenged in this way. But instead she was taking it so placidly.

"I'm sorry, Deb, but I'm going to have to pursue this case with or without your support," he said. "If that means—"

"You were suspended two hours ago, pending an investigation into your own conduct with regards to Archipenko, but also your paranoid behavior following Naomi's death," she said. "I'm sorry."

It was the most hollow apology Michael had ever heard.

"Can't you see what's going on here?" Michael asked quietly. "I mean, the Senate Committee on Intelligence? There's something criminal going on between Sittenfeld's bank and the government. To hide it, they've got you doing their dirty work. You're as culpable as the junkie they handed a machine gun to who killed that waitress. But with tens of billions hanging in the balance, I guess what's the life of one mother of three making eight dollars an hour plus tips?"

"Is this the tack you plan to take with this, Michael?" Deborah asked.

"Damn right it is."

"Then you're fired," she said. "Effective immediately. I'm sorry you can't separate your emotional connection to this case from your professional obligations."

Michael tried to read Deborah's facial expression, but she was a blank. An impassive executioner going through the motions.

"You know I'm going to—"

"The next step is jail, Michael," Deborah said, cutting him off as she moved to the door. "I'd be careful when it comes to threats."

Michael said nothing.

"By the way, you mentioned that Archipenko came to the restaurant to tell you about his investigation into Sittenfeld," Deborah said, hand on a stairwell door. "Nothing was found at the scene. Did he give you anything? Files? Paperwork?"

"He hadn't wanted to bring anything to an initial sit-down," Michael lied. "He wanted to 'scope me out first.' His words."

"Ah. We'll look at his place. Speedy recovery, Michael."

Deborah exited. Michael waited until the door was closed a full minute, then rang Father Chavez.

Having discussed heady things at the construction site, Luis didn't mind switching to other matters as he gave Sebastian a ride home. He learned that his father had been homeless for a while, moving from an apartment he was evicted from to a shelter to the streets to a worse apartment to another eviction to time in jail to time on LA's skid row.

"I waited to die," Sebastian said. "I was so sure it was going to happen, and I didn't mind. But somehow my heart kept beating. Eventually, I realized that God wasn't done with me. He still had a task for me on earth. I stayed at a shelter for a while. Did whatever construction came along, even if it wasn't carpentry. I'm as good with a shovel as I am with a hammer. I finally met a guy on a crew who let me stay in a room in his house. I was there eight weeks. Enough time to save for my own place in MacArthur Park. He was an angel to me."

"Did you attend Mass?" Luis asked.

"Not at all," Sebastian admitted. "I went to AA meetings and found God on my own. It wasn't hard at all. He was waiting with his arms outstretched. As if he'd been across the street staring at me and I couldn't see him."

"And the work is regular enough now?" Luis asked.

"The work? Yes. Good pay? Not so much. We're always getting screwed. But then I met this one guy who is on retainer for a couple of restaurants in Hollywood. He does electrical, plumbing, you name it. When he has a job, he comes to me first. Worked seven-day weeks four weeks in a row for him. Made a thousand dollars."

Luis did a quick calculation in his head. If his father worked ten-hour days, that broke down to $3.50 an hour.

"That's great, Dad."

"I'm not rich, but I am happy doing the work. When I'm not working, I start thinking, and that's when I want to take a drink and have to lean on God. When I'm working, particularly when it's somebody who treats me with respect, I don't need that drink at all."

They went quiet for a while, Luis wishing he had something to say to break the tension, but nothing came. By the time they were most of the way to MacArthur Park, there didn't seem to be any point, and he remained quiet.

"Up at that corner is fine," Sebastian said, indicating a spot on the park's southwest corner. "I'd invite you in, but I have nothing to offer you."

Luis pulled the car up to the curb. MacArthur Park was one of the least safe places in the city after dark—bodies of homeless junkies were routinely fished out of the lake—so he didn't feel great about dropping his father off there. But his father had convinced him of one thing over the past couple of hours: that he was a survivor first and foremost.

"Why don't you come by St. Augustine's this Friday night?" Luis offered.

"I told you," Sebastian replied. "Not into Mass. It's about my relationship with God. Not a building or its priests. No offense meant."

"I know," Luis said, nodding. "It's a spaghetti dinner to raise money to send the kids at St. John's to see the Space Shuttle."

"To see it go up?" Sebastian asked, surprised. "Isn't that in Florida?"

"No, Dad," Luis said. "They brought one out here. Put it in a museum. The kids can go look at it up close and dream about being astronauts."

Sebastian laughed. "In that case I'll be there. Thanks for the ride." He climbed out of the car and was about to close the door when he turned back to Luis. "And you'll talk to Osorio? And your friends in the police?"

About Nicolas.

"I will," Luis said, wondering if he meant it.

"I know you miss him," Sebastian said. "And I can see how angry you are about it still. But don't let that anger take over. When you do, that's when there's no room left for God."

With that, Sebastian closed the door and headed away. Luis watched him go for a moment, thinking on his words.

He was pondering this when his cell phone rang. The hour was late, but the caller ID was from UCLA Medical Center in Santa Monica. He answered and was surprised to hear the voice of Michael Story.

"Father Chavez, I need a favor. It's a matter of life and death."

VII

When Michael was done explaining exactly what he needed done, Luis couldn't say no fast enough.

"What you're asking me to do is not only illegal," Luis said into the phone, "it's also morally reprehensible."

"People have died for what's on that key drive," Michael said. "They're not going to let me go near the crime scene. But a priest who is there on behalf of the waitress's family looking for personal effects?"

It disgusted Luis to hear the words. "Forget it, Michael. This is where you go too far."

"I'll call the police on the scene myself," Michael said. "They'll know you're coming. They'll let you in."

"No way. And didn't you say you'd been fired?"

There was silence on the other end of the phone. Luis thought they were done and was about to hang up when Michael jumped back in. "What if all this is Oscar?" Michael asked.

"You're grasping at straws, Michael. Hanging up now."

"I'm not saying it is, but he's got connections all over this city. If it's not him, why's he got you telling me to get off his back? You don't think the two things are connected?"

"I don't. I'm sorry you got shot up, but—"

"Jesus Christ," Michael said, reacting to something unrelated to Luis's words.

Luis rolled his eyes. "What? You got a new angle you're working on?"

"Got a text from one of the officers on scene. The waitress's kids were with a neighbor, but they were too upset to be at home. So they were taken to their church. Guess which one?"

Luis was stunned. He was almost back to St. Augustine's, but the tone in Michael's voice made him miss his turn. "No way."

"St. Augustine's. You know her? Carrie Meallaigh."

Luis felt horrible. Of course he knew her. She was a Sunday regular, eleven-o'clock service. Sometimes she came with her best friend, Mary something, who also had a couple of kids. He'd even spoken to Carrie recently when she'd asked about summer camp at St. John's for her oldest son.

His horror at the situation quickly turned to anger. Was this God? Was this how he put something in front of Luis now? Or was this merely how the world worked when one ministered to thousands of parishioners?

"So, it's not a lie," Michael said. "You're the family's priest."

Luis hung up the phone and pulled the car to the side of the road. He climbed out and stared heavenward.

Why?

This he needed to know. Did God know he was going to refuse Michael and put a parishioner in the way of a bullet? Of course not. That wasn't God. That couldn't be God. But the fact that he found himself even asking the question made Luis realize how far gone he was, how abandoned he felt.

But in this moment he had to choose. Would he stand there and feel sorry for himself? Or would he do what he knew he'd have to do from the moment Michael had said it?

He climbed back into the car and rang Michael. "I'm on my way to the scene."

"I already called ahead," Michael admitted.

Santa Monica was cordoned off, and traffic backed up for several blocks as it was diverted through the neighborhood. Luis parked at a meter and simply walked the half mile down.

As he got closer, he saw the media vans, then the reporters providing coverage for the eleven-o'clock news, then the police line. He approached the first officer he saw, explained who he was, and was let in a moment later. He worried that the cameras might turn his way, given his collar, but no one seemed to notice.

Luis had been to crime scenes before, but none like this. Though he understood there was only one fatality, it looked like a massacre.

How could one person do all this? he wondered, eyeing the shattered glass, splintered tables and bullet-riddled walls.

He'd expected to see blood, but there wasn't much. A few marked-off spots on the sidewalk outside, another pool near the window. But then he saw a stain easily a foot in circumference and knew he was gazing at the spot where Carrie Meallaigh had left this world. It had the same haunting emptiness as the place where his brother had died. The same futility. The same uselessness.

Why, God, why? Luis asked, knowing he'd receive no answer.

He was handed shoe covers and gloves by a forensic tech and told that Carrie's purse was under the counter. He went behind it, found the bright-orange bag with fringe hanging off that he recognized from Mass, and held it tightly in his hand. He then knelt and prayed for her, hoping she would find peace and that, eventually, so would her children. The crime scene, bustling with activity a moment before, went silent as others prayed as well.

When he was done, Luis ducked low to find the key drive Michael had described, almost panicked when it seemed to be absent, then managed to extract it with his index finger. He palmed it, not daring to slip it into his pocket until he was out of the restaurant.

"Please extend our condolences to the family," an officer told him. "Maybe it helps them to know we got the guy who did it."

But did you? Luis wondered.

As he made his way to the car, he called the parish and told them he had Carrie's purse. He then hung up and called Michael. "Where are you?"

Fifteen minutes later Michael was in the front seat of the parish car, turning the key drive over in his hand.

"Is the owner alive?" Luis asked.

"So far," Michael said.

"What're you going to do with that?"

"Well, I need to get to a computer that no one's looking at. Somebody knew where Naomi would be when they killed her. That same somebody knew my whereabouts when they took a shot at me."

"You're sure they were aiming at you?" Luis asked.

Michael shrugged this off. "If not me, then the man I was meeting with. Whatever the case, for safety's sake I have to assume my phone and my computer are compromised."

"There's a computer at the parish," Luis suggested.

"Yeah, the last thing I want to do is bring this down on your head. But I have an idea. Drive to Bel Air. Helen moved to a spot on Outpost, but she's still having work done on the old house, and she's working out of her home office there. I need one of her old laptops."

Luis was skeptical but wound his way through the sleepy neighborhoods up to Sunset Boulevard regardless. He crossed the highway, dodging the construction, and pulled through the gates leading into Bel Air.

The Storys' old house was impressive by any standard. With a large grassy front yard, a patio, and pool in back with a view beyond, it was the polar opposite of the homes of the congregates that Luis was accustomed to visiting. Even dimly lit with scaffolding up for painters and no furniture to speak of, it was still a palace.

Michael retrieved a spare key from the garden and moved to the back door. "Never told Helen about this one."

As soon as the door opened, an alarm sounded. Michael hurried to the box to switch it off, but the combination didn't work. "I guess Helen changed the code. Borrow your cell?"

Luis handed his phone over. Michael called the alarm company and had them turn it off.

"At least I'm still on the authorized name list," he said, handing the phone back to Luis.

Michael led Luis up the stairs to Helen's old home office. Though it was filled with boxes, there remained a desk, chair, and two plugged-in laptops next to a phone charger that made the space seem even more temporary than it was. Michael booted up the first one and took a key drive from his wallet.

"Moment-of-truth time," he said.

Luis watched as Michael inserted the drive into the USB port. A prompt appeared on-screen asking if he wanted to download its contents onto the laptop. Michael agreed, and the transfer took only seconds. When it was done, he selected the "Downloads" folder and gasped.

Under the long list of items from Gennady's memory stick were thumbnails of sixteen photos that had been downloaded, presumably by Helen, the previous year. They were each of Michael having sex with a woman Luis recognized from newspaper photos as Annie Whittaker.

"Aw, Christ," Michael said.

Meaning, Luis extrapolated, that Helen must've seen these without Michael knowing it.

"She never said anything," Michael said quietly, confirming Luis's thoughts. "But she must've known the whole time."

"Did you take them?" Luis asked.

"No, somebody who was trying to blackmail me did. I thought all that had been taken care of before he got the chance to send them. Guess I was wrong."

Michael highlighted the photos and deleted the lot. He then emptied the recycling bin on the desktop. Luis figured it was a futile gesture at best but didn't say anything.

"All right," Michael said, sounding crestfallen as he went to open the first newly downloaded file. "Let's see what Gennady had on these folks."

"No, that's fine," Helen said into her cell phone. "Thank you for the call."

Oscar watched her as she hung up, then came back to the sofa, where he was waiting with two cups of coffee, her expression unreadable.

"Who was that?" he asked.

"Alarm company," she replied matter-of-factly. "Michael broke into the Bel Air house."

"What the hell's he doing there?"

"I don't know. Might've needed a safe place to shower or something after the shooting. The company sent a car by and said there's an '84 Caprice out front."

"That's Father Chavez," Oscar said. "My old partner-in-crime is now your ex's partner-in-crime."

"He knows you inside and out? This Luis Chavez?"

Oscar knew what she was asking. He put his coffee down and looked her in the eyes. "You can ask me if this is my doing if you want to," Oscar said. "I won't be offended, and I'll tell you the truth."

"I know it's not you," Helen said, putting her hand on Oscar's leg. "You're not that petty. Once you met him face-to-face, you knew automatically that you were the better man, and you stopped caring as long as you knew that I knew that, too."

Oscar scoffed and kissed the top of Helen's head as she nestled into him. "It's sad how well you know me."

"Nah. What did you say once? It's nice to be known."

"Yeah," Oscar replied wistfully. "It can be."

"You think your priest friend believes Michael that it's some kind of conspiracy?" Helen asked.

"It's hard to say. Luis is having some trouble these days. God's not answering his prayers or something."

"What do you mean?"

"I don't know," Oscar said. "He feels this bond with God. God tells him to do this, do that, whatever. He discovered this connection after his brother died and it's what keeps him on the straight and narrow. You think I'm a crook—well, Luis was the wild one when we were kids. If he was on the streets now, he'd run 'em. If he was in prison, which is more likely, he'd run that, too. But he got God."

"He believes all that? That some guy in the clouds is talking to him?"

"You don't believe in God?" Oscar asked.

"Maybe when I was little, but I haven't in a long time. I never know what to say when the kids come home and their friends have talked to them about Jesus and the Bible."

Oscar shrugged. "Much as I hate to admit it, Luis has done a lot of good in this city in the short time he's been back. Now, if that's God working through him, fantastic. If he's got some crazy voice in his head that happens to be his conscience? I'm fine with that, too. The result is the same."

"But what if the voice is gone for good?" Helen countered.

"I don't know," Oscar said, shrugging. "It's such a part of who he is. Without it, he's missing a big piece."

"Then I hope the voices in his head start talking to him again," Helen said, sounding flippant.

"Don't be so superior!" Oscar said, swinging Helen's legs aside and pinning her on the sofa. "You hook up with one Latin gangster and suddenly you know all the secrets of the universe?"

Helen laughed and cupped Oscar's face in her hands. "Maybe I do," she said.

"Fine," he replied, kissing her back. "Maybe you do."

But even as they embraced, Oscar's mind wandered to the Bel Air house.

What are you finding out there, Luis Chavez?

Luis stared at the contents of Gennady Archipenko's drives. The numbers were huge, but Luis didn't know what they meant. There were dollar amounts in accounts listed only by number linked to other accounts listed only by number.

"What is all that?" Luis asked.

"Currency exchanges and money transfers," Michael said, writing a steady stream of dates and amounts on a nearby pad of paper. "These are all high-dollar amounts that required the approval of someone in the executive chain of command at the bank."

"This Charles Sittenfeld?"

"Yeah. Currency exchanges are typically where a lot of money laundering slips through the cracks. People take advantage of fluctuations in the exchange rate between, say, the dollar and the euro to make a few bucks on occasion, but it's hard to get away with it for long. The big money-moving through here, however, is being done with the ease of someone taking twenty bucks from their savings account and transferring it to checking. It doesn't make sense."

Luis looked at the numbers. There were tens of millions of dollars flashing across the screen. "Could it be fake? Some kind of smoke screen for something else?"

"That's what I'm trying to figure out," Michael admitted. "A bank like this has to answer to the Treasury and even submit to congressional oversight. If they actually moved this much money around, they'd be caught. So either it's some kind of dummy operation to hide something else. Or people on all levels are looking the other way. I'm pretty sure this is what Naomi found before she was killed."

Michael pointed out a few other transfers. "Here's a more typical one," he said. "You've got a charitable organization in Senegal communicating with Sittenfeld here in Los Angeles. Because of the US government's watchdog programs relating to charities they believe may have ties to radicalism, they have to jump through a number of hoops to free up a half million in donations to be transferred to a bank in Yemen. But because they're a nonprofit and their status is valid in the US, they're ICE hoops, not banking institution ones."

"And all the big transfers are also from nonprofits?"

"So far," Michael said. "Or at least groups that are using that status to move their money faster."

"Sounds like you need to talk to Charles Sittenfeld," Luis said.

"Yeah, but he's been moved out of here for his own protection," Michael said. "If I could just find him."

Luis nodded and indicated the numbers from which the money originated. "They never come in from the same account numbers, do they? It'd require some serious infrastructure to pull that off, wouldn't it?"

"Yeah, or you'd need to control a single bank," Michael said.

"Sure, but the numbers are so wildly different. You've got different bank reference numbers peppered throughout. They're not the same banks." Michael turned to Luis, who simply shrugged. "You're the one who knows this stuff. I'm looking for discrepancies on a screen."

"Well, keep it up," Michael said. "I'll check into the reference numbers. See if we can at least get a sense of what country these are coming in from."

Michael switched to the e-mails Gennady had pulled from the bank's servers relating to Sittenfeld. Luis saw these were from as disparate a group as a Chinese industrial outfit working on building a new railroad in Kenya and a Russian natural gas company. Luis wasn't sure if any of this was related to money laundering, but he didn't put it past any large company to be completely free of corruption.

All of a sudden, he saw something on the screen that was so unexpected, so out of left field, he thought he might fall out of his chair.

"Hey, will you go back? Maybe one or two pages?"

Michael bounced back up through the inbox until Luis was again looking at a cache of e-mails sent around the same time a decade and a half before. They were all pieces of correspondence between Sittenfeld and one Nicolas Chavez.

"It can't be," Luis said aloud. "Can you open one of those?"

"Um, sure," Michael said, clicking the keyboard touch pad.

The e-mail opened, revealing a short note from Nicolas thanking Sittenfeld for talking with him on the telephone. It seemed to imply that Nicolas had been mollified by whatever Sittenfeld had told him, and the words back from the banker were cordial.

Luis had to look at the e-mail twice to confirm what he already knew. First of all, it was his brother's e-mail address from so long ago. Second, the e-mail was dated three days before he was killed.

"Are there more?" Luis asked, voice wavering.

Michael went to the beginning of the conversation. It was Nicolas following up on the call, a document attached to the note.

"Open that," Luis commanded.

When Michael did so, a poorly scanned image of a bank transfer authorization appeared on the screen. Sittenfeld's signature was on the bottom, as was a dollar amount in excess of $10 million. The party for whom it was being approved was not mentioned by name. There was only an account number listed.

"What is it?" Michael asked.

"Nicolas Chavez was my brother," Luis said, mind reeling.

"'Was'?"

"He was murdered a few days after this last e-mail."

Michael's face registered surprise. He turned back to the transfer document and scrutinized it more closely. "It looks like Nicolas came across one of the transfers somehow. Was he working at a bank?"

"No," Luis said. "He was still in high school. He didn't have a job. He spent all his time at . . ."

Luis didn't finish his sentence. It was almost too crazy to comprehend.

"Can you search for correspondence between Sittenfeld and a Bishop Eduardo Osorio?" Luis asked, taking a leap.

Michael did. Nothing came up. Luis couldn't believe how relieved he felt.

"So what is that?" Michael asked.

"I don't know," Luis said. "Nicolas never mentioned talking to some banker. But we weren't exactly close at the time."

This was true due to the distance Luis kept from Nicolas and his devotions at the time. Now, more than anything in the world, he wished his brother could've felt like confiding in him whatever he'd been doing in his last days. But he had confided in someone. He didn't know if Osorio, in his diminished state, would remember any of it.

Still, he had to try. If this wasn't God laying out a path for him to follow, he didn't know what was.

VIII

Michael was feeling woozy by the time Luis drove him back to his house in Silver Lake, the pain drugs wearing off and a sense of general weariness setting in. Luis parked and helped Michael limp inside, settling him on the sofa as he went to the kitchen to get water.

Michael stared into the darkness of his house, puzzling out where to even begin with all of this. He had to get to Sittenfeld, but the Senate Select Committee on Intelligence? He'd had to google it in the car to figure out whom they oversaw.

"Are you going to be okay?" Luis asked as he returned with a water bottle.

Michael nodded, taking the bottle gingerly. It had been Naomi's, one she'd brought over for when she went for a run around the Silver Lake Reservoir.

"I know what you think of me, Father," Michael said. "And you're right. I haven't always been a good guy. But this case is a new one on me. There's no clear bad guy this time. It's this phantom murder squad that makes hits look like accidents or random events. But somehow they're tied to Sittenfeld, and somehow he's tied to the government. I don't know about you, but if I don't go after them for what they did to Naomi, I don't know what I'm doing on this planet anymore. And if they had something to do with the murder of your brother, well . . ."

"I don't know what I'm doing on this planet anymore if I don't go after them with you," Luis said.

Michael nodded. "There we are then. You go talk to Osorio, and I'll try and find Sittenfeld."

Luis got to his feet and headed for the door. "I've got morning Mass and then classes to teach all day tomorrow. I'll drive over as soon as that's over."

"Sounds good. Be safe, Father."

"You too, Michael."

As Luis left, Michael wished he'd found something better to say. He knew his association with Father Chavez was a marriage of convenience. He got access to cases he might not have otherwise, and Luis had the ear of someone who could get things done on an official level when he uncovered them. That the priest hadn't blinked when Michael said he'd been fired made him think Luis had at least some faith in Michael's own abilities rather than those of his office.

This gave Michael an idea. He grabbed for his phone, held it in front of one of the numerous pages he'd printed from Gennady's drive at his old house, and took a photo. He scrolled through his contacts list, found the right e-mail address, attached it to a blank note, and sent it off to someone he thought could help.

Then he passed out.

Oscar stared at the mixing bowl, knowing he'd screwed up. Helen had decided the kids should stay at home from school, given that their father was all over the news and they were rather freaked out. He'd let her sleep in, saying he would make breakfast, but had already used regular white flour instead of whole-wheat flour for the children's pancakes.

Helen would kill him.

He'd been making a double batch, so he'd also used up all the eggs and milk. He couldn't start over.

"Are the pancakes ready yet?" Denny asked over the blare of the television.

"In a sec," Oscar called back.

The kids were watching their second animated movie of the morning. Oscar had caught a few minutes of it over their shoulders and thought it was pretty funny. He'd even looked up who did the voices on his phone and was surprised to see he'd guessed right about a couple of them.

Wait. What?

Oscar leaned against the counter, staring at his reflection in the glass of the kitchen cabinets. He wore a tank top that revealed the legion of tattoos running up and down his arms, across his upper chest, and around his neck. Who was he that he should worry about using the wrong flour when making breakfast for kids who weren't even his own? He wasn't some suburban dad. He wasn't *Michael*. He was Oscar Beristáin de Icaza, former Alacrán *cabrón*, master car thief, Echo Park OG—

"Thank you for letting me sleep in," Helen whispered into his ear as he felt her arms encircle his midsection, followed by a kiss on his shoulder.

"No problem," he replied. "I do have to get down to the shop at some point . . ."

"Don't worry," Helen said. "I called in at the dealership and canceled my day. I'll stay here with the kids. You've done plenty."

This concession wasn't enough, though. Oscar felt something boiling up in him. He wanted to pick a fight with Helen. It didn't matter over what. He needed to lash out and assert dominance.

She must've felt this tension in his body, as she retreated.

"Hey, I'm sorry about all the Michael stuff right now," she said. "I can only take so much of him in our lives going forward. The bare minimum feels like too much sometimes. But that's why it was nice to end the day with you last night—just the two of us. It was a big mess, it was exhausting, but we got through it together. Maybe tonight we'll find a different way to relax."

Oscar expected a sexualized image of Helen to pop in front of his mind's eye. When instead he visualized the night before, her body pressed against his as they fell asleep, he put his arms around her and kissed her on the lips.

"Sounds good," he said.

Helen kissed him back, then retreated to the bedroom. "Used the wrong flour again, huh?" she said as she ducked past the door.

Oscar sighed. *You've met your match, de Icaza.*

There was a knock on the front door. Oscar hadn't thought anyone who'd target Michael would head up his way, but he'd had a couple of his boys come up and keep an eye on the street. He didn't exactly like having people know where he lived, either, particularly as it was no longer within his domain of Echo Park, but he'd convinced the guys it was Helen's place, not his.

But when he looked through the keyhole, he saw the face of the devil.

"I already heard your footsteps," the man said calmly through the door, his thick accent suggesting an upbringing in Southern Mexico. "Open up."

Oscar wanted more than anything to keep this man out of his house. Wanted to put up a wall between them if he could. But his fingers simply went to the knob, turned it, and swung the door wide.

"Thank you," the man said, stepping over the threshold.

He was in his fifties, with a thick head of black hair that rose from his scalp, adding a couple of inches to his squat frame. He wore jeans, black cowboy boots, and a dress shirt. It was his face, however, that was unforgettable. With drooping jowls and sagging bags under his eyes, it looked like it was melting off his skull. His heavy eyelids gave him a sleepy Basset hound appearance, but the black eyes staring out from behind them were those of a demon.

"Help you, man?" Oscar asked, glancing up and down the street but seeing no sign of his boys or anyone the new arrival had brought with him.

"You've been looking for me," the man said. "I thought I'd drop by."

"I don't know where you get your information, man, but—"

"You were looking into the death of Naomi Okpewho. I'm the one who killed her. So I suppose you're looking for me."

The children had gone quiet. Oscar didn't think the children could hear the man's admission but didn't want to chance it.

"Why don't we speak on the balcony?" Oscar said.

"Okay," the man said.

Oscar ushered the man with the melting face, the very person he'd glimpsed on the gas station security footage he'd immediately destroyed, through the house to the balcony that overlooked Hollywood. Though he hadn't seen anyone arrive with the man, he was under no illusion that the fellow was alone. As they walked past the sofa where Helen's kids sat, each gave the stranger a look, then turned back to the TV. The visitor didn't glance their way once.

When they were on the balcony, Oscar closed the door behind him.

"Who are you?" Oscar asked. "Maybe if we were properly introduced we could talk business."

"People who know my name wish never to see me face-to-face. Those who don't, when they find out they wish they hadn't."

Oscar considered making a sarcastic remark, but some distant instinctual response warned him away. Like how animals instinctively knew a rattlesnake's rattle was bad news. This guy was that.

"If you were anyone else, Mr. de Icaza, I'd hack off your limbs and burn whatever's left of you alive in a barrel of oil while your family here asphyxiated on the smoke," the stranger said. "But you have an interesting alliance with the Chinese, don't you?"

Oscar did. Following a crisis with the Los Angeles triad, he'd been approached about opening new avenues of distribution to hotels and restaurants for triad-controlled liquor, produce, and linen suppliers. It wasn't the most profitable arrangement, but how this man knew about it, Oscar didn't know.

"What's it to you?" Oscar asked.

To Oscar's surprise, the visitor laughed. He kept right on laughing, too, clapping his hands as he did. But there was no joy in the laughter, only mockery.

"You are me," the man said when he'd finally recovered himself. "Me before the world took everything away. My family, my friends, my dreams. Anything that made life worth living. That's when I learned what real suffering was. But as you learn to withstand it, you also learn to inflict it."

The stranger nodded down the balcony toward the glass door that led to Oscar and Helen's master bedroom. Oscar looked, perplexed, but then noticed movement inside. He crossed the distance in two steps and saw a pair of men in black masks holding the half-dressed Helen down on the bed, a knife to her throat. Her mouth was only half-covered, but she didn't scream. He knew she didn't want to alarm the children, but as her gaze met his, he saw nothing but pure terror.

"What do you want?" Oscar asked, turning back to the man.

"It's not what I want but what you want," the stranger said. "I don't care if I walk out of here with my hands clean or stained with the blood of five corpses. Your triad partners would be upset, but if it came to that it would be manageable. But I am willing to let you convince me to allow you and your family to live."

And there it was. If Oscar murdered this man where he stood, then ran to the kitchen to retrieve the 9mm automatic he had hidden behind the refrigerator to deal with the stranger's accomplices in the bedroom, it would be the same as if he'd killed Helen himself. There was no telling how many others there were stationed around the house, either. He'd probably be dead within minutes, if not seconds, same as the kids.

The stranger had discovered his Achilles' heel. He was no longer the man with nothing to lose. Now he wanted something out of this world. Helen made his life worth living.

"I'm nothing," Oscar said. "Go ahead and kill me. I've got nothing of value to offer you. Nothing you couldn't get on your own. But that woman you're disrespecting in there right now is different. She's smart. She's connected in ways you couldn't dream. You think the Chinese care about me? Nah, they'd get themselves another Mexicano. It's her they care about. She's bringing them legit."

"Is this a threat?" the stranger asked.

"No, not even. This is a guarantee that when you're operating in Los Angeles and you need that local partner, I'm the one who makes sure your face doesn't show up on some gas station CCTV camera a few exits up. I'm the one who keeps guys like me from nosing around the auto impound. And I'm the guy who makes certain your junkie gets a ghost gun that doesn't fall apart three clips in. But also it means that when your boss or bosses need that LA hookup that goes over your and my pay grade, I introduce them to the crooked ex-wife of the city's chief deputy DA."

The stranger said nothing for a moment as he seemed to ponder Oscar's words.

"So willing to make your wife a whore," the man said. "Maybe there's a future ahead of you yet. One other thing I'd like to ask you if that's all right. This priest Michael Story reached out to—Luis Chavez. He is known to you, is he not?"

Oscar stared at him. Finally, he asked, "What do you want to know?"

A moment later the stranger tapped on the bedroom window, then moved to pass through the house back to the front door. Oscar waited for him to say something else but was blocked by the two men coming in from the bedroom, who followed him out.

"Wait a sec," he called after. "So, we have a deal?"

The man with the melting face turned back to him, the clumps of skin hanging from his jawline shivering as he did. He said nothing but didn't have to. Oscar closed the door, locked both locks, then raised the kick-proof jamb. He then remembered that the two men had found some other way into the house and knew the locks meant nothing.

He raced to the master bedroom, only to find himself looking down the barrel of a gun.

"Hold up!" he said, sliding to the floor.

But Helen didn't lower the pistol, keeping it aimed chest high at the doorframe, tears streaming down her face. She was on the bed with her back against the wall, a blanket wrapped around her torso.

Oscar inched up to the foot of the bed. "Put that down," he whispered. When Helen's eyes remained fixed on the darkness beyond the doorway, Oscar crept up next to her. "Hey, Helen. It's me. Come on. Look at me."

Helen didn't lower the gun but did turn to Oscar after a few more seconds. He held her gaze, then reached out his hand to take the gun. She wouldn't loosen her grip at first, but he kept her looking at him, and she finally let go. He placed the gun in a drawer in the nightstand, then wrapped his arms around her.

"He's gone," Oscar said. "We made a deal. He's gone."

Helen stiffened, turning to him with eyes afire. "You made a deal with him? I thought you'd killed him. But instead you've invited him into our lives? What the hell have you done?"

She pushed Oscar away and climbed out of the bed, making her way to the bathroom.

"Helen!" Oscar shouted, hurrying after her.

She closed and locked the bathroom door behind her. Oscar knocked but heard nothing except more tears. He considered knocking the door down but knew how little that would accomplish.

"Pancakes!" one of the kids, Marlo this time, called from the living room.

"One second!" Oscar bellowed before turning back to the door. "*Helen*. We have to talk about this."

But the soft crying had given way to real sobs. Oscar listened for a moment longer, then headed back to the kitchen.

Michael woke up the next morning to a number of waiting texts, voice- and e-mails. He sifted through them until he found the only one that mattered, a reply to his photo of the page from Archipenko's files.

It read simply, *Oh good. You're up.*

As he was trying to figure out what this meant, he heard a sound from the kitchen. He swiveled around on the sofa to see a woman in either her late forties or early fifties trying to work his coffee maker.

"Um, hi?" Michael said.

"Ah, I have to add water," the woman said. "Couldn't read what was right in front of me."

Michael got his feet and realized how unsteady he was. He caught himself on the sofa's armrest.

"Careful there."

Michael realized who she must be. "Where's Jeremiah?" he asked.

"Reassigned," the woman said, turning to extend her hand. "I'm Special Agent Joyce Lampman."

"Can I see some identification?" Michael asked.

Lampman indicated the kitchen table. Her badge, a business card, and a letter from the Bureau were laid out on it. He skimmed the letter, from someone he'd liaised with at the FBI's Los Angeles bureau at some time or another, which told him that Joyce was a solid citizen.

As he contemplated whether it was a forgery, Michael heard quiet footsteps coming up behind him. He turned as a man who looked as if he'd stepped out of the cage at an MMA match came up behind him. Even the fellow's chin looked like something he could beat a man to death with.

"We didn't have time to take Doug for a walk this morning, so he's full of nervous energy," Lampman explained without menace. "Besides, you seem to have a bit of a target painted on your back these days. Doesn't hurt to bring backup."

"You always break into people's houses?"

"When they don't answer the door or their phone for ten minutes when we come calling. Now, if we're wasting our time here, let us know, and we'll leave. If not, maybe you can tell us what's on your mind."

"I sent the FBI that note because I was hoping you'd be useful to me," Michael said. "I've come across something major. Only, my own office doesn't believe it and got shut down by the government. I turned to you because I was hoping you might have a work-around."

Lampman considered this for a moment, then started the coffee machine. It ground the beans, then poured her a perfect eight-ounce cup.

"Nice toy," she said.

"Bought it for my ex-wife, but she never used it, so I brought it here," Michael said. "Who has Sittenfeld?"

"CIA," Lampman said, then took a sip of the coffee. "He's not only outside of our grasp, he's outside our jurisdiction."

"They took him out of the country?" Michael asked, incredulous.

"They did, also to keep him out of harm's way should his old partners surface looking to silence him. We've been onto him for a lot longer than your late girlfriend. Only, we knew enough to stay off his radar. I'm sorry for your loss by the way."

"Why CIA?" Michael asked.

"Well, it turns out that our Mr. Sittenfeld and his bank didn't just launder money coming into the country, he also laundered it going out."

"What do you mean?"

"When CIA needed to, say, send a few million dollars of black budget appropriations money in 'logistical support' to rebels in Syria or an opposition candidate's dirty tricks campaign in Ecuador, they couldn't write a check for what some might construe as an act of war. So they used Sittenfeld to move money out of the country. Still want to know how deep this rabbit hole goes?"

IX

Luis pointed to an image of the solar system on the chalkboard. "You've probably all heard that it wasn't until 1992 that Pope John Paul II and the Catholic Church admitted that the earth revolved around the sun, but that's not entirely true. It took that long to say that it was wrong about condemning Galileo for saying so."

There were a couple of smirks from Luis's students. Luis shrugged.

"The church is not infallible," Luis said. "Not to quote the loyal opposition, but the Dalai Lama XIV suggests that if scientific advances proved elements of Buddhism wrong, it'd be Buddhism they'd have to change, not science. But what's important for you to know is that the church did at least consider the theory of a heliocentric galaxy when it was first proposed by Galileo. One of my favorite parables relates to this. Galileo was friends with a cardinal of the church, Robert Bellarmine, who was a professor of theology at the Jesuits' Roman College. Galileo was a very outspoken individual and told anyone who would listen that his telescopes and astronomical observations proved that the earth was in motion around the sun. Pope Paul V told Bellarmine to warn Galileo to stop preaching apostasy. Emphasis on *preaching*. He could believe anything he wanted. He simply couldn't try to convince others. Did Galileo listen? No. He kept right at it, until he was finally arrested and brought before the Inquisition."

The classroom smelled blood. Now he had their attention.

"Galileo brought with him his telescope and charts. He pointed the lens to the stars and said that if they only looked, they would see. The stars remained fixed in position. It was the earth that moved. But the cardinals refused. It was easier to put their heads in the sand. But then Robert Bellarmine, well into his seventies, rose to his feet and walked to the telescope."

Luis paused. He tried to remember when he last had the whole class this rapt.

"Bellarmine closed one eye and looked through the lens. He stared for a long moment, then finally pulled away and shook his head. He hadn't seen what Galileo said he'd see. Galileo was later forced to submit to house arrest, and his works were banned. The cardinals breathed a sigh of relief. But Bellarmine wasn't being willful. He'd grown blind in his old age, too blind to see."

Luis turned back to the chalkboard and tapped the sun.

"Sometimes people look away and reveal themselves as so lacking in their own faith that they fear something on the other end of a telescope will shatter it," Luis said. "But sometimes we look right at it but are too blind to see. Which is worse?"

Fearing a trick, the students didn't have an immediate answer but seemed suitably intrigued to think about it for the rest of the day. Luis had been pondering it since the moment he'd dropped off Michael the night before. The bell rang, and Luis dismissed the class, happy to have an off period.

The answer should be simple. The priests who chose not to look did so of their own free will. That Bellarmine was too blind was God's doing. But when Luis thought of it in terms of his brother, the young would-be priest who rose to look, and how it cost him his life, he wondered if it was so simple.

Pastor Whillans had told him the story, this after saying all he needed to know of man could be found in Joyce's *Ulysses*, and told Luis there wasn't an easy answer. At the time Luis hadn't believed him. Now he was beginning to.

What obsessed him the most about his brother's e-mails to Charles Sittenfeld was the maturity of the voice. Nicolas came off as a much older man, a sign of how much his involvement with the church had matured him. But Nicolas hadn't even had a bank account, to Luis's knowledge, much less any reason to contact Sittenfeld. The only thing Luis could think of was that it had something to do with Sacré Coeur's finances, but even that didn't make sense.

But from what Luis could glean about Sittenfeld from Michael and the files, the imprisoned banker had been well on his way into upper management at the time of the correspondence. He was already too high up in the corporate structure to be handling some minor account issue for the church.

He had to put it to Osorio.

By the time he'd finished the evening Mass and conferenced with the other priests, it was dark. Luis had called Father Belbenoit to say he was coming and was told that Osorio had been in poor health that day.

"But your visit may cheer him regardless," the priest had said.

Luis would've gone even if Osorio was on his deathbed.

As the other priests filed to the rectory, Luis retrieved the keys to the '84 Caprice and headed east of downtown. As he drove, memories of his brother flooded back to him. At first they were the familiar ones. The two of them at play in their small backyard. The first time they'd been allowed to walk to school together without their mother.

A surprising one also returned to him. It was of when Nicolas first invited him to pray. Nicolas had become a choirboy at age eight and was newly absorbed by his position. Being only six at the time, Luis had readily accepted the invitation.

"Now close your eyes and listen for God," Nicolas had said.

"I thought he was supposed to listen for me," Luis had replied.

"You don't ask for things. You can't make God do stuff. You put your faith in him and ask for his guidance in what is troubling you."

"Why can't I ask him for things?" Luis had asked. "He's God. He makes things happen."

"The Bible tells us not to put Christ to the test," Nicolas had chided. "That is not why we are here on earth."

Luis recalled this when he later came across the scripture Nicolas alluded to—1 Corinthians 10:9. He'd done as his brother suggested. He knelt. He prayed, or at least tried to. He'd listened for God. He remembered hearing many things that he would later understand to be his mind answering for itself. He also remembered feeling silly.

"Nothing happened," Luis had said. "Did he talk to you?"

"No," Nicolas admitted. "But I asked him to guide you into a better understanding of him. To let you feel his presence."

Luis then remembered the last time Nicolas asked him to pray with him. He'd scoffed, accused his brother of wanting to play dress up, and had walked away. Though this had been Luis's response for months, Nicolas would be gunned down less than a week later. Luis almost had to pull the car over as he recalled this agonizing memory. Knowing now what Nicolas might've been dealing with, he wished he'd said something different. Anything to open a door.

There was nothing he wouldn't give to pray with his brother one more time.

Luis was comporting himself when his cell phone rang. It was his father. He considered not answering but knew that would only invite more calls.

"Hey, Luis," Sebastian said. "What are you doing tonight?"

"Work around the church," Luis lied. "Preparing for Sunday."

There was a silence. "No you're not," Sebastian said, his voice wavering, as if unhappy to call his son out for lying. "I know that you're not. I know where you're going. God told me. He's worried about you. He thinks you shouldn't."

Luis closed his eyes. This was not what he needed to hear right now.

"Dad, God doesn't say that to people."

"He did to me," Sebastian insisted. "He knows you're going to see Bishop Osorio."

Luis was surprised, then remembered that he'd told his father that he would speak to Osorio about Nicolas. Still, to play this God card so blatantly felt crazy.

"Have you been drinking?" Luis asked.

Sebastian said nothing for a moment. "I can't believe you asked me that, Son."

"Why? You've been back in my life for a few days after being absent for years. I have your word that you've stopped, but listen to yourself. You sound delirious."

"Is that what you tell your parishioners when they hear answers to prayer?"

"I have learned over much time what is delusion and what is divine," Luis said. "That's not what's happening, Dad. You don't sound well."

"I am not well!" Sebastian said. "How can anyone be well when their Lord gives them such a direct warning? I didn't go to work today I was so troubled. I stayed in prayer throughout the day. I ate nothing! I drank nothing!"

And there it was. This was the crazy person Osorio had needed Luis to dispense with. Though his words weren't slurred, Luis recognized this version of Sebastian. The paranoid one. The unhappy one. It was all coming back. Only now he was an adult and didn't have his mother to run interference for him.

"All right, Dad," Luis said. "You should probably get some sleep. I will come over there in about an hour and we'll talk about it. All right?"

"Are you still going to Osorio's?"

"Yes, Dad. I have some new information. I'll share it with you tonight. Okay?"

"Not okay! Don't go over there!"

Luis hung up. The phone rang again, and Luis sent it straight to voice mail. When it rang a third time, he turned off the ringer and tossed the phone aside.

He was off the highway a few minutes later, nearing Osorio's Silver Lake house. It occurred to him that he'd been over here twice lately—once to meet his father on Sunday night, the next time to deliver Michael home. The idea of Michael Story and Bishop Osorio living only a couple of miles from each other was so strange, until he realized how quickly the area was being gentrified.

Soon there would be no more Osorios and four times as many Storys.

Chavez Ravine all over again.

Though the lights were off in Osorio's duplex, his bright-white Cadillac was parked out front. He checked the clock. It was barely eight o'clock. He could be over to his father's apartment before ten and hopefully back to St. Augustine's by midnight, giving himself at least five hours of sleep.

God, why hast thou forsaken me? he thought, only half-serious.

Luis locked up the Caprice and headed to the front door. He knocked, but no one answered. He tried a second time and heard movement from upstairs.

It was followed by a strangled cry.

Luis grabbed the door handle, but it was locked. He raised a foot and gave the door a couple of swift kicks. It held fast.

My kingdom for a hammer and a flat-head screwdriver.

He ran around the side of the house and found the back door locked as well. With no other choice, he picked up two stones from the garden, threw one through the back window, then chipped aside the remaining glass with the other.

"I'm calling 911!" a voice called through the night.

"Do it!" Luis yelled back, taking as much of the priest out of his voice as he could.

He climbed inside, finding himself in the kitchen, but saw no one. Hearing something on the second floor, he raced to the stairs, not knowing if he'd be met by a volley of punches or bullets. When he reached the landing, however, he found only the prone form of Father Belbenoit stretched on the floor. Luis turned him over and saw an inch-wide wound cut across his torso. It looked like a bloody sash.

Belbenoit angled his head to meet Luis's gaze and indicated a closed bedroom door. "Eduardo," he whispered.

Luis pushed the door open with his foot. On the bed was Bishop Osorio, clearly dead, his bedsheets stained with blood. Luis couldn't tell where he'd been wounded but doubted it mattered.

Belbenoit grabbed Luis's arm and pointed down the back stairs. "They . . . escaped . . ."

"I can't leave you like this," Luis said. "You're dying."

"Pray for me later," Belbenoit said, his voice barely audible now. "I'll take my chances with God."

Luis nodded, lowered Belbenoit to the carpet, leaving him to God without delivering last rites, and raced back down the stairs. He reached for his phone, only to remember he'd tossed it aside in the car and hadn't retrieved it.

Brilliant.

When he was back on the street, the night was silent save for the sound of distant traffic. He looked up and down the block but saw no movement. He took off running in one direction, hoping the arriving police would see his Roman collar and not shoot him on sight for fleeing a double homicide. He'd barely gone ten feet when he heard the muffled sound of a truck engine roaring to life a block up from Osorio's street. He ran to the nearest intersection and dashed up the cross street as fast as he could.

The good thing about growing up not far from here was that he knew the streets. When he reached the next intersection, he went over the area in his mind. Left ended in a dead end, while going right the street would wind all the way down the hill. He ran in that direction long enough to see a black Bronco, taillights dimmed, blowing a stop sign as it wove back toward the highway.

Bingo.

The other good thing about knowing the streets was that Luis remembered where there were pedestrian stairs between houses. The truck would have to stay on the roads, but Luis could cut all the way down the hill to Sunset Boulevard below, likely beating the truck. He wouldn't be able to stop it, but he would see where it was going and maybe even get a look at those inside. If he was really lucky and they were really stupid, he might catch a glimpse of the license plate.

Taking the stairs three at a time and fearing he might topple over at any moment, Luis made it to the bottom in record time. There was only one road that spilled onto Sunset, three short blocks from the entrance to the freeway. If it were him, this would be the route he'd take.

But as he caught his breath, there was no sign of the Bronco. He waited in the shadows of the nearest storefront, a shoe repair outfit with pairs of shoes literally cascading off shelves and piled in the aisles, and looked back up into the neighborhood and down the streets.

They couldn't have gotten past me, could they?

Seconds passed, then minutes. The silence of the night was broken by sirens, and he saw the distant flashing lights of approaching police cars. There was still no sign of the killers.

It didn't make sense.

It dawned on him that they must've anticipated that the police would be on their way. If they were the one car speeding from the scene, likely filled with blood-soaked passengers, they'd be pulled over immediately. The cops would've had reasonable suspicion without a doubt.

Instead they'd need a place to hunker down until the first wave of police passed.

As the first squad cars raced by, Luis looked back up to the quiet neighborhood. The Bronco was still there somewhere.

Hoping to keep a low profile, Luis moved back up the concrete stairs at an unhurried pace. The Bronco could be anywhere, he knew, but they'd have had to park in a hurry. In a neighborhood this crowded, it might mean a fender jutting out into the street or a vehicle parked in front of a driveway.

But as he walked, his senses heightened, the scent of exhaust fumes crept into his nose, providing him with a direction. He was sure there were other cars on the road that night, but this was the heavy stench of a gas-guzzling 4x4. He looked up and down a dark residential strip, bracketed on both sides with run-down houses framed by useless chain-link fences. He didn't see anything at first, so he took a few steps down the block, hoping his luck would last.

As the street curved around, he spotted it. The Bronco stood in front of a small house and, counter to Luis's theory, was perfectly parallel-parked. There were no lights on inside, no silhouettes. The vehicle was completely still.

For a moment Luis wondered if they'd gone two blocks, dropped the truck, and hopped into the real getaway to avoid detection. But as he stared at the truck, he could no longer be certain it was the one he sought. There were probably as many black Broncos in East LA as there were stars in the sky.

Still, he wanted to be sure.

He crept closer, kneeling low to the sidewalk as he scanned for a license plate number. As soon as he had that and maybe a quick look inside, he'd go back to the Caprice, call it in to the police, and ring Michael to tell him the latest. As he got closer to the Bronco, he noticed it still had its license plate. Not something he expected to see on a getaway truck.

He went around to the front of the truck and put his hand on the hood. He'd expected it to be cool but was rewarded with warmth. It had likely been stolen, used with the intention of sending police off on a wild-goose chase.

With the three killings thus far, this hit squad of Michael's had proven themselves perfect at setting a scene, whether it be staging an accident or doing their work through a junkie with a gun.

Who are *these guys?*

They had clearly anticipated every move the police would make. And what about him? It occurred to him in the last second before the blade entered his lower back and lifted him off the ground that he had walked into a trap. The pain was delayed by a microsecond of mere discomfort that soon erupted into a feeling of intense, devastating heat. As it consumed his every nerve ending, Luis's vision blurred and his heart rate accelerated. His body wanted him to flee, to run in any direction he could, but his muscles wouldn't respond.

As the blade was wrenched around, tearing through his flesh and making Luis feel as if he were being severed in half, the man with the knife leaned in close.

"Vamos a ver si su dios detiene esto, Padre," a voice hissed in his ear.

Let's see if your god will stop this.

Luis was thrown forward, the blade making the wet sound of the gutting of a fish as it was yanked free from his lower back. Luis, in agonizing pain, forced his eyes open, catching sight of his attacker reflected in the side of the car. He couldn't discern much. He was Latino, maybe forties, maybe fifties. As he faded into unconsciousness, he was struck by the fact that it looked like the man's face was melting.

PART II

PART II

X

When the bullet had entered Gennady's throat, he'd known he'd never be whole again. In the moment he thought he would die. It was as if a great clawed hand tore at his neck. If he moved in any direction, he feared he might snap his own spine, the pain was so great. He thought he'd been paralyzed or even partially decapitated. Then he'd mercifully lost consciousness.

When he awoke again, after several surgeries and an induced coma, the first thing he saw was Nina. She was gripping his fingers tightly and smiled.

"Papa!" she exclaimed.

He immediately let out a sob. Only it didn't resemble the anguished cry he'd expected. Instead it was strangled squeak of a suffocating mouse.

"You'll never speak again," Yelena explained to him after she'd shuttled the children from the room. "The bullet missed the major veins, arteries, and your spine by millimeters. You should have bled to death, but you didn't. You should be paralyzed, but you're not. For that I'm thankful."

At first, this didn't make sense. Gennady tried to respond and was punished by what felt like ball bearings moving around inside his neck. Yelena put a hand on his chest. Gennady waited for tears to glass her eyes, but they didn't. He was relieved. He pointed to a pad of paper and pencil on the nightstand. She handed them over and he began to write.

Michael Story? He scrawled.

"He also survived," Yelena said, bristling. "But why were you meeting with someone from the DA's office? We've already had calls to the house. Clients are worried you were selling them out."

Gennady wrote, I'll contact each directly. Say this was about my bank job only. Mention Charles Sittenfeld's arrest.

"How is that our business?" she countered. "You put your trust in a police officer?"

He knew she meant Michael but didn't correct her. Someone came into our house. Related to Sittenfeld. They cannot do that.

Yelena read this twice, then set the pad back down. Gennady waited for her to walk out of the room and out of his life, never to look back. Instead she took his hand and squeezed it tight.

"You're right, Gennady," she said. "I shouldn't have doubted you. Business is business, but family is off-limits."

Gennady nodded. He picked the pad back up and wrote a name and phone number on it, asking Yelena to call the person and have them contact him back via text once she'd set up a new phone for him that would only be for this purpose. She read the name on the page and frowned.

"Who is Miguel Higuera?" she asked.

Gennady wrote, He does what I do but has more connections. If anyone will know where to start, he will.

Yelena folded the piece of paper and put it in her pocket. She kissed Gennady on the lips, then headed for the door. "We'll see you soon," she said.

Gennady watched her go, then sank back onto his pillow. He wasn't sure he would've been able to take down all those responsible without her help. Now it was only a matter of time before they realized—too late—how imperiled they were.

"There used to be a million ways to launder money," Special Agent Lampman had explained to Michael at the beginning of their marathon debriefing in a small hotel conference room downtown. "My favorite will always be the casino scheme. Certain casinos used to be given some of the same privileges as banks. A high roller, a *whale*, wouldn't roll into town with suitcases full of cash. No, they'd wire the money into a temporary account with the casino, usually based overseas, and use it to draw chips at the tables."

Michael had nodded, though listlessly. On the way here, they'd driven past the exact spot where he'd last seen Naomi alive, last kissed her, last touched her hand.

"If they lost a hand and needed another ten thousand dollars in chips, it came right out of the casino account," Lampman continued. "Of course, they picked casinos where they tended to 'win,' so when they left they'd take back whatever was in that account in the form of a check. They could then walk it into any bank in the US or Europe and cash a check on gambling winnings that would normally be taxed. Money laundered."

"Not anymore?" Michael asked.

"Reined in somewhere around the end of the eighties to the beginning of the nineties," Lampman said. "It became harder and harder to find rogue governments, like Panama, who'd help out for a price. Heck, it used to be the only way a Swiss bank would open its records was if Justice could prove the money was linked to organized crime. Now they lift their skirts for anyone. Which leads us to Sittenfeld. Why don't you catch us up on your side of the investigation, and we'll try to fill in anything you might not know?"

Michael sighed, believing this was a way for them to get everything they wanted without giving anything in return. When they started laying out large chunks of the case, however, he realized that they'd been looking at Sittenfeld and his dirty dealings for a lot longer than he had.

When they were finally done, Michael outstretched his hands. "I know you're focused on the money-laundering side, but my case involves capital charges. They can't be made to go away. He was arranging to have his wife murdered! Money changed hands!"

But Michael knew he wasn't talking about Evelyn Sittenfeld right now. Not being able to prosecute Charles Sittenfeld meant there'd be no justice for Naomi. And he couldn't live with himself if that happened.

"You want to bet?" Lampman asked. "All it will take is convincing the spouse, the lawyer, and the LAPD reservist not to testify. And all that takes is money. If they want too much, CIA will lift back the curtain—a surprise audit, passport trouble, surveillance. Whatever it takes to make them see their way to ending their cooperation with the prosecutor's office. Your boss—sorry, former boss—will have no choice but to drop charges. I'd be surprised if there'd even be a civil suit after that."

"What's to keep him from doing it again?" Michael asked.

Lampman shrugged. "Nothing. But I imagine that'll be Europe's problem. Or some friendly nation out there he's done favors for. Used to be deposed dictators those courtesies were extended to. Now it's bankers."

Throughout the day Lampman's task force brought pages in to her from Archipenko's hard drive. Some she looked at, a few required instructions she hastily delivered to her agents, but her attention soon returned to Michael. A couple of times, however, she'd stepped out of the room, to return five, ten, or even twenty minutes later. Michael was exhausted by being made to sit still but truly had nowhere else to be.

He worried how this would all look to Deborah when she found out he'd been talking to the Feds but decided he didn't care. His future in Los Angeles was about finished anyway.

When Special Agent Lampman came back after being gone for a particularly long time, though, Michael was ready with an idea.

"If the CIA has Sittenfeld because he's involved in some kind of black budget operation with them, so be it," Michael said. "But I refuse to believe he's the only one at his bank who was involved. If we find out who all the players are, whose money it originally was and who laundered it into the United States in the first place, we can take what we know about Sittenfeld's operation and use it to see who those other bankers or even other banks are. Then we go after those Sittenfelds. They can't all work for the CIA."

"And how do you expect to determine who these other operators are?" Lampman asked. "From the best we can tell, it could be foreign governments, Russian oligarchs, drug cartels, terrorist organizations, even major stock swindlers. That's a pretty wide field."

"Yeah, that'd take too long," Michael said. "We ask Sittenfeld."

Lampman scoffed. "Brilliant plan. I see why you get all the head-lines around here but still somehow managed to get yourself fired."

"Leave that part to me," Michael said. "Just tell me that wherever they've got him stashed on this planet, you've got the budget to send me there."

Lampman sat up straight. "You're serious?"

"Sittenfeld has to be feeling rather confident about now. If I can get face-to-face with him, I think I can get what I need."

"No way they'll let you speak to him alone."

"Even if I'm his lawyer?" Michael asked.

Lampman turned to her left long enough for Michael to realize there must be a camera recording everything.

"You find a way in, and we'll send you anywhere on earth first class, all expenses paid," Lampman said, pointing a crooked finger at him. "I mean, you'll have to keep your receipts, but still."

"Done," Michael said, glancing to the window. "Give me forty-eight hours."

It had been dark outside for a couple of hours now, and his still-aching body had him looking forward to sleep. He wondered if he'd see Naomi in his dreams again.

Lampman had exited after Michael's last statement but came back in now, phone pressed to her ear. "What was the name of that priest you mentioned? The one whose brother had written to Sittenfeld all those years ago?"

"Luis Chavez. Why?"

"He was stabbed in Silver Lake. Two blocks from where they found the dead bodies of two other priests. It's about to hit the news."

"Christ!" Michael said, getting to his feet. "Who are the other priests?"

Lampman waited a moment as she listened for the answer coming from the other end of the line. "A Father Uli Belbenoit, and then a Bishop Eduardo Osorio. Either name ring a bell?"

Michael leaned against the conference room table, unsure how to process this. "Yeah, the bishop. The second Luis saw Nicolas's name in the Sittenfeld files, he asked for a search on Osorio. Nothing came back, but he was probably heading over to talk to him about all this."

"Looks like this hit squad is at it again."

"Yeah," Michael said wearily. "You said he was stabbed. Is he alive?"

"That's an excellent question," Lampman replied. "He was rushed to Kaiser. Went through several surgeries. Once he was stabilized, an ambulance arrived to take him to Cedars for even more work. He never arrived."

Luis thought he was dreaming. He stepped in and out of thoughts and conversations like a time traveler careening through the past. But when he recognized one as a memory, he leaped to something else, and the process had to begin again.

These moments were interspersed with lucid ones where he felt as if he was waking up but didn't know where he was or who was speaking to him. He felt confusion but no pain.

The only constant from waking life to the dreams and back was the image of his father. Sebastian materialized in some long-ago moments as he appeared now, an older man in voice and body. But then in contemporary ones he was the man he'd been twenty years earlier, faster and more agile. Quicker with a joke.

It was so confusing and propulsive that Luis felt as if he were hanging on for dear life as he was swept through the past and present. He had no control of what happened next and no sense of time. He wondered if this was what death was like and if time had slowed to the point that he was experiencing his last moments on the planet in a matter of seconds.

How would it end? Would the bright lights become gray? Individual objects and people blob into a single mass? What would be the last color he saw as his mind's eye gently closed?

Then all at once, life returned.

Luis's eyes opened, and he found himself in an unfamiliar room. It was warm, but a light breeze came in through the window. The room itself was unadorned, to the point of being almost bare, though the walls, ceiling, and floor appeared to be new. Luis perceived his body spreading out on the bed before him under a heavy woolen blanket, but it seemed detached. He raised his arm, but it took such a Herculean effort that he brought it back down to rest a second later.

He looked to the window, but there was nothing to see but sky. He glanced to the room's single door but saw only a doorframe with nothing attached. Beyond it was a hallway and some sort of open-air pavilion. He could hear sounds echoing up and realized he was on an upper floor of a building.

He moved his left arm, only to receive a searing pain in return. A needle was inserted into the back of his hand. A tube behind the needle ran up to a saline drip, hanging from a hook on the wall behind him. A stainless-steel table to his right was the only furniture in the room other than the bed.

He tried to move the wool blanket aside and found he was tucked into the bed by white sheets. He didn't think he was a prisoner so much as someone that needed to be immobilized. He turned back to his hand and had a terrible thought. It wasn't his. The color was wrong, faded and blanched, and the muscles weak and reduced. This was the arm of someone much older and malnourished.

He opened his mouth and realized what had felt like a dry stone held between his teeth was his dehydrated tongue. He tried to run it over his lips but found them cracked and dry. He craned his neck around to look for water and finally saw a crucifix with an image of the suffering Christ on the wall over his head.

I'm in a hospital.

It was his first coherent thought. He tested his legs and found them stiff and sore, as if he'd run a marathon. When he tried to sit up, pain erupted from his side with such ferocity that he thought the blade that had been driven into him was still lodged in his body. He lay quietly for a few minutes to catch his breath and allow the torment to subside.

Stabbed. I was stabbed.

The memories came back quickly now. The Bronco. Father Belbenoit and Bishop Osorio. The man with the melting face.

Nicolas.

He flashed back to the blade penetrating his flesh and recalled his body's spasms as he fell to the ground. The last thing he saw was the reflection of the man in the side of the car. But something had happened to this memory. He was now looking at it from the point of view of Nicolas lying shot in the street. Instead of the black Bronco, there was the house at 6780 Diaz Boulevard.

But where was he now? This didn't look like any of the many hospitals he'd visited in Los Angeles to tend to the spiritual needs of the sick and dying.

He closed his eyes, shut everything else out, and began to pray. He didn't know if he'd find God there, but he hoped to find more of himself. His mind was muddy and troubled. He needed to center himself.

He didn't know how long he stayed like that. He waited for someone to enter, but they never did. He heard people pass in the hallway, the sound of vehicles on the road outside, even what he thought was a faraway gunshot, but he remained alone. At some point he blinked and it was night. He blinked again and it was morning. The room remained unchanged. He was almost afraid to speak, fearing what might happen if he did.

What if the wrong people came?

When he opened his eyes next, he found someone staring back at him from beyond the doorway. It was an old man wearing a loose-fitting shirt and cloth pants and carrying a broom. He was looking at Luis as if waiting for confirmation as to what he'd seen.

Luis raised his right hand as high as he could, which meant about two inches off the bed. At the gesture, the old man turned and shuffled off down the hall.

Okay.

A moment later Luis heard two pairs of running feet hurrying down the hallway. Into the room burst a pair of middle-aged nuns in full habit. They raced to the side of his bed, overjoyed.

"*¡Padre! Usted ha regresado a nosotros. Es un milagro!* A miracle. You are with us."

Luis tried to speak, but no words emerged.

"You are in a hospital in Mexico," the older of the two nuns said in Spanish, as if reading his mind. "The town of El Tule in Michoacán. We have been so worried about you."

"How long?" Luis managed to croak.

"Twenty days," the nun said, checking Luis's pulse by a watch pinned to her habit. "I am Sister Vera Monte. This is Sister Marisol Klaveno."

Luis nodded by way of greeting. He tried to lift himself up again but was gently pushed back down by Vera.

"You need to rest," the nun said. "It is enough exertion for today that you have woken. That's very good. But right now efforts like that can be costly. Please. Lie back. Maybe sleep more."

Luis didn't argue. *Michoacán? How did I get there?*

He was asleep before he had an answer.

When another morning came, Luis awoke to find his father asleep in a steel chair at the foot of his bed, hand resting on Luis's ankle.

Is he why I'm here? Luis wondered.

His leg shifted, rousing Sebastian. When the older man saw that his son was awake, he smiled wide and clapped his hands.

"So, the nuns were right. Alive and alert. Thank God."

"One out of two," Luis said. "The sisters said I am in Michoacán?"

"El Tule," Sebastian said, slowly easing himself from the chair to rise. "A couple hours west of Morelia."

After steadying himself, Sebastian bent to unlatch the caster locks on each of Luis's bed wheels. He slowly wheeled the bed over by the window.

Given that the hospital he was in seemed fairly new, Luis was surprised to look out not over a metropolis but a midsize town of mostly one-story buildings stretching out a few miles. A truck passed beyond the hospital's gates, kicking up a cloud of dust the color of sand. Below the window was a courtyard, complete with concrete benches and religious statuary.

The other buildings in his sight line seemed small compared to the multistory hospital.

"Do you know this place?" Luis asked.

"It's farm country," Sebastian said. "This is the largest town for miles. An outpost in the shadow of the Pico de Tancítaro, off Highway 37, that'll take you all the way to Playa Azul. The farmers bring their produce into the city, as most of the work here is in packing and preparing for export. It's poor, but so is the rest of the area. Your mother and I came once for a funeral. Your great-uncle's."

This rang a distant bell in Luis's memory. The funeral was before either he or Nicolas had been born, but their mother spoke about attending, as it had been one of her only trips to Mexico after leaving in her youth.

"He was a priest, my great-uncle?"

"He was," Sebastian confirmed. "The fear was that you might be killed in the hospital. So I knew I had to get you somewhere far away but also safe. This seemed like a good answer."

"How did we get here?" Luis asked.

"Oscar. He paid for a private flight. We landed in Uruapan, and then an ambulance drove us here. This hospital, San Juan Diego, has close ties to the El Tule diocese. The local parish priest, Father Arturo, has been our primary benefactor, even making sure you had a private room. Sandra's uncle's name carries weight around here. Father Arturo has even put me up in his parish rectory, an apartment building a couple of blocks from the church, San Elias Nieves."

Luis stared out at the unfamiliar landscape, wondering how long he'd stay. He had to get back to his parish, to his life, to the real world. Mexico, particularly this far south, might as well have been on another planet.

"Did the killings stop?" Luis asked.

Sebastian nodded gravely. "Osorio and Belbenoit were the last. Many think you were kidnapped and are now dead. Only Oscar's pilot knew where we were going. Oscar said he didn't want to know."

Because he'd have to tell the devil, Luis thought.

"To preserve that," Sebastian said uneasily. "You shouldn't call the States, contact your parish, or ring that deputy DA. If someone's looking for you, I'd be afraid it could lead them—"

"Don't worry, Dad," Luis interrupted. "I have no intention of calling anyone back home."

Particularly as it seems God might've placed me precisely where I need to be.

XI

Michael relished the look on Deborah's face as she went over the letters in her hands. Her eyes flicked from the one in her left to the one in her right, then back again, as if to compare the wording.

And why not? Michael thought. *They practically say the same thing.*

"What is this, Story?" Deborah asked.

"A courtesy," Michael replied. "You did fire me, but I thought you should know—"

"Know what? That you found an end run to keep your name in the game? Fine. You've done that. Now you can leave this office."

She slapped the letters back onto her desk. Michael looked again at the letterhead, the first being from the director of the FBI's office and the other from the attorney general of the United States. He couldn't quite see the signatures on the bottom of each but knew they were authentic. It had taken some doing, but Special Agent Lampman had brought him onto the FBI investigative team as a civilian contractor.

As it turned out, Deborah hadn't necessarily meant her words to be taken as gospel when it came to firing Michael from the DA's office, so both Justice and the FBI had reached out to her for clarification. She'd backtracked, been made to reinstate Michael in order that he continue to be paid by the City of Los Angeles, and the two letters Michael presented to her confirmed that he was now a special liaison.

"They're using you, Michael," Deborah warned. "This is the FBI. They don't care about you. All they want is to glean everything they can from you, maybe make a few high-profile arrests, then ride back to DC."

"More than you're doing, Deborah," Michael shot back, folding the letters and returning them to his coat pocket. "And at least they're using me to try and prosecute a crime. CIA's using you to protect a criminal. You know who else was protecting a criminal? The guys who killed Naomi."

Michael turned for the door. He expected Deborah to retort, curse him, or make excuses. When none of this came, he glanced back to her. She was already facing away, staring out her window at the view of Grand Park.

"If you're going to leave, Michael, that was a great line to do it on," she said.

"I'm sorry. This one's personal to me."

"And it's not to me? I'm the one who plucked Naomi out of that mentorship program in the first place. You know why? Because she reminded me of myself. A young woman of color trying to kick ass in the big city going after the big fish. She didn't have a corrupt bone in her body."

Unlike the two of us, Michael inferred, completing Deborah's thought.

"That's why we can't let this slide," Michael said. "How many times have men like Sittenfeld gotten away with murder because of their connections? I'm sick of it. And yes, willing to sacrifice my career over it."

"So anything less makes me a sellout, huh?" Deborah asked.

"I didn't say that."

"You didn't have to," Deborah retorted. "But do you even have a plan? Other than 'get Sittenfeld while thumbing your nose at the government'?"

"I do," Michael said. "I'm close to implementing it, too. There's just one piece of the puzzle I can't find."

The third day after he first awoke, Luis rose from bed. On the fourth he made his first walking journey, going the dozen feet or so from the bed to the bathroom, which had gone completely unused up to that point. No matter how he tried to mitigate against the pain in his torso, it still shifted as he walked, driving the invisible blade inside deeper and deeper.

But the indignity of having to be changed by the sisters was too much. He had to be able to relieve himself. Unlike in a big American hospital, where every room would have had a bathroom, San Juan Diego's had one three doors down the hall. Halfway there he almost turned back to use a bedpan, but something yanked him forward like a cord. He was so unsteady as he drew down his trousers that he had to stabilize himself against the wall.

He'd begun to assess what had happened. He was supposed to be dead. There was no question of that. The blade had been aimed directly at his kidneys, a shot generally more lethal than a knife to the heart. It wasn't like the attempt on Michael's life, where a junkie was handed a machine gun down the block from a group of armored-car security guards. No sure result there. But the man who'd stabbed him had killed two other priests.

How could Luis have survived?

¿Un milagro?

A miracle was the one conclusion that made sense. All those platitudes about Nicolas (*His work on earth was done, so God called him home*) to Baby Cynthia (*God wasn't done with her on earth*) came to him at once.

God wasn't done with him yet. It wasn't his time. He had put this case in front of Luis for a reason.

But what is that reason?

When Luis was on the way back, he felt his legs might give out at any second and held on to the wall with both hands to guide himself. The hospital was three stories high and had a central atrium that let in light from a skylight, however dusty, overhead. It was strikingly decorative compared to the more functional buildings Luis could see from his window. Given the number of people he could hear moving in and out of the emergency suites below, as well as the rooms on his level, he wondered if the space would've been better served by having two full floors for beds.

Though they were always busy, Luis knew the sisters must've seen him on his journey to the men's room, but none offered him help. When he finally reached his bed and climbed in, he discovered why when Vera appeared in the doorway, delighted.

"Well done," she said, hurrying over to take his pulse. "If we helped you, you wouldn't push yourself as hard."

Ah.

"Has my father come in today?" Luis asked. "I wanted to talk to him about the town."

"No, he's working at the school again. Should be by at the end of the day."

"The school?" Luis asked, surprised. "Is he teaching?"

"Oh no," Vera replied, arranging the blankets around him. "It's still under construction. It's being erected behind San Elias Nieves. Though Father Arturo refuses to hear of payment for your hospital bill, your father offered to put hammer to nail as a means of recompense. Turns out he's quite the carpenter."

"He is," Luis agreed. "But I'm the one who owes Father Arturo a debt."

"He won't hear of that," Vera said. "He's very much looking forward to meeting you when you're back on your feet. Now rest."

Gennady hadn't known what to expect when he typed Miguel Higuera's address into his phone's GPS. He didn't recognize the street name and there'd been no zip code. So when it appeared that the house was in a tiny cul-de-sac high up in the hills off Mulholland Drive, tucked in alongside some of the most valuable real estate in the city, he was surprised. Miguel was a tech for Dzadour Basmadjian's crew out in Glendale who did a version of what Gennady did, setting up shell corporations and front businesses for the Armenian mob.

But that was like being an IT guy for organized crime. Not exactly the highest-paid person on the totem pole.

They'd met through happenstance. A partner of Basmadjian was so impressed with Miguel's work that he wanted to hire him to set up something similar for his outfit. Once Basmadjian told him that Miguel was strictly in-house, Higuera had passed along Gennady's name as a recommended outside contractor. Gennady had never heard of Miguel Higuera and was surprised the young man had heard of him but was nevertheless grateful for the business. When Gennady contacted Miguel to thank him, despite being wary of being in another's debt, Higuera joked over a secure IM line that the client would prove to be more trouble than he was worth.

This was eventually proven true, making Gennady curious about meeting this valued and prescient young man. Now, with his neck still visibly bandaged despite a high-collared shirt, Gennady made his way into the hills to finally sit with this mysterious tech head.

The last few weeks had been difficult for Gennady and his family. Getting accustomed to his inability to speak had led to a thousand problems, some minor, some major, but all with emotional consequences. Nina thought her daddy's silence was some kind of game, as he didn't look all that different, did he? So she tried to get him to talk but never could, frustrating her to no end.

Initially, Gennady's injury was simple to explain to people, as the shooting in Santa Monica was fresh in their memories and easily referenced. A few weeks and a couple more mass shootings in the press and the incident was a distant memory, requiring a few more hand gestures or Yelena's intervention. Gennady hadn't wanted to socialize anyway, staying at home with his family since the shooting. The trek to Higuera's house was his first solo excursion.

As he wound up Beverly Glen into the hills behind UCLA, Gennady went over what he wanted to ask Miguel. A quick inquiry had revealed that the tech freelancer seemed to have easy access to almost any computer system in the world, "tech freelancer" being a euphemism for "master hacker." That he didn't use his abilities to engage in blackmail or the illegal sale of stolen high-dollar software, as others might, told Gennady that Miguel was happy keeping off the grid as much as possible.

So why such an exclusive address then? Why not a shack out by the Salton Sea?

As he turned into the cul-de-sac and glanced around to the three small houses that made up the block, the answer was no more forthcoming. There were tremendous views of the neighboring canyon, particularly the one that matched Miguel's address. It easily cost a million dollars, despite the slightly seventies architecture and décor. It looked like the home of a pair of semi-hippie retirees, not a master crook trying to hide away.

Gennady parked and walked up to the front door. Though he'd communicated that he couldn't speak, he still worried about having to pass any kind of verbal test to prove his identity. He knocked and waited, but no one came to the door. He knocked a second time, but again nothing.

He was about to text Higuera when a teenage boy on a rusty bicycle wheeled past.

"Looking for somebody?" the kid asked.

Gennady pointed to his throat and shook his head to indicate he couldn't speak.

"You a salesman? 'Cause no one's home."

Disconcerted, Gennady took out his pad of paper and wrote, Looking for a friend.

"What's their name?" the teenager asked.

Gennady added, Friend is overstatement. We have a mutual acquaintance. I'm here about hiring them for a job.

"What's the name?" the teenager repeated.

Becoming aggravated but sensing the teen might have something to do with Higuera, he wrote, I have the address, not the name. I thought this would be a business.

"What business?" the teen asked.

They print T-shirts, he continued, wondering if this was some kind of a test to see if he'd blow Higuera's cover if this was indeed his home. I work at a law firm. It's for our softball team.

If this was some kind of test, Gennady had no idea if he was passing or failing.

The boy squinted up at Gennady after reading the latest. "Nobody like that around here. What happened to your neck?"

Gennady walked back to his car. He climbed in and was about to turn the key in the ignition when he saw the boy step into the house behind him.

Strange.

Before he could start the car, however, the engine roared to life on its own.

What the hell?

He grabbed the wheel, but it jerked from his hands, turning counterclockwise. Though the gearshift didn't move, the car rolled forward. Gennady stomped on the brake, but nothing happened.

Oh God.

He flipped the switch for the emergency brake, but the car kept moving. He tried it a few more times to no avail. When he looked back up through the windshield, he saw that he was inching closer to the edge of the cliff. He reached for the door to bail out, only to find it locked.

He was going to die.

That was when he spied the teenage boy approaching with an iPad. He sidled up to the driver's window and nodded to Gennady. "Why did you set up Michael Story?"

Gennady stared at the boy in disbelief. Ignoring him, he punched at the window. When it wouldn't give, he leaned back and kicked at it with both feet. It wasn't only shatter resistant but bulletproof, something he'd had done for both his vehicles. A decision he now regretted more than anything else.

"Did they get to you in some way?" the teen asked. "Make you some kind of offer? Anything?"

Gennady snapped out of it and shook his head.

"It's a hundred-foot drop," the boy said. "So unless you want your last words to be a lie, I'd lay it for me: Why did you set up Michael Story?"

"Gnnnh," Gennady groaned, his throat throbbing from the effort. The car was only yards away from tumbling over the edge now. *"Nnn!"*

"Come on now. You write something on that pad that tells me how they got to you and maybe—*maybe*—I'll send a few hundred thousand grand to your wife and kids. What do you think?"

Gennady grabbed the pad and wrote a single line. He slapped it against the window.

"'Go near my family and you die. No question.' Brave words for someone who can't even get out of a car."

Gennady sat in silence. He was done here. He could no longer see the patch of grass between the two houses. The car's front bumper was already over the edge.

"Okay," the teen said, touching a button on the iPad.

The car stopped rolling. Gennady stopped breathing.

"Park it over there," the teen said, nodding to a spot in front of the seventies house. "Then when you're done pissing yourself, join me in that other house."

The boy went inside the house across the street, closing the door behind him.

Gennady grabbed the door handle and, finding it unlocked, scrambled out of the car. He ran around to the other side, opened the passenger-side door, and plucked the 9mm automatic from under the seat. He made his way up to the door of the house the teen had disappeared into, ready to blow the kid away.

"Mr. Archipenko," the teen called from inside. "I told you to park your car. Then we can get down to talking about who sent that bullet through your throat."

Gennady hadn't known what to expect, but it had not been on his list of possibilities that the master hacker and tech expert for the Armenian mob would be a teenage boy—one who had threatened to kill him no less. He jammed the gun into his waistband, returned to his car, and reversed it into a spot in front of the house. He stood there for a moment, figuring he should hightail out of there, but was riveted in place regardless.

"Well, come in!" the boy said through the open door.

Gennady entered to find what looked like the teenager's oversized bedroom rather than a living room. Clothes were piled everywhere. The largest flat-screen television he'd ever seen dominated one wall, with multiple game controllers on the floor in front of it. Elaborate-looking bongs were set up on the coffee table like trophies. A stack of sneaker boxes stood in one corner, reaching all the way up to the ceiling. There were boxes and boxes of cell phones and iPads, with dozens more out of their packages and lying around the room.

Miguel was seated on the sofa, an iPad in his hands. He held it out to Gennady and indicated a chair. "You probably type faster than you write," Miguel said. "Use the text screen. Words'll come up on the television."

Gennady took the iPad and sat. Who are you?

"Miguel Higuera. But you knew that."

You know who is behind all this.

Miguel read this from the screen and nodded. "I have an idea. I don't know how all the pieces fit together, but I'm pretty sure I know who put that bullet in your neck."

Gennady was confused. He eyed Miguel a moment before typing. It was that junkie.

"Yeah, right. You think somebody shot you in the voice box by accident? These guys don't miss. They didn't miss when they killed Naomi Okpewho. They didn't miss when they killed those priests. And they sure didn't miss when they shot you in the neck. And it wasn't some junkie either. He was down the street. You got shot from behind. Angle of difference of about twenty-five degrees, but that's everything. Or didn't you realize that?"

Gennady had no idea what Miguel was talking about.

"The man who shot you is named Munuera, but no one calls him that. He was born in Acayucan or maybe Puerto Escondido or maybe Arriage in Chiapas."

What do they call him?

"Ah, many things," Miguel replied. "El Hombre Invisible he gets a lot, but everybody in a cartel tries to put on that name, right? He's also Cara de Fantasma and the Ten-Thousand-Dollar Man. This because he recruits the poorest of the poor to be hit men alongside him. They're like the Sinaloa version of Middle Eastern martyrs brigades. When you join, it's the equivalent of putting a bounty on your own head. When you die, your family gets the money. You'd think they'd let themselves get shot, but it becomes a pyramid scheme. You survive one job, and the bounty rises another ten thousand dollars. The most he's ever given out is fifty thousand, almost a million pesos."

He's with the cartels? Is he a boss?

"Not even close," Miguel said. "He's either too crazy or too shrewd to want any power. He prefers to be the most useful angry dog in the kennel. They say he looks like one, too. His face is all messed up with scars—maybe from burns, bad plastic surgery, or just all his bones fusing back at odd angles after he took a few bats to the face." Miguel pointed to a pile of equipment on a nearby table that looked both mechanical and electrical. "He's also the guy who modified Naomi Okpewho's car into a self-driving vehicle, which he then hijacked and drove off a bridge. I had it done to your car last night to see how easy it was. My boys were in and out in twenty minutes. I figure they did Naomi's car while she was eating dinner."

It was a lot to digest. Gennady had barely considered the drug cartels, as their control shifted so often. In the late seventies and early eighties, the prime movers in the drug trade were the Medellín and later Cali Cartels in the cocaine-producing regions of Colombia. After the death of Medellín boss Pablo Escobar and the dismantling of the Cali operation, the cocaine trade became more and more controlled by elements in Central America and up through Mexico.

Previously, Mexican drug lords had been relegated to transport, providing a means for South American drugs to reach their North American users. Times had changed. The sort of drug war that had turned Colombia into an inferno of murder and kidnappings in the eighties had now come to Mexico, resulting in tens of thousands of deaths over the past decade.

It didn't make any sense for these shifting regimes to all have partnered with Charles Sittenfeld, given how many years the man seemed to have been working as a high-dollar money launderer.

"Before you ask, no, despite uncovering evidence that some invisible someone made regular payments to offshore accounts controlled by Sittenfeld, I couldn't link those payments to any of the Mexican drug cartels past or present. I went back further and couldn't connect him to any of the Colombian cartels either. These guys are good, but they're not *that* good. So if we're agreed it's drug money, it means they went through that invisible third party. Best I can do is check when deposits were made to Sittenfeld and try to match the dollar amounts to transfers out of cartel accounts. But that's nothing you can build a case on."

So it's a dead end? Why is this 10K guy involved then?

"That's the ten-thousand-dollar question, isn't it? But there's always been invisible hands like you and me out there making connections between the bad money and the good. And laundering through American banks is as good as it gets. What you have to do is look for the original 'you and me' who put them together way back when. Find that silent partner, and you've got the story. Until then you've got nothing."

XII

It had been weeks since Luis had prayed through the Divine Office over a full day, from early-morning prayer to vespers. He felt compelled to set aside his own prayers for guidance and go through those prescribed by canon law. He remembered the breviary Bishop Osorio tried to give him and wished he'd been able to put aside his arrogance long enough to accept it. He did what he could from memory, which wasn't much.

When the sun rose the next day, the biting feeling of the phantom blade in his back had subsided, and he asked Vera if she thought it would be all right if he went for a walk around the grounds.

"Are you sure, Padre?" Vera asked. "The worry is that you might pop something. Not a stitch per se, but a muscle not fully healed. Maybe a vein? They recommended you stay in bed for at least a couple of months."

"My stasis may help my body, but it is doing more harm than good to my mind," Luis responded. "If I feel or hear anything pop, at least I'll already be at a hospital."

Vera shrugged and retrieved a robe for Luis to wrap around the cloth pants and shirt the hospital had provided. With that draped loosely around his torso, Luis made his way to the elevator.

The elevator proved to be the hardest part of the trek. Given the modernity of the rest of San Juan Diego, that the car bounced and hitched like a century-old freight elevator was a surprise. It was one more thing to add to the disorienting nature of his visit to Mexico. He thought of Mexico as hot, so being in a temperate climate almost identical to that of Los Angeles occasionally had him waking up thinking he was back home. The food was completely different than what he was accustomed to at St. Augustine's, but his mother had occasionally cooked the tamales, tlayudas, and chileajos of her youth in Oaxaca, and the carnitas, morisqueta, and churipo of Michoacán weren't so far off. He'd had trouble with some of the heavily accented Spanish he heard as well but only in the same way he did working with his parishioners and their many dialects.

But as he stepped out of the hospital building—if only onto the grounds—for the first time, he finally felt as if he had stepped into Mexico. The air felt different, and the scent of trees and dust, muted but detectable in his room, was omnipresent here. With the soil free from a man-made protective shell of asphalt and the sky unblemished by layers of pollution, Luis sensed this was what it smelled like to be out on the earth itself.

Michoacán—at least this corner of it—felt like an impermanent post the natural world could encircle and reclaim overnight, taking its tens of thousands of people with it.

The courtyard, which he had to himself, had two paths, a few statues of saints not unlike the ones placed around St. Augustine's, and a couple of benches. The hospital, which horseshoed around it, was then itself surrounded by a high white wall topped with short iron stakes. It stood in sharp contrast to the serene atmosphere of the rest of the small compound.

A truck rumbled past on the other side of the wall, though Luis could only see the exhaust and dust in its wake. The exhaust dissipated quickly enough, and Luis watched as the dust gently settled onto the wide leaves of the courtyard's plants, giving them a hazy yellow tint.

At a corner of the courtyard closest to the wall, Luis spied a pay phone. He was surprised at the sudden urge to contact Michael Story. He wanted to know if there'd been any kind of break in the Osorio case or information confirming that Naomi had been murdered, though he doubted there was. How could there be? The attacks had been precise and deliberate. And with Naomi's death believed to be an accident, seemingly unconnected.

Osorio. Uli. Naomi . . . Nicolas?

Charles Sittenfeld.

Luis was more certain than ever that this man, whose face he had never seen, was the key. And that someone had been willing to kill to safeguard him. To keep his secrets—and theirs—from coming to light. Luis felt a renewed sense of purpose. Not the kind born from the booming voice of God filled with confidence and authority, but a distant whisper.

He would continue to follow the path laid before him. Nicolas's death had led him to the church and now might lead him full circle to his brother's killer.

Maybe God placed me where I need to be and will let me figure the rest out.

The man who attacked him had such a distinctive indigenous Mexican-Indian accent, his words betraying an upbringing in the south of Mexico. Whoever was behind the deaths must have had authorization from someone south of the border, where Luis now found himself. The only organizations with that much power in Mexico were the cartels. And the cartels didn't lend out their top killers. That meant there was a connection between the cartels and Charles Sittenfeld. It stood to reason that their connection to the banker was money—the root of all evil. Perhaps the money that his brother had uncovered.

The only thing that didn't make sense in that equation, however, was that this meant his brother had flagged something to do with the Mexican cartels years before they were operating in a way that would generate the billions Sittenfeld had laundered.

"¡Buenos días, Padre Chavez!"

Luis turned to look for the speaker but saw no one.

"Up here, Father!"

Luis glanced to the hospital's second floor and saw a fiftysomething man with graying hair, a thickening paunch, and most indicative to his identity, a Roman collar, smiling and waving back to him from a window.

Father Arturo, Luis realized.

"Wait for me!" Father Arturo said, ducking back in.

Less than a minute later the priest emerged from the hospital, arms outstretched. "Father Chavez! At last we meet. It is so nice to see you on your feet."

"Father Arturo," Luis said, embracing the man. "I have much to thank you for."

"What is better than helping a brother priest?" Father Arturo asked. "Even more so, God is allowing me to repay the debt I owe to your mother's uncle, Ianis. It is fortuitous."

"You knew him?"

"He was a mentor to me!" Father Arturo enthused. "Many here in El Tule still speak well of him. He was one of the first great bishops to rise from Michoacán and from one of the poorest parts of the state. He never forgot what he came from and encouraged those who also emerged into success to lend a hand back."

"I don't know much about him, unfortunately," Luis admitted. "When I was a child, the names of these distant relatives went in one ear and out the other."

"But here you are now, a priest in his old parish," Father Arturo said. "Perhaps more remained than you knew."

"Perhaps," Luis allowed.

"I know they wish you to stay in your room and most definitely to stay on the grounds, but there is a wheelchair inside that door," Father Arturo said conspiratorially. "We could compromise by having you ride as I push. Not far, just to the parish. I would love for you to see what your father has been up to on our behalf."

Luis nodded. There was nothing he was more curious about.

Father Arturo fetched the wheelchair, an uncomfortable, spindly thing with half its spokes broken or thinned by rust. To Luis it was a chariot capable of carrying him farther from his hated bed.

"The ride might be bumpy," Father Arturo warned him. "I'll do my best."

Luis settled in the chair and looked back to the hospital, expecting to see an angry Vera looking at him, but there was no one. San Juan Diego wasn't particularly busy, though he occasionally heard the conversations and moans of other patients late at night, the cries of relatives when their loved ones passed on. Luis reflexively said a prayer for each even if he could not say their names.

The town was a reflection of its hospital. Though there were more people in the streets and in the neighboring buildings, it still had a ghost town quality to it. It was as if the place could easily sustain twice the population but folks had chosen to move on regardless.

"Everyone is at work," Father Arturo said, slowing the wheelchair to let an old pickup truck pass on the dusty road. "There are two factories outside of town and a distribution warehouse. The farms feed everything here, but there is still poverty."

Luis nodded, taking in his surroundings as best he could. The city was hilly and the roads all single lane. It was hard to differentiate which were private residences and which were commercial businesses, given the lack of advertising. They passed a restaurant with a single awning, which read "Tortilleria Gomez," with the hours of operation painted on an outer wall. Unlike an American restaurant, which would be overflowing with a myriad of ways to call attention to itself, that was it for Tortilleria Gomez.

Without so much competition, I guess you don't have to go overboard, Luis thought. *People know where the restaurants are.*

They turned a corner, though without street signs of any kind, Luis had no idea if he'd be able to retrace his steps. This made a small part of him—a remnant of the boy he had been long ago—a bit uneasy. But this was another city, another life.

As they continued on their way, that small part of Luis also noted that there were dogs everywhere. Dogs hurrying down the street, dogs barking from behind garage doors, and even dogs on rooftops. Maybe he'd be able to backtrack once he became familiar with their barks.

"We are nearing the center of town," Father Arturo explained. "The church is very old and unadorned, but it is still in the middle of things, near city hall, near the market, and so on. We don't often get tourists, but I have seen a few take photographs of our façade, and it is on the Internet and in certain guidebooks. The best ones, naturally."

They reached one of the largest structures Luis had seen so far, a construction site that took up half a block.

"Coca-Cola!" Father Arturo announced as if naming a saint. "Six hundred jobs! They've been promising it for almost a decade. We've been praying for it for twice as long."

"Why the delay?" Luis asked, staring up into the steel girders making up the building's two-story, warehouse-like frame.

"They were going to break ground a few years ago," Father Arturo explained. "Then the La Familia Cartel went to war against about everybody. The state was thrown into chaos. What business wanted to be exposed to that level of violence? They were the darkest years of our lives. But slowly order has returned."

"The cartel was eradicated?"

A beneficent smile, free of condescension, spread across the priest's face. "The head of La Familia was killed, and the cartel somewhat disbanded. But no, Padre. Not eradicated. A new governor was elected. New understandings were reached."

Luis didn't need clarification. Father Arturo changed the subject by pointing to a church spire rising over the nearby buildings. "That is my home. That is San Elias Nieves."

The church was a modest affair compared to St. Augustine's or, really, any of the cathedrals in the Los Angeles diocese. But compared to the other buildings on its own block, it more than did its job, drawing the eye and inspiring awe with the skyward reach of its spire. The façade was plain, save two statues tucked into niches, one of Jesus Christ and the other of the Virgen de Guadalupe. The outer walls were white and the roof pinkish tan, with rows of Spanish tiles. Over the large double wooden doors was a tympanum carved with the image of the Last Supper.

"It's beautiful," Luis said.

"Thank you," Arturo replied, beaming with pride. "We like to think that it serves a real purpose for its community here. There was once an older cathedral on this spot, but it fell into decay. There was talk of moving the rebuilt church elsewhere, but it was your great-uncle who insisted it stay in the center of town. We are part of our parishioners' daily lives this way, not a Sunday destination only. And now, with the school almost built, we can do even more."

Luis was impressed. A new hospital, the Coca-Cola plant, now a school. He'd understood a great deal of the Mexican drug war was fought in the states directly below the US-Mexico border—most over smuggling routes and territories impacted by sales to El Norte. Way down here in Michoacán it seemed miles away.

Father Arturo pushed Luis across the narrow street to the front of San Nieves. Rather than approach the double doors of the chapel, however, he wheeled Luis around to the side. Luis heard hammers at work and the buzz of a circular saw. Father Arturo took out his cell phone and presented a photograph. It was of the foundation of an L-shaped building about the size of San Nieves's basilica being smoothed by craftsmen, thick beams and wooden trusses arranged at regular intervals to support the second-floor eventual roof.

"This is two months ago. Two weeks before your father arrived, in other words. Keep it to one side of your mind."

"All right," Luis agreed.

Father Arturo pushed Luis down the alley between the church and the neighboring building. When they came around back, Luis gaped. The building he was looking at was almost complete. The framing of both levels was done, and walls were going up at the far side. There were pipes for bathrooms and water fountains. Two water heaters were in place. Windows, ready to be installed, leaned against a rear wall. In the middle of all of it was Sebastian, directing workers as he stood on a ladder, soon to return to work himself.

"My goodness," Luis said, surprised.

"We had a plan that we would finish half, cover it to wait out the summer rains, then finish it in the fall. The addition of your father's hammer and knowledge means that it will be completed in time for students in the fall. The community believes he's some kind of angel, and the support to christen the school in honor of his namesake, San Sebastian, has been total."

Luis almost couldn't believe his ears. His father, the drunk. His father, the man who left. His father, who heard voices that couldn't possibly be God.

His father, the savior.

"Dad!" Luis called out.

Sebastian grinned and came down the ladder. "Welcome! You like it?"

"It's amazing," Luis admitted.

"He works like a demon, up early and stays late," Father Arturo enthused. "We can barely keep him supplied with wood, he builds so fast. We have to take up another collection."

"They're predicating early rains this year," Sebastian said. "God wants us to hurry. Would you like a tour?"

Luis admitted that he would. Father Arturo and Sebastian went to lift the wheelchair into the school, but Luis shook them off.

"Let me walk in," he said.

It took work, but Luis managed to get to his feet and enter the schoolhouse under his own steam. The lot on which they had to build wasn't very large. The classrooms themselves, however, were each a good size and could accommodate at least a couple dozen students.

"There are six classrooms per floor," Father Arturo gushed. "The lower grades will be two-year. A kindergarten and first grade taught together, a first and second, a second and third. The upper grades will be alone. We are hoping to put together a scholarship fund so that those who do very well will be able to continue classes at St. Javier, the Jesuit high school in Uruapan."

"You'll need a number of teachers," Luis said.

"Is that an offer, Father Chavez?" Father Arturo quipped. "But yes, we already have the first three in myself and visiting Fathers Ponce and Feliz. There's enough housing at our temporary rectory, an apartment building about three blocks away, for all of us. Your father is staying with us there now."

"And who pays?" Luis blurted out without thinking.

Father Arturo didn't seem to mind, however. "The diocese in Morelia and then the archdiocese in Mexico City have been most helpful in providing for the teachers. The building is financed by our congregation, and we're hoping ongoing costs are supplemented by student fees, which we hope to keep at a minimum. We also hope that the archdiocese might favor us with at least some partial scholarships for those students most in need."

Luis looked from Father Arturo to his own father and back again. Who was he to say his father didn't hear the voice of God? God was clearly working through both men, and their passion and verve were as impressive as they were contagious.

"You're a force to be reckoned with, Father Arturo," Luis said.

"Thank you, Father Chavez. From what your father tells me, so are you. Perhaps, as you continue your recovery, you could come to San Elias Nieves and celebrate a Mass. It would be a blessing to us."

"I would be honored."

Father Arturo beamed, then seemed to remember something. "I can't believe I forgot this," he said, reaching into his pocket. "I was at San Juan Diego for a reason."

He handed a ziplock bag to Luis with a crumbling piece of paper inside. Luis opened the bag, unfolded the slip, and discovered a christening notice. The date was March 24, 1965, the location was El Tule. The name was Sandra Trueba, his mother.

"She was christened by your uncle in this very building," Father Arturo said. "And on the feast day of Saint Catherine of Genoa. How wonderful is that?"

Luis glanced to his beaming father.

Wonderful indeed, Luis thought. *It's all wonderful.*

First thing in the morning Michael made his way to the law firm of Wasser, Lustbader, and Rafson. Situated in a downtown skyrise, Wasser, Lustbader was one of the largest corporate firms not just in Los Angeles but in the entire Pacific Rim. This was almost not to be, however, as they'd suffered through a solid two decades of being the go-to firm for hospitals, pharmaceutical companies, and medical equipment manufacturers fighting malpractice suits that resulted in endless billable hours but little in the way of growth. The partners were content to grind their junior associates down to nubs as long as they were paid their dividends and bonuses, but didn't blink as these same associates quit to form more nimble, expansion-oriented firms capable of taking Wasser, Lustbader's business out from under them.

That is, except for Paul Ravet.

During the late seventies and early eighties, as Japanese economic power rose around the Pacific Rim, Paul Ravet looked farther east and believed China could be next. One of the rare men in American corporate culture who didn't look down on the Chinese, Ravet saw what was coming: a nation poised to rapidly industrialize and potentially do the same to the United States across multiple marketplaces that Japan had done with cars.

At the time China wasn't interested much in talking to a Los Angeles–based corporate attorney. The government didn't favor Chinese investment in American firms and didn't welcome American interest in their own. Ravet understood. America had spent much of the twentieth century misunderstanding China, both over- and underestimating the authority of its leadership and its supposed subjugation by Moscow.

Conveniently, Ravet didn't care for politics. He saw several companies already using Chinese labor in the tech sector and knew Americans couldn't be far behind. So he began petitioning the Chinese Ministry of Commerce for trade permits, customs information relating to double taxation, and reciprocal law accreditation. He went largely ignored. When he finally received a rejection, he celebrated it as a form of acknowledgment.

Then one day a shipment of Brazilian oil destined for the Chinese port of Qingdao ended up in Long Beach mired in the kind of red tape only an American lawyer could cut through. Ravet was contacted by a Chinese government official, helped free the oil, and extracted a high fee for his services. Another request followed a few months later. Within a few years he personally oversaw the visit of the California governor to Beijing and opened even more trade avenues.

Paul Ravet was also Michael's mentor for the handful of months Michael had gone into the private sector after completing law school. Though Michael was one of many first-year associates who resigned from Wasser, Lustbader within only the first few months, he'd already earned Ravet's trust and respect. As he rose in the DA's office, he kept in contact with Ravet, relying on him for advice now and again.

But now Michael presented himself at Ravet's office at seven in the morning without an appointment. This went so against the grain that he knew he risked offending Ravet's sensibilities. He also had no choice.

"He's prepping for a big meeting in Shanghai all day," Ravet's second assistant, Caitlin, told Michael. "You can probably ring him early next week."

Michael took a seat. Caitlin didn't make eye contact with him for the next four hours. Finally, after a brief intercom exchange, she rose, nodded his way, and escorted him through Ravet's door.

Ravet didn't look up from his tablet as Michael entered. Michael indicated a solid-gold ox standing at the corner of Ravet's desk.

"That's new?"

"From a group in Taipei," Ravet said. "Turns the heads of the PRC types when they see it, but it's good for them to know I'm playing both sides."

Michael didn't want the lecture on Chinese-Taiwanese business culture Ravet seemed poised to deliver and decided to be direct. "Are you acting counsel for Charles Sittenfeld?" Michael asked.

Ravet raised an eyebrow.

For the murder-for-hire charge, Sittenfeld's defense was being handled by Leslie Radden, a safe choice given the gendered charge. But Michael knew that wouldn't include whatever charges or noncharges the CIA would have whisked Sittenfeld out of the country to discuss.

There had to be at least someone in Sittenfeld's circle being consulted on this, too.

"Weren't you fired?" Ravet finally asked.

"My official notification reads that I've been suspended."

"So who do you work for now? Don't tell me it's Justice. Aren't they tired of all the interagency sniping?"

"So that's a yes?" Michael asked.

Ravet put his tablet down, leaned back in his chair, and studied Michael for a long moment. "What do you want, Michael?"

"I want Charles to stand trial as an accessory to the murder of Naomi Okpewho and Carrie Meallaigh. Barring that, I want him to give up his third party. There's a cartel connection—"

"Is there?" Ravet said, cutting him off, as if to suggest Michael was entering dangerous territory.

"There is, but Charles hid his hand well. He never did anything that could prove a link between himself and those making billions off narcotics. The problem is we've got this Byzantine maze he's constructed. We know who is on one end and who is on the other, but have no clue as to the Minotaur hiding within. I want to ask him who that is so that I might go after them."

"With the full authority of the Justice Department, the FBI, and the Office of the District Attorney of Los Angeles?" Ravet added mockingly. "And what do you have to offer him? Immunity at trial?"

"I found his money."

Ravet smirked. Then the smirk faded. "What are you saying?"

"I have a pair of associates who do what Sittenfeld does. Only, they're better than him in a couple of ways. They called me up this morning, talking about a third party that hides behind all these randomized account numbers. They can't get to that guy, though, so they decided to go after Charles himself. It turns out he has exactly 348,972,450.23 dollars spread across multiple accounts in—that cliché of all clichés—the Cayman Islands by way of three shell companies in Delaware, two in Nevada."

Michael waited for Ravet to consider this. "You can't get at it, Michael," Ravet retorted. "I don't know what you're threatening."

"We found it. We could steal it," Michael said. "We could make it look like it was being seized, then remove it, then close the accounts. By the time it was done, he'd have no legal recourse to get it back either."

"You are describing a serious crime, Michael," Ravet said, getting to his feet. "You need to leave."

"Okay, okay," Michael said, heading for the door. "By the way, *you* have a couple of accounts in the same exact bank as Sittenfeld, almost as if you advised him on where to keep his money if he wanted it safe. If he has hit squads going after people who could put him behind bars, what do you think he'd do if he found out his lawyer's former associate was responsible for the heist that cleaned him out? Murder-for-hire seems to be his thing."

"Now you're fishing," Ravet said. "You couldn't possibly go after the money."

"No, but his wife could. Or the CIA. I've heard the Austrian government is angry with him for some reason. Could tell them even. Pretty sure Sittenfeld, wherever he is, is thinking once he's done with CIA he'll happily retire somewhere with his third of a billion dollars. I wonder who he'd start ratting on if he suddenly knew that nest egg was gone. How many people, how many *governments*, have been introduced to him over the years by—I don't know—persons like yourself in ways that might interest CIA? His ability to do business has functionally been destroyed. I wonder what happens to all those others now?"

For the first time in a long time Michael was in his element, and he was relishing it. He watched his former mentor's expression change as the older man mentally examined his dwindling options.

Ravet stared angrily at Michael. "CIA can't know."

"I'm fine with that," said Michael.

"You'd have ten minutes to speak to him," Ravet said. "Not a second longer."

"Still not hearing anything I'd object to."

"And if you touch that money or anyone else's money, it won't be a junkie with a machine gun that comes after you next time," Ravet said icily.

Michael paused. "Amazing what you can get accomplished when you threaten not someone's life but their social standing and lifestyle, ain't it, counselor?"

XIII

There was no reason that Luis could determine why San Elias Nieves should have a spontaneous feast that night, but he got the sense that the congregation was overdue. It had started small, a dinner that would take place in the small yard between the construction site and the rear of the church, where a courtyard had been proposed. Then one of the volunteer construction workers called a neighbor about bringing pork. Another rang up his wife, who called her sister about making carnitas and morisquetas. A third texted his bandmates and asked Father Arturo if dancing was appropriate.

"'Rejoice in the dance, both young and old together,'" Father Arturo had replied.

Somewhere along the line it was decided that they were honoring Sebastian Chavez for all his labor, and then everyone was invited.

Knowing he wouldn't be allowed to duck out, Luis returned to the hospital to rest for the afternoon. His doctor came by in the early evening to see if his extracurricular visit to San Elias Nieves had done any damage.

"You're in good shape, Padre," the doctor said. "Will I see you at the church dance later?"

Now it was a dance?

"I believe so," Luis said.

"Great. My wife is already cooking. You should've seen the clinic we had before Father Arturo built this hospital."

"He built the hospital?" Luis asked.

"Well, not him personally, but he knew there was a real need in the community. So he set about raising the funds. Took him three years, some help from the archdiocese in Mexico City, but primarily he got the money from the community."

Like the school, Luis thought, surprised the impoverished community could sustain the perennial layout.

"The church can do a lot when it puts its mind to it," Luis said.

"That it can," the doctor replied.

Luis fell asleep for a couple of hours, waking when his father entered.

"It's already started," Sebastian said. "Parishioners filed over even before sundown. People brought chairs. A couple of benches and some boards became a stage. There's more food than I've seen since I've been down here."

Luis thought about his congregation at St. Augustine's. There were several congregants whose social life revolved around the church, so this wasn't so unusual to him. What did stand out was the entire community helping out. Los Angeles was many things, but united when it came to a citywide religious preference it was not. Being in a town, however small, that was universally Catholic was a first for Luis.

"Will you pray with me before we go?" Luis asked Sebastian.

"Of course."

Father and son prayed together before Luis went through his own evening prayers, utilizing a breviary he'd borrowed off Father Arturo. In the absence of God's voice, the rigor of the Divine Office made him feel closer to his brother priests around the world and back through history in a way that was similar to being alongside God. It wasn't the same, but he felt a part of a whole regardless.

Sebastian had brought Luis some clothes he'd picked out for him at a small mercantile across the street from the hospital. They consisted of a pair of black jeans, a western shirt, cowboy boots, and one of Father Arturo's Roman collars. It was as unusual a getup as Luis had ever worn, made even more unusual by the fact that he'd lost two whole pants sizes over the course of his weeks in bed. He'd never been overweight per se, but now he looked downright sickly.

Seeing what Luis was reacting to in the mirror, Sebastian shrugged. "You'll look better once you've got some real food in you," he said.

What made Luis happiest was having the collar. He'd reached for it so many times over the past few days, only to find it absent, like a phantom limb. He needed it, another piece that made him whole, and he was glad Father Arturo had one that could be made to fit.

When he was ready, his father brought the rickety wheelchair and helped him into it. The hospital was already fairly busy, something Luis knew was common on any Friday payday. When they passed Vera at the downstairs nurses' station, Sebastian grinned at her and nodded to the door.

"Coming to the party?"

Vera rolled her eyes and got back to work.

Once they were off hospital grounds, Luis was amazed to see how many people filled the streets. Father Arturo had been right. The town emptied out by day, sending its workers far afield. But now everyone was home, and the tiny restaurants, bars, and clubs were alive with lights and color. The roads themselves were filled, too, as young men in the flatbeds of slow-moving trucks called out to friends and whistled at girls as they cruised the blocks.

When they reached one club that Luis had thought earlier was boarded up and closed, there was now a line of middle-aged men outside.

"It's a disco," Sebastian explained. "You go in and you buy tickets to dance with girls." As if suddenly realizing he was speaking to a priest, he quickly added, "It's all quite innocent, though. Nothing sensual."

Given the number of men lined up outside, Luis doubted this but didn't comment. They passed another club, where someone Luis initially thought was an Elvis impersonator was singing. When he realized the song was by the Smiths but done in a Cumbia style, he saw that the crooner was emulating the English singer Morrissey.

"Have you heard of Morrissey?" Sebastian asked, nodding to the singer. "I heard someone say he was from Chile. Very popular here."

"From England I think," Luis replied.

"I knew you'd know him!" Sebastian declared. "I looked for his tapes but couldn't find any."

Luis tried to imagine his father listening to the Smiths or popular music in general and couldn't. It was at moments like this that he was glad to have left the secular world behind.

Luis noticed that there were no streetlights, the town lit only by the glow from the surrounding homes and businesses. It cast everything in a strange blue, orange, and green light when not in shadow. This might have been intimidating to a man who couldn't run from danger if the constantly changing food smells weren't so inviting. Luis felt like a Pavlovian dog, a new scent appearing to make him salivate every few yards or so. The locals didn't differentiate, either. There were as many people seated for food at the storefront restaurants as there were for people cooking on small grills right on the sidewalk.

What was also interesting to Luis was a sort of absence of social hierarchy. People wore their nicest clothes, but there were no showy standouts, folks who looked as if they had more money than anyone else. The neighborhood and the town itself would have appeared impoverished to the foreign eye, but the people would not. It reminded Luis of his neighborhood growing up.

When they reached San Elias Nieves, a number of people were already milling around outside, taking pulls off bottles of beer or smoking cigarettes. Boys flirted with girls without saying a word, and the girls flirted right back. It was so pastoral Luis thought he'd stepped into a Norman Rockwell version of a telenovela.

It suddenly occurred to Luis that there was one thing he hadn't seen in the town.

"You know, I haven't seen a single cop since I've been here," Luis said.

"Oh, they're around," Sebastian said. "They don't leave the barracks without a reason. When they do, it's a long line of trucks, men in masks in the back, guns out like it's a parade. You've never seen such a noise. Of course, it's after the fact—picking up a dead body, towing a burned-out truck. They don't have the power here."

"When I was under, I heard gunfire."

"Everyone around here has a gun. Sometimes it's to scare the dogs away," Sebastian said, nodding to one of the mutts on a nearby roof, barking at the passing pair. "When it's trouble, you know it. The bullets sound less certain. Do you know what I mean?"

Luis did.

The crowd parted as Sebastian pushed Luis down the alley to the back of San Elias Nieves. Father Arturo, a plate of food in his hand, smiled as they approached.

"You made it!" he enthused, then waved a hand to the crowd. "Everyone, if you haven't met him, this is Father Luis Chavez, visiting us from Los Angeles, and his father, Sebastian Chavez, the architect of our success!"

A cheer went up. Bottles of beer appeared almost magically in their hands. As one the crowd descended on Sebastian. Parents introduced their children who would be attending the school. Others came to shake his hand and compliment his carpentry work. Luis watched his father beam through all the attention, but he was never less than humble or gracious.

Over his lifetime Luis had felt many things about his father. He now added a new one to the list: pride.

"Come! Eat!" Father Arturo told Luis, shooing him out of the wheelchair. "Put that somewhere else tonight. If you need an arm to lean on, I'm here for you. But it's time to get up."

Luis knew the priest was right and stood. He steadied himself, found the right angle to keep his knees from buckling, and saluted Father Arturo with his beer.

"There you go!" Arturo said, clapping Luis on the back. "Now, a proper meal."

For much of the next hour Luis ate shredded pork and rice and even drank bottles of Sol, a beer he hadn't tasted since his youth. Father Arturo introduced him to the two other priests currently visiting San Elias Nieves, as well as a third, a Father Barriga, who had arrived from Zamora in anticipation of teaching at the school.

"You teach, do you not?" Father Barriga asked, his accent so thick Luis pretended to be hard of hearing in order to make the man enunciate more clearly.

"I do," Luis concurred. "It adds a dimension to my faith. I can't imagine living without it in my life now."

"But it must also be so terrifying, no?" Father Barriga asked. "Los Angeles, all those gangs, that endless violence. How many students must you lose?"

Luis was a taken aback. *No, no. Mexico is the place with all the violence and gangs, no?* But then he thought about it, how there was a plague of violence across his city, resulting in the unsolved gun deaths of hundreds if not thousands of youths across the years. Like this priest, who'd become inured to the everyday slaughter in Mexico, Luis had come to feel the same way in Los Angeles.

"I try to be honest with my students," Luis said. "This generation is so savvy, so skeptical of the institutions of their elders. A false note can end their relationship with the church even if you don't mean it. I try to present the strengths of our faith without ignoring the weaknesses. But most of all, I want to be an example of what I get from it."

Father Barriga eyed Luis with curiosity for a moment, before breaking out in a grin and taking his arm.

"I'm glad to hear such wisdom from someone so young in the clergy," Father Barriga said. "When I grew up, the sisters that ran my school were all about dogma and discipline and mortification. Then I look to a man like the pontiff, who slips away from the Vatican at night to comfort the homeless, the ill, the sinners, and sinned upon. That's when I remember that we're a church of love, not regulation. We're to be a beacon for these boys and girls who look out their window and see nothing but blood and wasted lives."

Father Barriga excused himself. Luis glanced up, not realizing that their conversation had led them into the unfinished school. Through the roof beams, Luis could see the stars. It took him a second to realize what was amiss. Then he reminded himself how much farther south he was. The constellation Dorado, out of sight in California, was in full view in Michoacán.

The stars, a reminder of heaven, always made him feel closer to God. He allowed himself to be carried along by this feeling. Though he still felt outside of God's presence, the memory of star fields past filled him with joy.

He stayed there for a few minutes, staring up through his father's unfinished roof, until the band returned from a short break to begin a new song. Preferring silence, Luis hobbled away from the school to the back door of the church. The jeans his father had brought him were feeling tight against the padded bandage on his left side, and he relished the idea of a moment or two alone in a pew.

He swung open the door and moved down a narrow hall, passing a small bathroom that seemed to double as a sacristy. The chalice and paten were on a shelf above the sink, a box of a thousand communion wafers in a cabinet above the toilet.

Necessity, the mother of invention.

As he stepped into the chapel, he found himself alongside the altar. He was immediately struck by how unadorned it was. The walls were as white on the inside as they were out, with a holy water font by the front door that seemed to have been whitewashed as well. The pews were old and functional. The pulpit from which Father Arturo preached was a music stand with a purple sash with a cross stitched onto it hanging over it. The altar was equally simple, with a pair of candles and a reliquary. On the wall alongside the altar was a poster of the Virgen de Guadalupe pressed in with thumb tacks.

There was a single confessional against the far wall that looked much older than anything else in the building. Luis decided it must've come from the earlier church at El Tule.

What was impossible to miss was how rich the place was with purpose even when empty. The ceilings were stained with the smoke of endless candles, the backs of pews discolored by the hands of the rising faithful from the front row to the back. The wood in front of the altar where the congregation knelt to take communion was worn away by so many knees. The aisle between the pews was laid with red carpet. Its middle was threadbare, though its edges looked new.

Luis was reminded of a story Father Whillans told him of celebrating a Mass in a church in a poorer neighborhood in the north of Paris. It had been built after World War II, when building supplies were hard to come by. So the locals constructed it using cinder blocks and purple cubes of glass. It was wholly functional, the opposite of, say, Notre Dame, a few miles to the south. But the strength and will of its congregants was felt the moment one stepped in, cast in the purple glow. Whillans had said that the experience changed his life.

You learn quickly the difference between a church built for its people and of its people, Whillans had said.

Luis felt as if he finally understood this notion. What must it be like to face a congregation like this one, where you didn't only recognize faces and names but entire lives?

"Ah, I know that look."

Luis turned as Father Arturo entered from the front of the building.

"Sorry, I was admiring—"

"I know what you were doing," Arturo said. "How wonderful it would be to cast aside the cares of a big-city parish and come here to do the meaningful work, no?"

Luis scoffed, but Father Arturo smiled, as if knowing he'd hit the nail on the head.

"That's what's so good about trusting God, no?" Father Arturo continued. "He puts you where best you can serve. When I am envious of the great cathedrals of the Morelia diocese or in Mexico City, I will remember the look on your face and think that there are those who admire this, too."

"I'm glad you brought that up," Luis said. "I've been meaning to ask you something about this place. I, too, believe God sends me where best I might serve." He indicated the injury to his torso. "The man who did this, who killed Bishop Osorio and Father Belbenoit in Los Angeles, I want to find him."

"In Michoacán? Maybe this village itself."

"Perhaps he'll find me," Luis said. "He meant to kill me. He's someone who takes pride in finishing a job."

Father Arturo had a strained look on his face. "You are perfectly safe here. I mean that. Perfectly safe."

"I wasn't saying this was a confrontation I was hoping to avoid," Luis added. "But how is it that you can guarantee my safety?"

Father Arturo seemed to be considering his reply when the back door of the church opened and Father Ponce hurried over. He said something to Father Arturo, who blanched, then nodded back to Luis before following the other priest out of the chapel. Luis went after them.

"Padre!" The speaker was a twentysomething man in a crisp black Stetson and new clothes. He swept Father Arturo up into an embrace and nodded to the unfinished school. "This is incredible! A miracle! You've done so much! How long has this been your dream? Easily as long as I can remember."

Luis glanced around the party. Everyone had gone silent and was watching the interaction. The Stetson-wearing man seemed to have brought an entourage with him of about a dozen similarly dressed young men. They looked more ready to take the nightclubs of Puerto Vallarta by storm than a church picnic.

"It is a miracle," Father Arturo quietly agreed.

"And will be finished by the summer I heard," Stetson said. "First students by the fall."

"That's the hope," Father Arturo replied.

As Stetson turned, Luis noticed the pearl-handled automatics tucked into the back of the man's waistband. He'd been around guns enough to know which parts became worn with use no matter how many times they'd been cleaned. These weapons were not for show. This man, whoever he was, was the local "authority," legal or otherwise.

"And who's this?" Stetson asked, nodding to Luis.

"The priest I told you about," Father Arturo said. "Father Luis Chavez. From Los Angeles."

"Ah, Father Chavez!" Stetson said, arms as wide for a stranger as they were for Father Arturo. "I am Victor Canales. I've looked into you. Did you really intercede on behalf of some thousand *esclavos* up there? Risking your life even?"

Victor was referring to the incident that had first put Luis and Michael Story together. Luis had gone undercover following the murder of a farmworker. This had only been six months after he'd been ordained.

"There were many who interceded," Luis said.

"A *humble* priest!" Victor roared, playing it up for the crowd, who seemed to recognize this routine. "And you, with your incredible ability to not die at the hands of a hit man? It's also you who we have to thank for bringing your father down with you to build this mighty school?"

Luis didn't respond. Victor barely seemed to notice, as he had already turned to Sebastian. He put an arm around his shoulder and pointed to the school. "This is something, maestro. It's beautiful! I need you out at my ranch. The house is falling apart. It could use a master's touch."

Father Arturo visibly tensed. This wasn't a request.

"Of course, any of my work can wait until there's a roof up there," Victor added, pointing to the stars. "But then a visit?"

Luis looked to his father. Sebastian appeared both annoyed and befuddled. He met his son's gaze, then turned to Victor.

"A house?" Sebastian replied with mock surprise. "I'm sorry, I still have the echo of a million driven nails sounding in my head. I have seen this thing you call a house, el Jefe. You mean to call it a *barn.*"

Father Arturo gasped. He wasn't the only one. Victor eyed Sebastian closely, obviously surprised at the older man's remark. But then Sebastian grinned, and Victor burst out laughing.

"A barn! A *granero*? How dare you! I'll have you know, I *live* in that barn! I take my girls into that barn!" Victor cried, scowling. "I live"—*snort snort snort*—"in that *barn*! Are you saying I'm a barnyard animal?"

Victor made more pig sounds, to the delight of the assembled children and the relief of their parents. Then Sebastian took Victor's hands in his own and held them tightly, probably tighter than the *chico malo* had ever had his hands held. He tried to free them, but the master carpenter's hands, Luis knew, were like a metal press.

"I would be *honored* to work on your house, el Jefe," Sebastian intoned gravely. "Whatever you need done, I will do. Your support of San Elias Nieves and this school is the real *milagro*. Any small thing I can offer as thanks, and I will do it."

Victor's expression went from annoyed and amused to humbled and almost reverential. He nodded quickly and took off his hat. "You are the miracle, Señor Chavez," Victor said, finally able to withdraw his hands. "Finish your work here—all of it—and then we'll talk about my barn."

"Thank you, el Jefe," Sebastian said, bowing his head. "We will make you proud and keep you in our prayers."

Victor nodded and looked around the newly solemn gathering. The gratitude of the congregants mirrored Sebastian's, and Victor appeared moved. Luis suddenly realized the chess game Sebastian was playing here. Victor reached into his pocket. Instead of a gun, he withdrew two thick money clips and handed them to Father Arturo.

"For you, Padre," Victor said with gravity before turning to Luis. "And of you, son of the carpenter, may we ask a blessing for myself and my friends?"

Luis nodded as Victor and his cadre knelt like schoolchildren. He made the sign of the cross, said a blessing he didn't feel, and backed away. Victor rose, nodded to Luis and Father Arturo, and then led his fellows away.

Once they were gone, Luis looked back as his father with even more pride than before. Not only was he able to defuse a potentially dangerous situation, he'd picked a crook's pocket and made it seem like it was the villain's idea.

"You should've been a priest, Sebastian," said Father Arturo, articulating Luis's very thoughts.

"Maybe, maybe not," Sebastian said with a shrug.

The weight of the evening landed on Luis all at once as his adrenaline levels began to ebb. He sought his wheelchair and took a seat. He hadn't been in it for more than a few seconds when he felt his father's hand on the push handle.

"Let's go," Sebastian said, sounding every bit as exhausted as Luis felt.

As they made their way back through the unlit streets to the hospital, Luis fell as quiet as he'd been when he'd driven his father back to MacArthur Park a few weeks earlier.

How quickly changes the hand on the wheel, he mused.

"I hope you don't judge me too harshly for extracting money from that man," Sebastian said, sounding contrite. "Father Arturo was right when he said we are building faster than we can keep supplied with lumber. If we really are to finish by the summer rains, we have to get all the building materials here."

"I didn't judge you," Luis said. "Favorably, if at all."

Sebastian considered this. "Maybe that's worse."

Luis scoffed. "Who was that guy? The local cartel flunky who makes sure the police stay in their barracks and guarantees my safety?"

"This isn't America," Sebastian hushed Luis. "Just because he let us walk out of there, doesn't mean he's not a big man around here. You curry favor with the big man by ratting out those who talk about him." Sebastian nodded to the nearby darkened walls and doorways. "These are inches thin. The whole town is a microphone."

"Even in English?" Luis asked, switching from Spanish for the first time in days.

Sebastian sighed. "He may as well be mayor. He controls the drug trade here and in the neighboring areas. When you have this much poverty, you have many users. Not all of it is shipped to the States, you know. He's also Father Arturo's son."

Luis eyed his father with surprise. "His *son*?"

"From before he was a priest," Sebastian explained. "This isn't common knowledge, however. Father Arturo only told me because he knew I wouldn't be here for long."

"It seems the kind of thing that's hard to conceal," Luis offered.

"True, but people have seen what happens when you talk out of turn. It's one of the reasons Father Arturo goes by his first name only."

Community fund-raising, Luis realized. *That's how you get a hospital and a school built. And the bad guys get to think they're all Jesús Malverde Robin Hood types, taking from the rich to save the poor from themselves.*

The evening's silence was suddenly interrupted by gunshots. They were close, only a few blocks away. They were followed by the roar of a truck engine.

"Down," Sebastian ordered.

Luis ducked as Sebastian pushed the wheelchair to the side of the road and helped Luis limp into a doorway.

"Probably not coming this way, but best not to chance it," Sebastian said.

But the words had barely gone past his lips before more gunshots rang out, these even closer. They sounded like air guns being fired into an empty oil barrel, all metallic echo and punch, hardly the cinematic *rat-at-at* Luis grew up hearing at the movies. A dull glow illuminated the end of the block, growing wider and wider, until an aged Ford bounced into view.

"It's coming straight at us!" Luis said.

"Sebastian!" Luis hissed in warning.

"Stay *down*!" Sebastian cried.

Bullets smashed into the truck from behind, shattering its windows and blowing out its tires even as other rounds bashed great dents in its steel frame. More bullets whizzed past, ricocheting off the nearby buildings, one striking the doorway only inches above Luis's head.

Someone pressed the truck's accelerator all the way to the floor. With a last bellow, it bounced off the street, clipped a building, and plowed into the wall a few feet from where Luis and Sebastian were crouched. The air was suddenly filled with the stench of gasoline and antifreeze as the truck tried to burrow farther into the building.

Luis heard footsteps race up to the truck. He rose to cry out, but Sebastian yanked him back down. The driver's-side door was opened and several bullets fired into the cab. Luis watched as the light pouring in from beyond the truck was now tinted red by blood splattered on the shattered windshield.

The gunmen came around to the other side and swung open the door, but no shots followed. The door was slammed back, and the gunmen disappeared into the night.

Luis got to his feet and hurried around the back of the now-whining vehicle to get to the driver's side. He opened the door, threw it into park, and silenced the engine.

The driver, a young man, had slumped sideways onto the passenger seat. He'd been shot so many times Luis could barely make out any identifiable features. Then he noticed the boy's clothes and recognized him as one of the young men who was flirting with the girls in front of San Elias Nieves earlier that night.

Sebastian opened the passenger-side door and almost immediately closed it back. Luis saw why as a few lights came on down the street, illuminating the passenger-side floorboard. A young woman lay in a fetal position under the dashboard. Judging from the blood on the side of the door, however, Luis figured she'd been mortally wounded in the initial fusillade.

Over what? Luis thought as tears filled his eyes. *What on earth, Lord? Why did they have to die?*

He looked back to the passenger-side floorboard and saw that the dead girl, her eyes half-open, seemed to be asking him the same question. *How did it come to this?*

Luis stepped away from the truck, overwhelmed with anger and sorrow. When he felt a hand on his shoulder, he shook it off, then saw it was Sebastian.

"Let's go, Son."

Luis stared at the bullet-riddled truck for another long moment, then walked away.

XIV

Michael was surprised to learn that Charles Sittenfeld had a favorite among his mistresses. Her name was Livinia and she was from the largest island in the Swedish archipelago. When Sittenfeld was removed from Men's County in downtown Los Angeles by CIA and told he would be moved out of the country, he said that he wanted to meet up with his paramour, who had left the country the day after he'd been arrested.

CIA said that would be fine.

Michael, naturally, was dumbfounded by this, particularly after learning that Sittenfeld had flown to Sweden on the taxpayer's dime. Not only this, he'd been put in a hotel in downtown Stockholm when he'd first arrived to the tune of almost a thousand dollars a night. He'd since been moved to more permanent quarters outside the city, where, according to Ravet's latest, he was enjoying his time hiking and skiing, dining with food brought in from the city that was selected by his young female companion (a lawyer no less), and, a few hours a day, was taking time out of his busy schedule to dictate to his CIA handlers what he knew of international money laundering.

"I've had guys like that in custody," Special Agent Lampman told Michael as she drove him to LAX. "They act like they're dictating their memoirs. So much of it sounds rehearsed or memorized, like they've been waiting to tell someone their juicy story for years."

"But isn't he self-incriminating?" Michael asked.

"He's probably got some kind of ironclad immunity on anything he talks about," Lampman said as she pulled up to the departures gate at LAX. "Don't you wish you'd become an engineer or something useful?"

Michael climbed out of the car and considered this. The past few days, as he and Lampman had jumped through endless State Department and congressional hoops, he'd come to an awful realization. He was flying halfway across the world to ask a banker for information about the murder of his girlfriend—information the CIA likely already had, and that may have even been known to them before Sittenfeld's arrest. If the government was in any way functional, he wouldn't have to make this trip. Lampman could have gotten on the phone with the right person, asked the question, and called it a day.

But no. Sittenfeld was a voluntary informant for CIA, operating outside the jurisdiction of the United States. Michael would be traveling as a special liaison for the law offices of Wasser, Lustbader, something that had been arranged by simply reactivating his long-dormant employee profile. He would then be allowed access to Sittenfeld in an interview that could last no more than ten minutes.

Ten minutes, and then he would return to the United States on the next flight out.

Oh, and none of it would be actionable, as it was gathered independently during a voluntary interview, though secondary warrants could be arranged. In theory.

That was if Sittenfeld actually said anything of value.

"I don't get it," Michael said, leaning into the passenger-side window of Lampman's car. "It sounds quasi-legal on paper, but what on earth does this have to do with justice?"

"You remember how President Obama rode into office talking about how he was going to dismantle the extralegal prison at Guantanamo Bay? He was the *president*, and it still took him almost two full terms to get through all the legal morass to get anything accomplished there. Sittenfeld is a banker who has made the donors behind some of the most powerful men in politics very, very wealthy over the years. Worse, he knows where their bodies are buried. You're lucky you're even getting on this plane."

Michael wanted to kick the car door in. The saddest part was that he knew she was right. But he thought about Naomi, and his focus returned to him. This was a situation designed to make sure none of the little people ground up in the process saw anything resembling justice.

But Michael thought he might change the game in Naomi's favor.

"I'll call you from Stockholm," Michael said.

"Only if it's good news," Lampman said.

Michael thought she was still joking, her persona of the office wise-acre seemingly never to slip. When he caught the look in her eyes, one born of years of investigations that resulted in quagmires like this one, he knew she wasn't.

"Will do."

Michael flew first to London, a ten-hour flight, then raced across the unfamiliar airport to the SAS terminal for a two-and-a-half-hour hop to Stockholm. Once there, he retrieved his rental car, a small compact that he thought was completely ill-suited for the frozen conditions, and set off for Sittenfeld's romantic hideaway.

Being in a foreign country did nothing to assuage Michael's strange feelings about all the subterfuge. A part of him wished it felt James Bond–ish, but in reality he felt like an errand boy. It took him back to his days at Wasser, Lustbader, with his daily commute, not to their shiny offices downtown but to a medical documents warehouse in Los Feliz or Glendale. His days spent going through what added up to mountains of files, hunting for the one clerical discrepancy that could dismantle the opposition's case.

Perhaps his mind was on this instead of the road, as he got lost more than once trying to find his way. Stockholm, it turned out, wasn't so much a single city as a group of islands and peninsulas connected by bridges. His English-language GPS remained ever patient but equally insistent that he was going the wrong direction with every turn.

When he finally made his way to the E4 motorway, which led up-country for a hundred miles, he breathed a sigh of relief.

Though he'd dressed warmly, it was still a shock to his system to have flown from an eighty-degree day in Los Angeles to one that was a mere five degrees above freezing. The car's gauge displaying the temperature in Celsius as three degrees above zero somehow made him feel even colder.

After about a half hour's drive through what in the summertime would've probably been idyllic countryside but in winter might as well have been the North Pole, he finally saw the turnoff for his destination.

Thank Christ.

The location turned out to be a compound of three old, beautifully architected wooden chalets connected to one another by covered pedestrian walks. Other than the narrow road leading in, the spot was completely surrounded by woods. Michael pulled to a stop in front of the center house alongside two other vehicles, one a van that he took to belong to Sittenfeld's CIA minders, and the other an expensive BMW. Smoke rose from a tall chimney.

Before he had even climbed out, a middle-aged woman emerged from the house, bareheaded and without gloves, and strode down to meet him. He clambered out and shook her hand.

"I'm Brigitte Ekedahl," she announced. "Ministry of Justice. Here to make sure everything goes according to protocol. And you are?"

"Michael Story, Los Angeles district attorney's office," he offered. When she merely smiled back patiently, he sighed. "Adjunct counsel, Wasser, Lustbader," he corrected.

"Nice to meet you, Mr. Story," she said, shaking his hand without a hint of irony. "How was your flight?"

Good. My late girlfriend and I talked about flying to London once. We even talked about all the places she wanted to visit. She looked amazing in haute couture, so we even discussed an extravagant shopping excursion.

"It was fine," Michael said. "Is Sittenfeld inside?"

"He is. He's anxious to speak to you. He's been out on a hike this morning and—"

Michael turned on her. "I have a recording of that man explaining in graphic detail what he wanted done to his wife to allay suspicion after her murder. If she was shot, it could be anyone, he says. She had to be beaten. He was 'okay' with sexual assault. Anything to make it obvious he, in his advanced age, couldn't have done it. When asked if he wanted her perhaps knocked unconscious first, he declined, saying that it could 'lack authenticity,' particularly the way one's muscles contracted when faced with real terror. Shall I go on?"

Michael wasn't sure what Brigitte Ekedahl's reaction would be. He half expected her to walk him back to his car. Instead he saw something change in her face. She hated being here, too. Perhaps hated being used by the Americans as much as she was surely being used by her own government. More importantly, she didn't seem to have been privy to the details of Sittenfeld's murder-for-hire case.

"Do I have to worry about you approaching this interview with anything less than a professional deportment?" she said for the ears clearly listening to them both.

"Not at all," Michael replied.

"Perfect," she said, a distant smile returning. "Then let's get this done."

The inside of the house was as incredible and inviting as the outside. The fireplace, filled with burning logs the size of tree trunks, was large enough inside for a man to stand up straight. The wooden furniture matched the house itself, and Michael wouldn't have been surprised to learn it had been built by the same person. Brigitte led Michael through the house to a large dining room, where at long last Michael found himself in the presence of Charles Sittenfeld, and a woman who Michael assumed was his girlfriend.

Michael had never seen Sittenfeld in the flesh, but his photos—the same few reprinted ad nauseam in the newspapers—didn't do him justice. He looked ten years younger than his booking photo. Slimmer with more vibrant skin. His eyes lit up as he spoke to the young woman next to him, growing even brighter when she smiled.

"Mr. Story, I presume?" Sittenfeld said, rising to his feet.

He was almost six feet tall, wore corduroy pants and a sweater over a polo shirt. His hair was thinning but was cut in a way that accentuated where it was still full. He wore stylish glasses that looked European in design and made Michael wonder if he'd been shopping in Stockholm.

This is what $300 million looks like? he wondered.

Then he realized that what the man controlled, had access to, or could put together in a moment's notice was a hundred times that. That was all it would take to make this sweater-wearing would-be wife killer if not a king, a minor noble among the world's elite. An untouchable made man in his own modest way.

Michael punched him in the face.

Growing up, Michael had never been that physical. He was not much of an athlete, and the only team sports he took part in were the academic decathlon and a locally televised high school quiz show, *Star Academic Challenge*. That hadn't changed in high school, college, or law school. The punch he sent into Charles Sittenfeld's face was the first he'd ever thrown.

Which is probably why it glanced off his cheekbone and knocked his glasses off rather than broke his nose or teeth or something more dramatic. Still, the girlfriend shrieked. Sittenfeld stepped backwards, lost his balance, and fell on his ass, a sight that more than ameliorated the pain the punch had delivered to Michael's still healing forearm. Michael saw that, tellingly, Brigitte didn't move to help him up, despite being closest. He waited for CIA minders to come flooding in, but they didn't, much to his surprise.

"What the hell?" Sittenfeld said, hand to his reddening cheek.

"The money you laundered originated with Latin American drug cartels," Michael said evenly. "First the Colombians, then the Panamanians, now at least two competing Mexican operations—the Gulf Cartel and La Linea of the Zetas. Of course, I can't prove that, but it'd be a pretty amazing coincidence that these organizations would withdraw and transfer money from the accounts they pay all their bribes from in the exact dollar amounts that days later showed up in your own accounts, wouldn't you say? So who is the person your bosses think you're working for and who is sending the money through?"

As his girlfriend crouched next to him, Sittenfeld looked up in anger. "What're you talking about?"

"This isn't your scheme. That wouldn't make sense. The cartels have shifted over the years, but the money remained consistent. You get a cut, sure, but someone else does, too. You're a middleman. Who is doing the actual laundering? Who is getting the money from the cartels to your banks without anyone raising so much as a finger?"

"Is that what you've come all this way to ask?" Sittenfeld replied indignantly.

Michael cocked his fist to punch the semi-disgraced banker again. Sittenfeld raised a defensive arm and clambered to his feet.

As if that will do him any good.

"Paul told me what you threatened to do," Sittenfeld protested, feeling his jaw to see if anything was broken. "You're a thug."

"So are the men who killed my girlfriend to hide your crimes. So was the man who tried to murder me a few weeks back and ended up killing a young woman named Carrie Meallaigh. So are the literally thousands of people who have carried out as many murders over the past several decades in the name of the money you are using right now to finance your ridiculous lifestyle here in Sweden, when you should be, at best, rotting in jail, at worst, hanging from the end of a noose. Your money is steeped in blood. You're not a money launderer, you're a war profiteer. But you're not alone. I might not be able to touch you, but I can get the others. And I don't care how long I have to stand here to get what I came here to get. You're going to tell me."

Sittenfeld stared at Michael for a long moment. He looked from Brigitte to the young woman from Gotland, who'd already begun taking steps away from him, and then went to a nearby desk and withdrew paper and pen. He wrote a name and a series of numbers on the paper, then handed it to Michael.

"This is the account commissions were paid into. Pretty sure it's a dummy account that was used by someone else like me to funnel the money out again, but you'll get your answer."

Michael took the slip of paper and walked out.

In the driveway he found that a second van had arrived, but there was no sign of its driver or any passengers. Even their footprints were covered by a light snowfall that had begun while Michael was inside.

"If you didn't have to turn right around and get on another plane, I'd offer to buy you a drink," Brigitte said, jogging down the steps after him as she pulled on a coat. "He's already on the phone with his lawyer in Los Angeles."

"Doesn't matter. He can't sue me in an American court, and I doubt I'll be back here anytime soon to face trial in Sweden."

"That's too bad," Brigitte said. "There's a museum in Stockholm you'd like."

"A museum?"

"It houses a single artifact, a great Swedish warship called the *Vasa*, built in the early seventeenth century under the instruction of King Gustavus Adolphus," Brigitte explained. "Though the shipbuilders countered his every request to build the boat bigger or add more cannon or sails, the king was the king and had the final say. They finally completed this monstrosity, meant to be the most imposing warship of its day, and launched it on August 10, 1628. It sank a thousand three hundred meters from the dock, killing thirty people in front of a crowd of thousands. It was so large that the tops of the masts were visible above the waterline even as it settled on the seafloor. The king had them sawn down to extinguish the humiliation."

"It was raised?" Michael asked.

"Yes, then brought to this museum," Brigitte said. "It's probably the only museum in the world dedicated, ultimately, to the hubris of power. It's worth seeing, Mr. Story. Or maybe you've had enough hubris for one day?"

Michael smiled, exchanged information with Brigitte, and watched as she drove off. By the time he climbed back behind the wheel of his own rental car, Special Agent Lampman had written him back about the information on Sittenfeld's piece of paper that Michael had texted to her earlier.

The bank turned out to be a small private financial institution in the heart of Mexico City. It had a sterling reputation and was favored by foreign companies who wanted that dedicated personal touch, but with boots on the ground in the heart of Central America. Part of what had endowed it with such prominence was that a controlling amount of its ownership rested with Mexico City's Catholic archdiocese, the largest in the world, which ministered to the needs of the city's seven million Catholics.

XV

Luis had stayed close to the hospital in the days following the shooting. He hadn't done so out of fear for his life as a witness to the shooting, but because he didn't want to face Father Arturo. He still didn't know how he felt about Arturo using drug money to build a hospital and a school for his church. The fact that he'd taken the funds from his own son was also troubling. So he confined himself to his room, prayed from the breviary, and focused on getting back to Los Angeles.

He'd managed to get on a computer downstairs in one of the administrative offices to read the stories in the Los Angeles press about Bishop Osorio's murder. It had been international news, with even the Vatican weighing in. Osorio was praised for continuing to live in a "crime-ridden neighborhood" to "maintain his connection to his congregation" even though it had cost him his life.

Crime-ridden neighborhood?

Father Belbenoit was relegated to two or three sentences, but little more. He'd had a sister back in Lyons, who'd taken his body back to France for burial. It was suggested that he died trying to save Osorio.

The motive was reported as robbery. There were no suspects. Luis's own stabbing wasn't mentioned as, he surmised, there was no body in a hospital bed or morgue drawer. He searched for information on Michael Story, only to find that his profile was still on the county district attorney's website. He'd considered contacting him but wasn't sure it was worth risking his own exposure.

Sebastian came by every morning, every day at noon, and every night to check on his son, but their conversations had taken a turn for the superficial.

"Got a shipment of lumber, good Mexican cypress—*sabino*—from Yucatán," Sebastian would say. "But the nails! The nails were bent! Worthless, all of them. Worse, I stepped away, and one of the other workers used them. We had to undo his work and destroy the nails. One step forward, two back."

Luis commiserated but could tell Sebastian was flagging. He figured his father must've known about Father Arturo and where the money was coming from but had managed to conjure some fiction that made it all right with him in his head. When his own son was endangered during a shoot-out, likely perpetrated by gunmen whose pay came from the same pocketbook as his construction materials, the fiction was shattered.

While Luis couldn't be sure that Victor Canales's outfit was responsible for the deaths of the two people in the truck, the quiet word around the hospital was that this was so. This was why no real investigation had been pursued. An aunt of the dead girl had ranted and raved out in front of the hospital's morgue to a police detective for the better part of half an hour, before she herself was arrested. That was the last Luis heard of it.

When Sebastian arrived one evening, he mentioned in passing that Father Arturo's relationship with his son made him call into question his own with Luis and Nicolas.

"Were there things I could've done differently that would have meant Nicolas would still be alive?" Sebastian asked. "You can say that you wouldn't have found the church that way, but maybe you would have. Maybe you wouldn't have drifted into gangs."

Luis assured him that this wasn't the case, but Sebastian waved him off. "It's not something we can know. But it weighs on me."

When Sebastian left, Luis called Vera and asked to be moved to a communal room.

"Why? Father Arturo has arranged the private room for as long as your recovery takes."

"I am grateful for his generosity," Luis said. "But it is too luxurious. My comfort is impeding my recovery."

Vera raised an eyebrow but could tell that Luis was sincere. She checked a nearby dry-erase board and selected a room. "There is an open bed downstairs in the post-op ward. You can move there if you like."

"Thank you," Luis said, returning to his room to collect his few personal items.

His new roommates turned out to be friends of the youth shot dead in the truck. Both eyed Luis with suspicion when he entered. This deflated after he introduced himself.

"Ah, you were the man stabbed by 10K," the older of the two patients, a young man with close-cropped hair and a thin mustache, said.

"10K?"

"Munuera, but let's not say his name. I'm Rogelio. This is my cousin Oswaldo. The guy you saw killed was his brother."

"What was his name?" Luis asked.

"Sergio," Oswaldo said. "How'd you survive 10K anyway? Don't think of him as one who misses a target."

Luis had heard his purported killer's nickname first from one of the nurses, then from Sebastian. He hadn't been sure that this was the man whose face he'd seen reflected in the side of the Bronco until one of the orderlies heard Luis's description and confirmed it.

"Not sure how I survived," Luis admitted. "Which generally means it was the hand of God."

Oswaldo scoffed. "Yeah, because my brother was such a jerk and deserved to die for flirting with a girl Victor had his eyes on."

"I'm sorry," Luis said. "I didn't mean it that way."

Oswaldo shrugged. "I mean, can you believe a guy like that? You think some girl's hot, got it going on and so on. Then she goes to share a cigarette with somebody that's not you, and that's it. She has to die. Either fall at your feet or that's that. I mean, Sergio—I can get that twisted logic. Guys fight over girls all the time, and my brother probably even knew Victor had his eyes on her and wanted to prove something. But shooting up the girl like she was nothing? That's crazy."

Rogelio eyed his cousin warily for a moment, then shook his head. "It's all crazy. But we're more accustomed to some crazy than others." He turned back to Luis. "Hope you recover quickly."

"Why's that?" Luis asked.

"I heard 10K and his crew were in Michoacán. But don't worry. They don't know you're here or you'd already be dead. Either that or they've heard the good word that the hospital is neutral ground. I think it's 10K's bosses, one of the splinters off the Zetas Cartel, that's poking around Canales's bosses, you know? They look for where the rival cartel is the weakest. Right now that's El Tule. Might be another reason Victor wants to shoot up people—to show what an unpredictable badass he is."

"I hope it doesn't devolve into an all-out war," Luis said.

"What do you care?" Oswaldo interjected. "You get paid either way. Paid to pray for everything to stay on the straight and narrow. Paid to put people in the ground."

And paid to assuage any vestiges of guilt the narcos feel.

Michael's words returned to Luis. *Government's watchdog programs relating to charities. They're a nonprofit. ICE hoops, not banking institution ones.* It suddenly all made sense to him. Luis knew exactly how the cartel cash moved from the drug lords to the US banks without alerting the government.

Luis didn't reply to Oswaldo and settled into his new bed. He found that he couldn't sleep, however, as his mind returned to Father Arturo. He realized he'd been wrong to avoid the priest.

Toward sunset Luis rose from bed, changed into street clothes, and made his way out into the courtyard, past the gate, and into the town itself. He was unsteady out of the wheelchair but knew he had to make the journey without it.

As he moved through town, nothing seemed to have changed since the shooting. People milled around, walked in and out of bars and cafes, and chatted amiably as if nothing had happened. The gaping hole in the building where the truck had struck it had been covered over with two large boards screwed into the wall. The broken stones in the road and the bullet hits in the nearby walls, now at a remove, could've been caused by anything.

The dogs on the roofs continued to bark and continued to stay well off the ground. Luis figured they might've had the right idea all along.

As he turned onto the next street, one he'd self-titled the Avenida de los Perros de Techo, he could hear the sound of the tiring hammers losing a race with the setting sun. When he reached San Elias Nieves, he found the chapel door open and slipped inside.

The chapel was illuminated by more candles than usual. The votive rack was filled to capacity as about forty candles sent thin plumes of smoke to stain the ceiling above. Luis wondered how many of them had been lit for Sergio or the girl, whose name he still didn't know. If Rogelio was right and 10K had been sent to Michoacán to wage war on Victor, there'd soon be many more.

There was a creak from within the nearby confessional, and Luis realized he wasn't alone. He genuflected and crossed himself toward the altar and took a seat in the pews to wait. A moment later an older woman emerged from the confessional and walked down the aisle, blessing herself with holy water as she stepped out into the street. Once she was gone, Luis moved to the confessional himself.

"Forgive me, Father. It's been several weeks since my last confession."

"You're forgiven, Father," Father Arturo said wearily from the other side of the screen. "But why do I sense you're here for my confession, not the other way around?"

Luis said nothing. Father Arturo fell silent for a moment as well, then sighed. "I was sorry to hear about your brush with calamity the other night."

"I'm sorrier about those who were killed," Luis replied. "I thought the local authority was meant to keep order."

Luis heard the bench on the other side of the confessional creak as Father Arturo stiffened.

"You've got it all figured out, don't you?" Father Arturo said.

"Not yet I don't," Luis said. "How much money goes to you, how much to the archdiocese, then how much goes on to the United States?"

Father Arturo rose and exited the confessional. Luis went after him. Father Arturo was halfway up the aisle to the altar before turning on Luis.

"It's easy to look through some lofty prism at me and decide I've compromised myself. But I'm no more compromised than any other clergyman in this country save the noble few who have stood up to the drug lords and swiftly paid with their lives. The same goes for the police, the government, and even the army that can't handle the cartels any more than they can provide for their own people. Who steps into that void for their communities? We do. We're hanging by our fingernails, but without us there's nowhere for anyone to turn."

"So collaboration and complicity is the answer? Even when it means mass murder?"

"Tell me, Father Chavez, what would you do in my place? What's your perfect solution?"

"I'd expose the links between the church and the cartels. There are two things that keep the cartels running with impunity. One is fear. The other is the money they pay those they can't scare. Not much you can do about the former, but a lot you can do about the latter. You're in a unique position to expose the whole arrangement. The money flows through the archdiocese. We need the records."

"Then what? Take it to the Policía Federal Ministerial? Or to the regular police? The press? What happens when we choose wrong, and no matter what kind of a crusader the person has painted themselves to be on the outside, they turn out to secretly be in league with the cartels?"

"The answer isn't to do nothing," Luis said. "Or haven't you read your Bible?"

Father Arturo seethed, his eyes burning into Luis. "You are asking me to condemn myself, which is one thing, but also my son. That isn't something I can do."

Luis shook his head. "Your son has condemned himself. But maybe what you've done is worse. You're telling yourself that it's okay because there will be children educated with their money, they'll have a place to worship, they'll have a hospital to go to when they're sick. But what kind of life will they lead if they, too, must live in fear? You're perpetuating a nightmare that is about as unholy as can be. You need to help me stop it."

Father Arturo shook his head. "I wish I had been born in America. Maybe then I could afford these high-minded ideals of yours. But this is where I live, and these are the problems faced by my parishioners. The Catholic Church in Latin America has long served at the pleasure of whoever or whatever was in power, because that's what it takes to stay close to the faithful. The one real criticism of the sainted Pope Francis is that during Argentina's Dirty War he kowtowed to the government and looked the other way during their worst abuses, even when it involved the imprisonment of other priests. We do what we have to do in times of trouble, like the ones we face now. So tell me, how can I listen to you when what you're asking forces my congregants to face these troubles alone?"

Luis didn't have an answer. Father Arturo turned and walked out of the chapel.

"I can't believe this! You are my savior! *Our* savior!"

Oscar allowed the man opposite him, a less-than-successful restaurateur named Raul Bega, to continue his praise, which included emphatically slapping the table between them, for another moment. The truth was Oscar could barely stay still. He had no interest in bailing out the restaurant. The only feature of the establishment that garnered his attention was the front door, which he glanced feverishly toward every few minutes. This was fear.

And he hated it.

"This is the kind of deal that binds people together," Raul continued, oblivious. "You and I are family now. There's nothing you cannot ask of me. Nothing."

Can you take a machete to the man who threatened my family and all of his henchmen?

"Glad you feel that way," Oscar said, pushing away from the table. "You see how this works to your advantage then?"

"How could I not?" Raul said. "I'd have to be blind."

Oscar nodded. Time to lower the boom.

Raul Bega ran four family-style Mexican restaurants that he'd inherited from his parents. Theirs was a celebrated Chicano success story. They had as many photos of themselves with movies stars and political figures on the walls of their flagship restaurant on Alvarado as they did laudatory plaques and certificates from the city. Raul Bega Sr. had passed away five years ago. The widowed Mrs. Bega had retired to a hillside estate in La Jolla, where she enjoyed the attention of a harem of personally selected boy toys. Raul, meanwhile, had run the family business he'd inherited into the ground. With a lack of vision and no head for figures, he'd spent money on all the wrong things and never the right. He was now $8 million in the red.

Then came Oscar. The solution he offered Raul was a partial buyout by Oscar's "silent partners," a restructuring of the restaurants' debt, and a move to new vendors, from food services to liquor to linens, owned by his new partners. This unexpected lifeline was the only thing keeping Raul Bega from bankruptcy.

The restaurant's front door opened. Oscar swiveled in his seat with alarm, only to see a pair of cooks arriving for the evening shift.

"Just in time!" Raul piped up. "Can you prepare something for my guest? He's helping with our revised business model."

The cooks knew exactly who Oscar was and seemed to regard the news that he was involved in the business with trepidation. Yes, they'd keep their jobs, as the restaurant wouldn't fail, but they'd work for a gangster. Oscar nodded—*you do your jobs and I'll do mine*—then shook his head to Raul.

"No time for food, but I thank you," Oscar said. "I grew up eating at your family's restaurants. Always a special occasion. I am thrilled for the opportunity to return the kindnesses your parents showed me."

The cooks seemed surprised at Oscar's deferential tone, then headed back to the kitchen, likely to begin the grass fire of gossip born from what they'd witnessed. Raul beamed back.

"Have your partners eaten here?"

"They have not, but I look forward to bringing them," Oscar said, trying to imagine his triad pals out for a night of margaritas and bottomless guac. "There is one last point to the deal that we need to discuss."

"Oh?" Raul said, impressing Oscar with how quickly he detected danger. "Don't tell me they wish to increase their ownership share?"

"Not at all," Oscar assured him. "Their exposure here is the maximum they would ever take in the restaurant business."

"Then what?" Raul said, relieved. "As I said, you're family now, so ask anything."

"I'm glad you said that," Oscar began. "My partners would like you to introduce them to your brother."

Raul looked sick. His younger brother, Raphael, had eschewed the restaurants his family owned to strike out on his own. He'd started a restaurant in Century City a few years back, dedicated to authentic Oaxacan cuisine, which, despite fantastic reviews, shuttered within a year. He'd started a different one, this with an expanded menu, down in Hermosa Beach eighteen months later. It closed two years later. But his next one, built in West Hollywood near the Pacific Design Center, took off. Six months after it became LA's "it" spot, he opened a satellite version with the same menu in Fairfax. Two years later there were six in Los Angeles, a seventh in San Francisco, and a branch being opened in Caesars Palace in Las Vegas.

Unlike his parents or older brother, Raphael didn't want to be the face of his restaurants and took no photos with politicians or celebrities. He did, however, donate to their campaigns and causes.

"My brother and I do not exactly see eye to eye when it comes to business," Raphael said carefully. "He does things his way and I—"

Run your restaurants into the toilet, Oscar thought.

"Of course," Oscar interrupted, nodding. "I know this and my partners know this. Your brother doesn't need us any more than, to be completely frank, we need him. What we're talking about is one meeting, in which we could pitch a streamlined strategic partnership that would take his businesses one step closer to maximizing their profitability."

It wasn't a dishonest pitch. The triad supplied the same brand of oven cleaner that Raphael's current vendor did. Delivered the same bulk produce and meats and spices from the same wholesalers and laundered tablecloths, aprons, napkins, kitchen towels, and uniforms in the same fashion. Only, they cut out the middleman by owning their own trucks and, well, using cut-rate, fresh-off-the-boat Chinese illegal labor, and had determined that they could save Raphael Bega easily half a million dollars a year.

All Bega had to do was accept that his new partners, at some point, might be tangentially implicated in a criminal enterprise he'd otherwise know nothing about.

What surprised Oscar the most was that the triad had needed little convincing, given their more typical reticence.

You get Raphael Bega on board, and I'll be able to pitch you to anybody in the city. No more taco stands and burger shacks. I can walk into Mastro's and tell them they're idiots for not working with you.

He proceeded with their almost immediate blessing.

But even as the words "maximizing their profitability" escaped Oscar's lips, he knew this wasn't who he was. He belonged under the hood of some car back in Echo Park. Sure, he enjoyed watching Raul Bega squirm. But the other nonsense? Never.

Oscar waited for Raul to call his brother. That was part of the deal. It had to happen right then. The call was also to include nothing about Raul's deal. Only raw numbers and what Raphael could gain by this arrangement. Oscar's job was to get Raul out of the way, set that first meeting with Raphael, and close that deal without the older brother screwing it up.

"He wants to talk to you," Raul said, face full of shame, as he handed Oscar the phone.

"Hey, how are—?" Oscar began.

"These numbers you had my brother recite over the phone even remotely accurate?" a blustering Raphael Bega barked.

"I can show you the breakdowns but also provide you with a list of our satisfied partners."

"I know who you are," Raphael said. "And I'm pretty sure I know what you're promising my brother. If it's worth all that to get some deal in front of me, how stupid would I be to not to hear you out?"

"Fantastic," Oscar said. "I'll arrange a time for you and me—"

"Nope," Raphael shot back. "You're just the guy who conned my brother. I want to see your bosses. Got it?"

Oscar resisted every impulse to throw the phone through the front window. "Got it," he said.

"Have them call me," Raphael said, then hung up.

Oscar looked across the table to Raul and didn't feel so high and mighty anymore. They were both middlemen now. Raul shrugged, but Oscar saw pride returning to his features.

"You screw this up, and the next time your mother goes to get her Botox injected there'll be something far worse in that needle," Oscar threatened.

"Far worse than anthrax?" Raul snipped.

Oscar kicked the table over. The crash of the settings and shattering glasses was nothing compared to the look of fear on Raul's face. The two cooks appeared in the kitchen doorway, one holding a carving knife. Oscar pulled his jacket and showed that he had a 9mm automatic in his waistband, one which he was licensed to carry. The cooks retreated, and Oscar went to the front door.

Once out in the sunlight, Oscar squinted up into the sky and waited for a cascade of bullets to tear his body apart. When this didn't happen, he took out his phone, and texted his driver—one Helen had insisted on hiring following their home invasion—to ask where the hell he was.

Immediately after hitting "Send," three dots appeared on the screen, signaling the imminent excuse to come. As Oscar moved to put the phone in his pocket, message unread, he picked up movement in his peripheral vision. He whirled around, hand on his gun, only to see Michael Story approaching from the parking lot.

"I just need a minute," Michael said.

"Where's my driver?"

"I'm having a friend from LAPD detain him in case anyone's got eyes on you right now. No one'll think you were voluntarily talking to law enforcement."

"How thoughtful," Oscar said, but knew it was good thinking.

"Where's Luis Chavez?" Michael asked.

"Like I'd tell you."

"We were working together when he got stabbed," Michael explained. "It was in its early days, but Luis felt there was enough to go on to pay a visit to discuss the matter with Bishop Osorio."

"Discuss what?"

"I have reason to believe someone within the Catholic Church has been helping launder Latin American drug money through Los Angeles banks for the past thirty-odd years."

Oscar stared at Michael. He couldn't believe his ears. "The church is laundering drug money?"

"Sadly, it's not without precedent," Michael said. "Just last year the Vatican's Financial Information Authority closed something like five thousand fake accounts at the Vatican Bank being used for nefarious purposes. There was evidence of possible money laundering and tax evasion tied to the Sicilian Mafia after they arrested all those priests in 2012. And it wasn't too many years ago that the pope's banker, Roberto Calvi, had bricks put in his pockets and a noose around his neck before being thrown off a London bridge while on the run for potentially laundering millions through the Vatican's banks."

"Yeah, but that's Italy," Oscar said. "You really think the archdiocese of Los Angeles is in on this? I mean, I'm not particularly devout or anything . . ."

"No, but I think the one in Mexico City might be. We're beginning to associate individual priests and parishes with cartel money transfers.

The problem is that we can't then see where the money goes on from there. It's completely closed off to me. My associates couldn't even get a foothold into the financials of the archdiocese. Luis, on the other hand, could do it easily."

Oscar scoffed. "How many times can you and Luis play Hardy Boys without one of you getting killed? Helen told me you'd been canned. And yeah, I'm sorry about your girlfriend, but that's what happens. The cartels aren't a joke. They're not some white-collar criminal hiding in plain sight that fears getting busted for tax evasion. These guys are killers who'd rather shoot you than listen to an excuse. They don't screw around."

"I know," Michael said. "But if the church is acting as a middleman for the cartels, getting at them could be a real way to strike at the drug lords. This could be billions. Even better, we could be taking down a bank or two with them. Banks that think they're too big to be bothered with the illegality of laundering drug money."

Oscar thought about the man with the melting face. Would he come for Michael next? Or would Michael win the day, as he inexplicably always did, and maybe Oscar wouldn't have to keep looking over his shoulder all the time?

"Why do you think I know where Luis is, much less how to get in contact with him?" Oscar asked.

"Because you care a lot about your friend," Michael explained. "Enough to arrange to have all flight plans and records for his emergency trip down to Michoacán scrubbed. Only, the plane was sighted by the FAA and its approximate flight path recorded. Didn't take a lot of detective work to piece together who hired it and for what."

"Bravo," said Oscar. "Let's pretend I could get word to him. You're hardly his favorite person. What do you want me to say?"

"That I have a line on his brother's killer. Or more accurately, a lead on a way to find out who hired him. You got that?"

Oscar stared at Michael in surprise, then finally managed to nod. "Got it."

"Good," Michael said. "Get a contact number for him. I'm working with an old friend of his. He can make sure any of our communications are secure."

With that, Michael headed away. As he watched the chief deputy DA march off, Oscar tried to calm his accelerating heart rate. It had been half a lifetime since Nicolas Chavez had been buried. Enough time to convince Oscar he'd stay that way.

How wrong he was.

XVI

After speaking with Father Arturo, Luis had drifted out to where his father was working. Sebastian called down to him, indicating one of the other workers.

"This is Octavio," he announced. "He's invited us to dinner."

Luis wasn't in the mood to socialize but nodded anyway. He waited below for the work to finish, then followed his father and the other workers to Octavio's house, where a feast was waiting.

"Octavio's wife is Purepecha," Sebastian explained, introducing Luis to Octavio's assembled family members. "She wanted us to taste the food of her culture as well."

The night was warm, and they ate outside, sitting on wooden benches pulled up to long tables, picnic-style. As Luis had come to expect, dish after dish appeared from the kitchen and made its way around the table. He tried everything, eating to the point of bursting. It turned out to be the birthday of an aunt, which made Luis feel better about accepting such largess, though it was clear that Sebastian was the guest of honor.

Toward the end of the second hour of the meal, Luis turned to his father and put a hand on his shoulder. "We need to talk."

As if having expected to hear something like this, Sebastian nodded idly and raised a silencing hand. "After dinner. On the walk back."

Luis sank back onto the bench in time to see two more platters emerge from the kitchen. He suddenly noticed that the birthday-celebrating aunt was glaring down the table. Luis followed her gaze to the woman seated beside Sebastian. Her eyes aglow, the woman, whom Luis took to be the celebrant's sister, laughed easily, a hand on Sebastian's shoulder. Luis looked back at the glaring aunt and recognized it for what it was: jealousy.

While amusing, it meant what Luis had to say to his father would be that much harder.

It was almost midnight when they finally left Octavio's house. There had been multiple waves of good-byes, several embraces, a few promises to return, and even, Luis glimpsed, a clandestine kiss planted on Sebastian's cheek, which was promptly returned in kind. But when they were on the road again, Sebastian turned serious.

"So, what is it?"

"I have told you perhaps that I am somewhere outside God's voice right now," Luis said.

"You have," Sebastian said. "And I have prayed to him to find a way through to you."

"Yes, but that is something of me, not him. I am at fault somehow, but I don't know how to rectify it. The trouble is I need to understand right now how I am to enact his will."

"How do you mean?" Sebastian asked, face coming in and out of the orange glow of muted house lights.

"I'm afraid the villain here is God's church," Luis said. "They're not just taking donations from minor cartel enforcers. They may be actively laundering money into the United States on behalf of the major drug lords."

"The church? How can you be sure?"

"I can't," Luis said. "Not without investigating further. But if I'm right, this could embarrass and humiliate the church, doing significant damage to its relationship with its parishioners. What I need to know from God is whether I am to pursue this or not. Too many people could be affected if I'm wrong. This cannot simply be a decision left to my heart. Will you pray on it?"

Sebastian looked embarrassed, even befuddled. But then he nodded. "I will, Luis."

"Thank you, Father. Depending on what I am to do, I should tell you that El Tule might become a dangerous place for you."

"I know this, Luis. But I won't leave until the last brick is laid for that school. I have to finish it. That is the task God has given me."

Luis nodded painfully, wishing things could be so cut and dried for him. They parted ways at the small apartment building that served as San Nieves's rectory. Luis made his way back to the hospital on his own.

"You didn't bring any beer back, did you?" Rogelio asked as Luis entered, more to cover for Oswaldo hiding a pornographic magazine than out of a real desire for alcohol.

"Was I supposed to?" Luis asked.

"Always!" Rogelio replied, pausing the portable DVD player in his hands. "What's wrong with you?"

Luis shrugged good-naturedly before climbing into bed. "What're you watching?"

"No idea," Rogelio replied. "Guy who sold it to my mother said it was a kung fu movie, but I have yet to see anyone kicked through a wall."

Luis laughed. He was hoping Rogelio might switch it off and let him get to sleep when the sound of gunfire erupted from outside. Luis and Rogelio dove out of their beds as Oswaldo turned his over and dropped behind it.

"Stay down!" Rogelio said, crawling to the window. He peeked out and blanched. "They're coming over the walls. They're after someone."

The window exploded as gunfire shattered the glass. Rogelio ducked away from the shards raining down over the room. Luis scrambled behind Oswaldo's bed as the splinters embedded themselves in his mattress.

Vera, on her hands and knees, appeared in the doorway. "Everybody to the back of the building. The laundry. Those doors can be locked. Quickly!"

Oswaldo nodded. "The doors are thick, too, and muffle the machine sound. Let's go."

Rogelio hurried across the floor, hissing in agony as broken glass chewed up his bare feet. When he got to the far side of Oswaldo's bed, Luis retrieved the spare wheelchair that had been brought for him and quickly helped Oswaldo lower his cousin into the seat.

"All right, get him out of here," Luis said as the trio emerged into the hallway, the gunfire now echoing up from within the building.

"Where are you going?" Rogelio asked.

"To see if any of the patients upstairs need help," Luis said, turning to head away before the cousins could protest.

As he raced up the stairwell, the gunfire grew louder. The shooters were using automatic weapons, both assault rifles and pistols. Luis heard mostly panes of glass shattering, followed by distant laughter. This could mean that the gunmen were more interested in tearing up the building than doing any killing, or at least that was his hope.

When he reached the second floor, Luis found the first few rooms empty, the patients having already evacuated on their own. In one of the last he checked, however, he found a terrified young woman, heavily pregnant, cowering alongside someone he took to be her mother. The older woman had covered her daughter with a heavy blanket to keep her safe from flying glass but had been cut in the process. As blood streamed down the side of her face, her daughter was attempting to staunch the bleeding.

When the daughter saw Luis, she panicked, then saw the collar. "Can you help?"

Luis hurried over and saw that the pregnant woman was still in her teens. Though her mother was gritting her teeth, it was clear she was in agony.

"We have to get out of here," Luis said, grabbing a pillowcase. "Press this against your face."

The mother did so as Luis led her pregnant daughter to the doorway. The gunmen had entered the atrium below, and their automatic weapons now boomed in the hollow space like great kettle drums. As Luis tried to determine where they might go next, the power went out.

"Oh!" the pregnant young woman said.

"Quiet!" Luis whispered as the guns went silent.

For a moment the entire building was as still as a graveyard. Then a voice familiar to Luis, one he'd last heard whispering into his ear as he sliced his torso with a blade, spoke from below.

"We are here to help you," the man with the melting face, Munuera, said. "We have learned that your district has been overrun by criminals, and the police are doing nothing about it despite knowing the identity of everyone in the gang, including its boss, Victor Canales. That changes tonight! We're here for Armando Morales, Juan Luis Carrillo, Eloy Paez, and anyone else who has pledged allegiance to Canales. You give them to us, and we will go. Protect them, and you will die. Understood?"

As Luis's eyes adjusted to the darkness, he peered down the hallway, looking for the door that led to the back staircase. He had no faith in Munuera's pledge to leave once he had the men he'd named. It was up to him to get the women to safety.

"Did you hear me?" Munuera shouted, the end of his statement punctuated by a blast of machine-gun fire that tore into the hospital's ceiling.

Luis turned to the two women and nodded toward the stairwell. "Let's go."

Keeping as low to the ground and as close to the walls as possible, Luis and the pregnant woman helped her ailing mother hurry down the dark hall. Luis had been banking on using the gunfire as cover, but suddenly it ceased, and everything was silent again. Luis indicated for the women to go still. It wasn't enough.

"Up there!" a voice said.

Bullets blasted into the short guard wall overlooking the open atrium, muzzle flash illuminating the walkway like a strobe light. Wood paneling showered over them as large chunks of the ceiling cracked apart and fell to the ground. The pregnant woman got to her knees as if to run, but Luis yanked her back down.

"They can't hit us," he hissed in her ear. "Angle's wrong. They're trying to flush us out."

The young woman didn't look any less terrified but stayed in place. Luis eyed the stairwell door, unmarred by gunfire, and nodded toward it.

"Crawl," he ordered.

The older woman didn't move. Her daughter leaned over and spoke softly to her, until she finally inched forward. The gunfire became more sporadic, aimed at all points on the upper floors. Luis figured the gunmen had lost track of them and were shooting at random. Unfortunately, he saw too late that the decorative finial on the short wall included gaps at the corners. As he and the two women passed by, they would be momentarily exposed.

"Hurry!" he exclaimed.

The pregnant woman saw the problem right away and crawled faster, but the gunmen below must've seen the movement.

"There!" came a cry, followed by concentrated machine-gun fire.

The mother screamed as Luis put his arms around her and carried her the last few feet through the stairwell door. As soon as they were inside, Luis looked over the rail to the lower floors. He wasn't sure how far the stairwell was from the laundry rooms but didn't think it was close. To make matters worse, bullets were already pinging off the bottom steps.

"Roof," Luis said hoarsely.

The three hurried up the steps, Luis now hoping the door to the roof wouldn't be locked. A few seconds later and he was rewarded to find it not only unlocked but already open. He went through first to see if any of the gunmen had made it that high, and found a handful of patients, doctors—including Luis's—and nurses, all cowering in different spots around the roof, all waiting for the violence to end.

Luis raised his hands to show he meant no harm, then led the women from the stairwell out to a spot alongside a large rooftop air conditioner. Luis felt someone's eyes on him and turned to see a young man gazing at him from across the roof. He recognized him as one of the men who'd been with Victor Canales the other night. He looked much younger now, illuminated by only the moon. He couldn't have been more than fifteen or sixteen. The terrified look on his face told Luis he was assuredly one of the men named by Munuera.

The bursts of gunfire lasted for a few more minutes before the air grew quiet again. Looking past the roof, Luis tried to make out which floor the gunmen were on, based on the lightning-like muzzle flash bouncing off the nearby buildings.

Suddenly, bullets tore up through the roof, nearly hitting them. The young pregnant woman screamed and jumped. Luis put his hand on her mouth to muffle the sound, but the clanging of footsteps on the metal stairs echoing up from the stairwell indicated that the gunmen were already on their way to the rooftop.

Dear God. Please spare these people.

The thought had barely formed in his head when the stairwell door swung open and two men with machine guns emerged. They were both soaked in sweat, and one had blood splattered up his pant leg. One appeared drunk, and the second one's wild-eyed expression suggested he was fueled by something more than adrenaline.

"Where is he?" the drunk asked, raising his gun. "We know he has to be here. He's nowhere else."

Luis's doctor stepped forward and shook his head. "It's only patients and employees up here," the doctor said. "No one you named."

The drunk raised his machine gun and fired a three-round burst into the doctor's chest. As everyone on the rooftop screamed, the gunman walked to the mortally wounded doctor and fired a final shot into his head.

"Who's next?" the shooter asked, waving the gun around. "Or are you going to make me shoot you all?"

Luis was about to rise when he caught the young man they were seeking trying to get his attention. The teenager pointed to the two shooters, signaling for Luis to hold. When they finally turned and had their backs slightly toward them, the teen motioned for Luis to stand.

"If you must shoot someone, shoot me," Luis said, getting to his feet.

The two gunmen turned, raising their weapons, then paused when they saw Luis's collar. This was all the teen needed. He launched himself at the drug-fueled shooter, grabbed his wrist, and turned the gun on his comrade. He forced the gunman's finger to pull the trigger, and a single bullet blasted into the drunk man's hip, sending him spinning away, his gun falling from his hands.

The crazed gunman cursed and elbowed the teen in the face, regaining control of his weapon. "Not smart, *pendejo*."

The teen, whose nose was shattered by the first blow, ducked behind his attacker and grabbed his arms. Luis raced at the pair, only to have the gunman shrug off the teen, aim his weapon at Luis, and squeeze off a couple of shots. Luis barely had time to duck away but tripped and landed flat on the roof.

The gunman squared off this time, aiming for Luis's heart. *"Te crees la muy muy."*

Luis stared at the barrel of the gun, holding his last breath. But when the bright light exploded from the muzzle, it was aimed upwards. In a flash the boy had grabbed the gunman and yanked him backwards, sending them both over the edge of the roof. The rooftop erupted in fresh screams as Luis hurried over and saw the two broken bodies on the concrete below.

Luis raced back to the drunk gunman, now held down by two of the doctors, and picked up his mislaid machine gun, aiming it at his head.

"Don't speak and don't move."

The gunman complied. Luis aimed the gun toward the stairwell to await the arrival of the gunmen's confederates, but he could already hear the distant sirens of the approaching police. Luis saw the utter lack of concern on the drunk man's face and felt a rage growing within himself.

The man smirked.

Luis wondered who the police were coming to protect.

In all, there were nine dead and twice that number wounded, including Rogelio and his cousin, who both suffered crippling injuries to their legs. That they hadn't been executed, like the doctor, was practically a miracle in Luis's mind.

When the police spoke to Luis, he could tell right away that it was for show. Not because the men were necessarily corrupt but because they were terrified. The destruction at the hospital was far more than they were accustomed to dealing with. The shift in power in El Tule had come quickly, and there was no telling who or which institution would be targeted next.

"You saw them shoot the doctor?" the federal police subinspector asked Luis.

"I did," Luis replied, offering no embellishment, reverting to a tactic drummed into him in childhood when dealing with police.

"What was said?"

"The man who shot the doctor said they were looking for someone. The doctor said there were only patients and nurses there."

"And then he was shot?"

"I think so. It happened quickly. I might have gone into shock."

"Some said that you then rose and stood up to the men," the subinspector said.

"That was somebody else," Luis lied.

"What did this somebody else look like?"

"No idea. It was dark."

The subinspector gave Luis a pained *work with me* expression. Luis stared blankly back.

"Did you know the boy who carried him over the side of the building? Had you seen him before?"

"No," Luis said.

Knowing it was a lie, the subinspector stared hard at Luis. Luis said nothing. Without a word, the subinspector walked away.

Luis tried to track down the pregnant woman and her mother but was told by a nurse they'd been driven to a hospital in Uruapan.

"Near where they got Canales," the nurse added.

"What do you mean?" Luis asked.

"10K," the nurse replied. "Canales's boys were caught unaware by the attack and scattered. That's why some of them even ran here. But Victor got tipped off and was on his way to Morelia when they ran him off the road, shot the two guys with him, and carted Victor away."

Without the nurse saying it, Luis knew exactly what this meant. He'd be tortured to death, his body likely to be found in horrifying condition at a later date. Whatever they eventually interred would be a horror show.

"You know he's got one of those elaborate mausoleums waiting for him in Morelia," the nurse said, her voice dipping lest she be accused of talking out of school. "He had it built last year. Showed me a picture once. Very pretty. He knew this day would come."

Luis nodded. But his worry had been for Victor's father rather than Victor himself.

Setting out for San Nieves, Luis found half the town in the street outside the hospital. They all wore the dazed expression of the walking wounded. They might not have been in the building during the gun battle, but they understood what it portended. War had come, and the first strike had been at the one place they'd believed they might be safe.

For the umpteenth time Luis wondered how anyone could live under conditions like this. The answer came to him immediately. It wasn't so different from the lies he lived, proselytizing when he couldn't even hear the voice of God anymore. They faked it, too. Pretended like everything was going along as normal when it was anything but.

Like Father Arturo.

Luis closed his eyes. How could he have accused Father Arturo of doing exactly what he had done? The pain of this humiliation made him wince. He was a fool.

When he reached the church, he found the chapel doors locked. The back door was locked as well. He considered the idea that Father Arturo might've gone elsewhere to pray but then spied the priest through a window. He was on his knees in front of the altar, arms outstretched, face skyward, weeping. There was a gun on the floor a few inches away.

Scrambling to grab a screwdriver from the now-empty construction site, Luis went to the back door, stuck it between the jamb and strike plate, then stomped downwards on the handle. The jamb cracked and Luis pushed the door open the rest of the way. He hurried down the narrow hallway to the chapel, only to find a stricken Father Arturo pointing the gun at him.

"It's me!" Luis said, ducking away.

Father Arturo stared at Luis without recognition for a moment. He lowered the gun. "You broke in?"

"I can fix the door," Luis said. "I feared for your safety."

Father Arturo eyed the gun, then set it aside. "I can endure anything but this," the older priest said. "I don't know what I'd do if they hurt him." When Luis looked at the gun, the priest shook his head. "Not that," Father Arturo added.

"I wanted to apologize for what I said yesterday," Luis began. "You were right. I have no idea how you survive all of this. I had no right to judge you."

Father Arturo nodded idly. "No, you did not. But what does it matter now?"

"I don't know," Luis said. "But I will pray for your son."

"You were on the roof when the Morales boy grabbed the gunman?"

"I was. He saved the lives of everyone on the roof. It was maybe the bravest thing I've ever seen."

"I'm glad he saved the patients, but if you're trying to convince me that my son might share some similar last shred of humanity, save your breath," Father Arturo said. "Victor's heart is black. Do you know how many coffins I've prayed over filled by his bullets? But he's my child. There was time for him to repent. If he goes to God as he is, unrepentant and unsaved, I have failed him in every way possible. So I pray that he is returned to me long enough to save him, but not so long one more person dies in his wake. If that is something you can pray for, then join me."

PART III

PART III

XVII

When Luis exited San Nieves, he walked the three blocks to the clothing store where his father had bought him the clothes he'd worn to the picnic the week before. When he'd gone to retrieve his belongings in his hospital room, he'd found a short note with a phone number at the bottom of it, along with the name of the store, instructing him to call.

As the shop owner guided him to a quiet spot in the store's tiny back room, Luis knew without dialing who would be on the other end of the line.

"Is this Lazarus?" Michael Story asked after picking up following ten rings. Luis said nothing. "I remember reading somewhere that Lazarus was Jesus's brother-in-law, if you believe he married Mary Magdalene and was more ill than dead when Jesus of Nazareth went to raise him from the dead. You could argue that death might have been preferable to living as a resurrected in-law of Christ with some sort of obvious brain damage."

Luis continued to say nothing. Michael sighed.

"At least tell me this wasn't you last night," Michael said. "The hospital shooting down there."

"That wasn't me last night," Luis said.

"I knew it was you!" Michael exclaimed. "If there's shit in the road, you'll step in it."

"I was going to call you," Luis said. "I've found at least a piece of what we've been looking for."

"I'm sure you have if you're igniting cartel wars," Michael said. "And I think I've got the other big piece here. All that's missing are the pieces that connect the two. But I have a pretty good idea of where to look."

They traded information for the next twenty minutes. Luis had questioned his role in all of this, but the shooting at the hospital the night before solidified his resolve. God wasn't speaking to him in the traditional sense, but his hand was clearly present. His response to Luis's question was to demonstrate again how monstrous the cartels were, whether they were run by Victor Canales or operating under the orders of the man with the melting face and his band of 10K-ers. If there was anything to be done to stop them, he had to do it. "After we identified the church as the go-between, we've gone back through—"

"We?" Luis asked.

"Myself, Gennady Archipenko, and your old friend Miguel Higuera."

Luis was surprised to hear Miguel's name but didn't say anything. It was the murder of Miguel's uncle the previous year that had sent Luis undercover into the farm fields. Miguel's mother was later killed by the same people. Whether Luis could've prevented this or not, the boy owed him less than nothing. He had no idea why he'd be helping the chief deputy DA.

"Go on," Luis urged.

"Anyway, we've gone back through Sittenfeld's correspondence over the years with that information in mind. So far we've identified a handful of priests associated with the Mexico City archdiocese, including two bishops and a cardinal, from whose accounts money was transferred up to Sittenfeld's bank from Mexico. The problem is these are a smattering of what look like tests, barely a quarter of a million dollars all told. Sittenfeld knew how to obliterate his tracks on this end. So we need access to the accounts of the priests themselves."

"And you can't hack the archdiocese?" Luis asked.

"It's on a closed network with an internal server. A lot of security to protect church records, but I guess we know why now. But if you managed to get to the archdiocese yourself and could access the server locally, Miguel assures me he could take it from there."

I'm sure he can, Luis thought.

"Then what? You're an American deputy DA. You can't exactly prosecute the archdiocese of Mexico City."

"No, and nor would we want to. They'd lawyer up and keep this out of the courts for the next twenty years. I mean, ideally we'd get Sittenfeld to turn witness and take a jury through it, but that's not going to happen. Our play is with the banks. If we can line up the transfers of all the middlemen from within the church and see who they were sending money to, we can go after the banks here. Kill the messenger, and they'll find another messenger. Stop the banks laundering cartel money, and you've done something."

Luis looked down at the note in his hand. The only writing beyond the phone number were the initials NC. Nicolas Chavez.

"What's this got to do with my brother?" Luis asked.

"There was a flurry of money transfers and calls in Sittenfeld's records between his last correspondence with Nicolas and the day of Nicolas's death. I think Nicolas found something and, perhaps in ignorance, brought it up to Sittenfeld. I think he may have arranged, or at least had something to do with, setting up your brother's murder."

It fell into place like a reclaimed memory. Luis felt numb knowing, from what Michael had said previously, that prosecuting Sittenfeld for the crime would likely be as impossible as going after him for Naomi's death. But maybe if Luis could discover the triggerman, the various intermediaries, the money that changed hands, somebody somewhere could make it right.

A single witness to tell the tale.

"By breaking into these accounts, we can track that name down?" Luis asked.

"The shooter was probably paid in cash, so there might not be a name," Michael admitted. "But if someone in the cartel or—well, if someone in the cartel wanted him dead, we'll probably see some money changing hands. You get me and the FBI what we want, and I'll make for damn sure we get to the bottom of your brother's case, too."

Luis didn't need Michael to clarify that it could've been someone within the church itself.

"Give me the names of the priests. I'll contact you back when I'm set up."

"Great," Michael said. "Got a pen?"

"I'll remember."

Michael did so. Luis didn't recognize a one of them. Their names burned into his memory regardless.

Michael had taken the call in a phone room Miguel had recommended off MacArthur Park. After he hung up, he texted a number that Miguel had given him a quick version of what was said. When he was finished, he removed the SIM card, snapped the cheap flip phone in half, threw it in the phone room's recycling bin, and then headed out into the morning. He was going to call Special Agent Lampman next and fill her in, but then they'd both be stuck waiting for Luis to ring back. He decided he'd wait and hopefully deliver the FBI some actionable information later, but then—what? He'd still been quasi-fired, or at least had fallen out of favor with Deborah. He hadn't even begun to think about lining up his next job. He was sure Helen would understand if he was late or short on child support, but that didn't make him feel any better.

As he neared his car, he realized he didn't even have anywhere to go. He'd driven all the way down here to make the call but had the rest of the day free. He could go for a run or to the gym, whose membership he would soon have to cancel. Maybe he should spend the day reaching out to old colleagues to discuss his next move.

That'll do, he thought, already mentally working out how to frame the situation for others. *I needed some time off. The cases were killing me. Too much political pressure to do my job properly. I resigned in protest.*

He figured he'd go with a version of the last two.

So when his cell phone rang and he saw that the caller was within the mayor's office, he wasn't so much alarmed as amused. *Oh, you haven't heard? Yeah, I was fired.*

It might even be fun.

As he raised the phone to his ear, he saw Deborah Rebenold looking back at him. Rather, it was her photograph on the front page of that morning's *La Opinión*, visible through the glass of a nearby newspaper vending machine. The headline was in Spanish, and Michael's translation abilities were poor, but one word stood out: *resignación*.

"Hello?" asked a voice on the other end of his phone.

"Sorry, this is Michael Story. How can I help you?"

There was a click, and the mayor's voice came on the line. "Did you know about this, Story?"

"Finding out now, sir," Michael said, banking on the fact that the mayor could only be calling about Deborah. "What I can't figure out is why I'm learning this from a newspaper and not a phone call."

"Then we're on the same page," the mayor said, though Michael couldn't imagine he meant the pun. "What we've pieced together so far is that *La Opinión* got the story. Called Deborah sometime last night about it. And rather than call me, you, or anyone else that matters, went on the record right then with her resignation."

Michael scanned the article, looking for anything that might shed a light as to the why. He was fairly certain the first three paragraphs were full of words like "*La Opinión* exclusive" and "interview with Rebenold," but the fourth had the meat. There was a mention of triad lawyer Jing Saifai. She and Deborah went way back.

"How could you be prosecuting a case against the triad without knowing your boss was colluding with them?" the mayor asked, clearly having had the benefit of reading the entire article.

I did know.

"As far as I could tell, her interest was strictly oversight. She knew what we were doing, called a couple of plays, but that's it. I had free rein."

"There's nothing you would've done differently without her involvement?" the mayor asked, his tone suggesting it was Michael's future, not Deborah's, that hung in the balance.

"Not one thing," Michael said. "That's why it's such a surprise."

"She might've known you'd be suspicious," the mayor surmised. "All right. Be at my office in two hours for the press conference."

"Press conference?"

"You're the new interim district attorney of the great City of Los Angeles. And like it or not, one of your first assignments is going to be going after your former boss. Congratulations."

Michael couldn't believe his ears. He was about to reply when he realized the mayor had hung up. For a long minute Michael stood on the curb staring into the middle distance, wondering how on earth something like this could happen.

Then he pocketed his phone and glanced out to the skyscrapers of downtown to the east, all thoughts of Luis, the conspiracy, even Naomi momentarily pushed aside. Everything he'd ever wanted had been handed over on a silver platter.

Praise God.

Victor Canales's body was found that evening. He'd been bound and tortured, his body then cut into five pieces before being dumped not in El Tule but on the steps of Uruapan's city hall. Luis didn't understand the significance until he asked one of his father's coworkers at the construction site.

"Victor's bosses control this region: Uruapan, Morelia, and much of the rest of Michoacán," the worker said in a hushed tone. "10K's bosses want them to know they're coming for him next. Maybe they get a couple of the younger guys to switch sides, leak intelligence in hopes of staying alive."

Luis glanced up to his father, who worked away on the roof. Sebastian didn't look back. Luis turned and headed into the church. There he found Fathers Ponce, Feliz, and Barriga circled around Father Arturo, who was speaking quietly. Luis hung back until they were done. When the three other priests exited, Father Arturo spied Luis and waved him over.

"My name and relationship to my son is going to be in the *Reforma* tomorrow," Father Arturo said. "I've been told it's already on a couple of blogs that follow cartel violence. I don't know how they found out, but they did. My days in Michoacán are numbered. The diocese won't let me stay if they think I'll be targeted for reprisals or a danger to my congregation. But of course, why should my congregation trust me anyway?"

Father Arturo scoffed and sat back down.

"I understand more than you know," Luis admitted. "I, too, have held back the truth from my congregation. I have lost touch with God. There is no connection. I go through the motions even as I know it is me and not him acting as this vessel. Do you understand?"

"I do," Father Arturo said. "I'm very sorry."

"Which is why you should stay. You owe your congregants an explanation, your loyalty, and an apology. Your compromises are your own business and sins. What you owe God and his people is something you pledged long ago. You can't turn your back on that. What you were or weren't able to do for your son is the past. What you do now is what matters to God."

Father Arturo eyed Luis suspiciously. "Which includes what? There's something *you* want."

"As you suggested, you've got only a few hours left before your name becomes a headline," Luis said, leaning in. "Before that happens, I need you to bring me to the archdiocese in Mexico City. Tonight."

"For what?"

"I need access to their internal network. Financial records, e-mail accounts, personnel records. I have the names of six priests who are allegedly colluding with the cartels to launder money into the United States. Now I need the proof."

Father Arturo looked thoughtfully at Luis for a moment, then patted his wrist. "Only six?"

"So far."

"I've only been there a couple of times, but enough to know there's a lot of security," Father Arturo said. "They log everyone who uses even the research computers in the library."

"That's why I can't do it alone. I need you to come up with a reason that gets both of us through that door."

Father Arturo considered this. "I've got a way in. Let me make a call."

"Nina wet her bed again," Yelena explained. "It wouldn't be so bad, but the mattress cover was still drying in the bathroom after I washed it the night before. It ruined the mattress."

Gennady closed his eyes and put the phone to his other ear. The shooting and his subsequent hospital stay had rattled everyone in the family, but Nina in particular. During the first few days she saw his injury like a game. If she worked at it, she could trick her father into speaking. After a couple of weeks of this, however, reality set in, and his wound quickly went from a novelty to a real source of fear. If it had happened to her daddy, couldn't it as easily happen to her?

Can you have a new mattress delivered same day? Gennady typed into a text screen.

"That's the plan right now," Yelena said. "But it would be different if you were here."

Gennady didn't doubt it. Before he'd even come home from the hospital, Yelena had begun to make plans to fly to New York, where they could stay with her aunt, who lived off Prospect Park in Brooklyn. Nina had loved exploring the vast park the Christmas before, taking her father on trips to hunt for evidence of dragons, whether foot or tail tracks, eggs, or would-be scorch marks. But when Gennady had told his wife he needed to stay behind for a few extra weeks, they'd gotten in the worst fight of their marriage. Yelena left the next morning.

I'll be there, Gennady typed.

There was a knock on the downstairs door. Gennady checked the security camera feed and unlocked the door via remote.

I have to go right now, Gennady wrote. FaceTime in the morning so I can see the kids and they can see me?

"Of course," Yelena said. "I love you."

I love you, too.

Gennady hung up the iPhone and went to the stairs. Miguel was already making his way up the steps, swaying back and forth from the weight of multiple satchels.

"You know, it's impossible to find a parking space down there," he said.

Gennady shrugged and led Miguel into the home office. Miguel opened the satchels and placed a number of laptops, routers, and a server box out around the room. He eyed Gennady's Internet connection skeptically. "What is this? AT&T or something?"

Gennady shrugged again. He was getting good at that. Miguel went back to the stairs.

"I'll be right back," Miguel said. "Actually, you'd better come with me so I don't get shot for trespassing."

Gennady followed Miguel out of the house, the younger man holding a heavy loop of cable under his shirt. They walked down the canals, Miguel glancing right and left, but for what, Gennady had no idea. It hadn't been Gennady's first choice to even do this from his house, given that it had already been hit. But once he learned how many extra security guards his fretful neighbors had paid to patrol the perimeter of the canals, he figured familiarity trumped an unknown quantity.

Miguel indicated a Mediterranean-style minimansion that took up much of the end of Gennady's block.

"Think anyone's home?" Miguel asked, but in a way that suggested it didn't matter much.

Gennady shook his head. The retired couple who owned it also owned a place in the Trastevere in Rome and spent most of their time overseas. Miguel jogged down the alley between the Mediterranean and the bungalow aside it, unspooling cable as he went. Gennady looked up to the closest windows, wondering who was watching. No matter how random and coincidental they were on the surface, the vandalism of Gennady's house and the wound to his neck were connected in the minds of his neighbors. He caught them looking at him, their eyes full of accusation. He was no longer a member of the community but an outsider in need of excising. His perfect three windows on the Neva were no more.

No matter. He'd find them again elsewhere. He just couldn't leave without salvaging his reputation first. That was everything in his line of work. People got hit. That was the price of doing business. How one responded was what mattered.

Miguel reappeared, trailing cable. "Let's go."

When they arrived back in Gennady's house a moment later, Miguel checked his computers. "Excellent. Much faster now."

Gennady typed on his iPad. Won't my neighbors complain?

"By the time anyone knows what I did back there, we'll be long gone," Miguel said cheerfully. "Don't worry about it."

Gennady nodded and typed. Michael said that you know this Father Chavez.

"I do," Miguel replied, though his tone was guarded. "He tried to help my family once, but things got worse. Maybe it was his fault, maybe it wasn't, but that's the kind of thing that strains a relationship, you know? When he offered to help me out after, I walked the other way."

Gennady didn't need to know the rest of the story. All he knew about Luis Chavez was that he'd be down in Mexico City at another computer and that Michael Story trusted him. That he was a priest mattered not at all. If there was anything he'd learned in his line of work, it was that no one makes money off the church for long except the church.

Once the laptops were arranged haphazardly around the room in a way that resembled an impromptu Wall Street trading desk, Miguel sat back.

Think anyone will know what we're up to on that end? Gennady typed.

Miguel laughed. "Oh yeah. They'll know immediately. Aren't you glad you're fifteen hundred miles away?"

XVIII

Father Arturo didn't have a vehicle, but a pickup truck described as reliable was lent by one of Sebastian's coworkers. Luis couldn't remember the last time he'd driven a stick shift and was initially reluctant, but got the hang of it relatively quickly. He hoped he wouldn't have to reverse.

The drive from El Tule to Mexico City was over six hours long. There was almost no traffic on the road to Uruapan, though Luis imagined it would pick up once they were past Morelia. He'd been unconscious on his initial drive in, so Luis took in their vast, empty surroundings as they went. He was reminded of the long stretches of low scrub that ran between Los Angeles and San Bernardino or farther out to Arizona. Only here in Mexico, without the constant barrage of billboards, gas stations, and fast-food joints, it felt so much more remote.

Father Arturo said little as they left El Tule and got underway. Luis understood why about an hour later when he nodded matter-of-factly out the window as they neared a bridge.

"That's where they ran Victor off the road," Father Arturo said.

Luis said nothing.

Three hours in and the topography changed. It became even less green, more rolling hills and flat valleys, the mountain roads even more precarious the higher they got. When they passed a sign indicating that Mexico City was 250 kilometers away, Father Arturo offered to drive for a while, but Luis declined. The drive had a calming effect on his nerves.

Also, as a Los Angeleno, he'd spent plenty of time behind the wheel of a car, but mostly in the city. Long drives out into the country were few and far between. He didn't know when next he'd be in Mexico, if ever. He wanted to soak it up. The mountains grew higher and the roads more isolated, slowing the drive as they neared Tuxpan.

Before the sun went down completely, he could see the great forested mountains of the Sierra de Angangueo, where sign after sign announced them as the winter home of the *mariposa monarca*, or monarch butterfly.

They were a few dozen kilometers from the Mexican state border when they spied a detour up ahead. Luis could make out the dark-blue uniform of the Policía Federal on a man waving a red lantern alongside two fiery barrels. He indicated for Luis to pull to the side of the road. Luis slowed, but Father Arturo grabbed the wheel.

"Are you insane? Go around."

"They're blocking the road," Luis said.

"Go around!"

Luis saw almost too late the pickup trucks parked off the highway, their beds bristling with the barrels of guns. They weren't police. Or maybe they were, which might've been worse. Whatever the case, it was bad news. Given the revelations about Victor Canales's parentage, it was possible Luis was driving the very person they were looking for.

He spun the wheel and bounced into ongoing traffic. A lone truck swerved to avoid them, but Luis thought the blockaders wouldn't shoot if they thought they might hit the driver. He was wrong, as he heard the sharp report of distant rifle fire echoing from the other side of the highway.

"Get down!" Father Arturo said, grabbing Luis's shoulder and shoving him down so that he could barely see the road ahead. Luis expected to hear the ring of metal hitting metal as the bullets hit their mark, but the sound never came.

Luis righted himself and continued to accelerate, one eye on the rearview mirror, until they were a good five kilometers down the road. Once satisfied no one was following them, he slowed the car, though could not do the same for his rapidly beating heart.

"10K's guys?" Luis asked.

"No telling," Father Arturo said, shrugging. "Could've been anyone."

Unimpeded and unpursued, they kept going toward Mexico City, now completely enshrouded by night, the darkness only broken by the soft glow behind the mountains in the distance. Luis was overcome as they crested the ridge-ringed basin to behold a vast, impossibly dense city stretching out as far as the eye could see. It was like being on the moon, believing all was still and silent, then looking over the edge of a crater to discover a great civilization.

It was the largest city he'd ever seen in his life, its immensity overwhelming. He could imagine living there his entire life and not seeing every corner. As they pushed closer to the city itself, trees and earth ringed the highway. In his home city, humanity had conquered nature and wrapped her in a shroud of concrete and asphalt. Here, as in Michoacán, there was compromise.

Father Arturo spotted the exit for Madero Street and nodded. "That way."

They left one traffic jam, only to merge into another as they pushed into the heart of the city. Father Arturo nodded in a northerly direction. "Too bad you traveled all this way but can't visit the Basilica of Our Lady of Guadalupe."

Luis hadn't even considered this. The story went that in 1531 the Virgin Mary appeared to a peasant named Juan Diego, telling him in Nahuatl, the language of the Aztecs, to build a cathedral to her on that site. He went to the Mexico City archbishop and told him what he saw but wasn't believed. He returned and received a second vision, as well as a gift of Castilian roses, a flower native only to Spain. He gathered them in his cloak and took them to the archbishop. When he opened his cloak to present them, on the inside was an image of the Virgin of Guadalupe. The cloak, in a gilded frame, hung in the basilica.

It is too bad, Luis silently agreed.

The seat of the archdiocese of Mexico City was located in the Catedral Metropolitana de la Asunción de la Santísima Virgen María— the Metropolitan Cathedral—the largest church in Latin America. As Luis crossed República de Guatemala, he could see even from the back that it seemed to stretch on for block after block.

"We're not in the sticks anymore," Father Arturo explained.

Coming around the side of the building, the two priests entered through the front doors and into the cathedral itself. Luis kicked himself for believing such grandeur was only found in Europe, the towering ceilings rising high above the pews, stretching the length of a football field from a gilded altar. Even the pipes of the organ shot skyward from its position beside the quire.

A midnight Mass was being celebrated, and though hundreds were in attendance, they were dwarfed by the building, making it look like a small, intimate gathering. The priest used a microphone and amplifier to address the solemn assemblage, as if there were thousands.

"What's crazy is that this spot was once sacred to the Aztecs," Father Arturo said. "The Spanish built right over it. Took over a hundred years."

"God lives where God lives," Luis replied.

They watched for a moment longer, before Father Arturo signaled Luis that it was time to go. "This way," he said, indicating a hallway off to the side.

The church offices of the Mexico City archdiocese were as large and expansive as that of a major university, albeit one lined with paintings, gold plates, and tapestries dating back a half millennium. Even at the late hour, priests and nuns moved from office to office, answering phones, printing up itineraries, and placing orders.

As they stepped into the building, Father Arturo revealed his plan. "There is a Father Manka here. He is an American. He visited El Tule when he first arrived and invited me to visit him at the archdiocese."

"And you're sure he'll be here?" Luis asked as he opened a heavy wooden door for Father Arturo.

"I telephoned him before I left," Father Arturo said. "I told him you were interested in seeing if there was any more information about your mother."

This gave Luis pause. It was a passable lie, but that was why it bothered him. He hated to casually exploit his great-uncle's memory for the commission of sin. There would be a day of reckoning for all of these things he had done.

"We need a computer with access to the internal servers, password protected or not," Luis said. "We then hand over control to Miguel."

"Sounds easy."

"It is. If you're willing to betray the church," Luis said succinctly.

"From what you have described, it's not the church but a handful within it that have abused the church's power to do this. I look at it as we're righting a wrong."

Luis wished he was as adept at rationalization.

They approached a desk, where a young priest sat. He didn't look much older than a teenager, and his immediately eager-to-please manner reminded Luis of the late Father Belbenoit. Father Arturo explained who they were there to see, and the young priest picked up a phone to find out where he was. As if he'd been waiting in the wings, a middle-aged priest of surprising height—easily six foot seven or eight—emerged from a nearby doorway and smiled in greeting at the two visitors.

"Welcome," the priest said in American-accented English, shaking Luis's hand after greeting Father Arturo. "Jim Manka, originally from the States as well. Upper Peninsula Michigan."

"Los Angeles," Father Chavez replied. "Born and raised."

Father Manka led them through the doors into the archdiocese's inner offices. The heavy Baroque décor continued, causing Luis to wonder what it must be like to work in such a place where every day you were surrounded by centuries of history. He thought it must be wonderful.

They reached a door that required Father Manka to wave a key card over a pad. It unlocked, and he ushered them in. Luis had counted half-a-dozen cameras in the hallway. There were three at this door alone. Father Manka saw where Luis was looking and sighed.

"The archdioceses, ours and others, have proven naïve when allowing outside researchers into the archives. There have been thefts of letters, documents, but plates from rare books in particular over the years, some as souvenirs, others to sell on the open market. As you might imagine, some of these works are priceless, and to razor them out of a centuries-old text is an offense so much more than a violation of trust."

Luis nodded. He wondered how Father Manka would characterize what he and Father Arturo were there to do.

They passed through another door and into a modest-sized white room furnished with tables, chairs, and reading stands. A priest stood behind a desk typing away at a computer as Father Manka led Luis and Father Arturo to him.

"Fathers Chavez and Arturo, this is Father Cicero," Father Manka said as the priest moved to meet them. "He will assist you with any records you need."

Father Cicero smiled and indicated the shelves behind him. "Everything is stored back here. We ask that you wear gloves when going through it." He pointed to a bank of computers at the end of the white room. "You can look up whatever you need there, write down the cataloging information, and bring it to me. I'll bring it out to you as soon as I can find you."

"Thank you so much," Luis said.

"When I found out who your great-uncle was, I couldn't wait to be of any assistance," Father Cicero said. "He was an amazing man and inspiration."

"Thank you," Luis said, burning with guilt.

Father Manka walked him over to the computer stations and popped the lid on a thumb pad alongside the keyboard. "Fingerprint check."

Luis waited for Father Manka to activate it with his thumb, but the Michigan priest nodded to Father Arturo. "I can't log in here and also be logged in at my desk. But I checked, and luckily you're already in the system, Father Arturo."

Father Arturo stared at the pad as if placing his finger on it would seal his fate. Then he pressed his thumb onto it anyway and the workstation came to life. On the pad itself a tiny picture of Father Arturo appeared, alongside his name and home parish.

"Piece of cake," Father Manka said. "I'll be right down the hall if you need anything. Please stop by on your way out to tell me how it went."

"Will do," said Father Arturo.

Luis sat down at the computer and took out his phone. Father Arturo pulled a chair up next to him.

"How is this computer supposed to get us to these priests' bank accounts?" Father Arturo asked. "It looks like a simple archive catalog. It's not even connected to the Internet, is it?"

"It's not the computer," Luis said. "It's that thumb pad. Miguel told me to look out for anything that might check back with the internal servers. That's what he needs. We're going to use this catalog for exactly what we said."

Luis placed his phone alongside the thumb pad. He opened a text window and wrote a single word: ahora.

Now.

Luis took a breath, unplugged the thumb pad, and inserted the cord into the phone. When there were no alarms or flashing lights, he let himself resume breathing. Almost immediately an image of Father Arturo's thumbprint, along with his name and photo, appeared on his phone.

We're in.

Below the thumbprint, an app opened on Luis's phone, and text scrolled rapidly down the screen. Father Arturo looked on in amazement.

"Your friend is hacking into the servers with your phone?"

Luis sent Father Arturo a silencing gaze, then settled in to discover what he could of his great-uncle.

Gennady watched as seemingly thousands of images flashed briefly on Miguel's computer screens, until one by one they lit up with the faces, thumbprints, names, and home parishes of six priests. To the Russian, the faces looked downright generic, an assortment of DMV snapshots rather than the portraits of men who had spent the past three decades or so orchestrating a massive Latin American money-laundering scheme.

Father Marcelo de Hoyos—Diocese of Tuxtepec, Archdiocese of Antequera, Oaxaca

Father Cornelio Colombo—Diocese of Tlaxcala, Archdiocese of Puebla de los Ángeles

Father Maximilliano Gaviria—Diocese of Ensenada, Archdiocese of Tijuana

Father Heraclio Bonilla—Diocese of Cuernavaca, Archdiocese of Mexico

Father Joao Arellano—Diocese of Veracruz, Archdiocese of Xalapa

Father Adalberto Pardo—Diocese of Nogales, Archdiocese of Hermosillo

Miguel tapped a couple of keys on his tablet and nodded to Gennady. "Here we go."

Gennady typed, How'd you do that?

"Convinced the security system on the archive computer that Father Chavez's phone was the thumb pad. Now, if I can keep my data miners invisible enough to pull these guys' records, we'll get somewhere."

Hard to believe they need this much security, Gennady wrote.

Miguel stared at Gennady with surprise. "Hey, who has more to hide than the Catholic Church?"

There was more information on Bishop Socorro Trueba than Luis could've looked over in a lifetime. He finally decided on a selection of letters his great-uncle had exchanged with Pope Paul VI to begin with. Father Cicero, it turned out, had already put them aside.

"I thought this was where you might wish to begin," Father Cicero said. "Amazing man, Pope Paul. Traveled wide, living up to his pontifical name."

Luis nodded and took the letters back to a table near the catalog machine. He put on the white gloves Father Cicero had laid out on the desk for him and paged through them. The letters concerned Pope

Paul VI's recent visit to Bogota, Colombia. When the pope wrote back asking about Bishop Trueba's parish, the return letter from Luis's great-uncle was more personal. Socorro spoke of the Indian poor in the area that he hoped to minister to. The letter then took a surprising turn, calling out the church's responsibility in the matter due to the religious colonization of the Aztecs, stripping away their religion and replacing it with Catholicism.

In our arrogance, we believed we could elevate the lives of these indigenous people simply by presenting them with evidence of God. But in doing so we were complicit in the dismantling of their great and vast civilization by the Spanish. We must make reparations for this sin in whatever way we can.

It was a radical idea, particularly for its time and even more so coming from a bishop. In California there were plenty of American Indian activists who protested against the canonization of the Franciscan Junípero Serra for his role in the genocide of Native Americans. But here in Mexico, where the adoration of the Virgen de Guadalupe had cemented the hold of Catholicism, a bishop was writing the pope to say the same thing. The response, disappointingly, came from a cardinal and not the pope. There were assurances and references to God in his wisdom.

There was no evidence that Paul VI had written back.

See where you get it? Luis imagined his mother saying.

"Father Chavez, you should look at this."

Luis turned to Father Arturo, who watched images flying across the phone's screen.

"There's so much information," Father Arturo said.

"Easier to hide things that way," Luis said.

But then something changed. The names of other priests replaced those that had initially been on-screen. More e-mails were opened and more accounts. The amount of money shifted as well. In the earlier currency transfers, there seemed to be records in the tens of millions or more. Now they were in the tens or hundreds of thousands or even less but coming from even more accounts. Faces of dozens more priests flashed across the phone screen.

"Who are these priests?" Luis asked.

"I thought I recognized one or two—" Father Arturo said, then cut himself off.

"What's the matter?" Luis asked. "Michael said he only got a few names on that end of priests funneling money to Sittenfeld. This might mean there were dozens if not hundreds more from all over the country."

Father Arturo turned away sharply, as if he'd been slapped. Luis looked down to what had appeared on-screen. It was Father Arturo's photo again, with the name of his home parish. A bank page was opened, revealing transfers in Father Arturo's name of thousands of dollars over several years, sent from El Tule to the Mexico City archdiocese.

Luis turned to Father Arturo in surprise.

"You asked how it worked. Well, now you know."

Miguel shook his head as the information rolled across the multiple screens.

"Wow, I thought *I* was good at my job," Miguel said. "It's nothing compared to this scheme. Have you ever seen so much money? They make us look like amateurs."

Gennady stared at the different faces flying past and wrote. Not just the six priests?

"Nah, man, that's what's craziest. Father Heraclio Bonilla? Father Adalberto Pardo? I ran cross-checks. They fooled me. Those guys don't even exist. They've got work records, photographs, fingerprints, bank accounts, e-mail accounts, home parishes, and everything else. But they don't seem to have ever physically existed. Six virgin births in cyberspace, complete with endless paper trails. Must've been something Sittenfeld set up for them."

And all these other priests?

"A nationwide network of bagmen. The local cartel chieftains come to them with money, they send it to the archdiocese. Some are involved in a single transaction, some handle many a year. Hard to say who knew what they were doing, who looked the other way, and who was truly complicit with the cartels. But at the end of the day, all that matters is that the cartel never could've gotten all this money into American banks without the help of the church. And that's crazy."

Gennady wasn't certain "crazy" was the right word.

Unlike his younger counterpart, he didn't feel any sort of rah-rah admiration for Sittenfeld's scheme. Seeing all the billions flying past filled him instead with revulsion. These were men of faith, men allegedly above reproach, but because someone saw an opportunity to make money, they'd been twisted and converted. He needed air.

But as he turned to head for the stairs, Miguel's voice held him in place. "Wait, what the hell's this?"

Gennady looked back as one by one the screens began to freeze. Miguel stared for a second more, then went to the back of his remote server and yanked the cords. He grabbed one of his phones and typed out a text.

"Get out of there, Luis," he whispered urgently, mashing out the note with his thumbs as quickly as possible. "Oh crap. It's not going through."

What's going on? Gennady typed to Miguel.

"One of the records was a trap, a fail-safe. And I walked right into it."

"Everybody knew," Father Arturo said, leaning back in his chair. "It was like having two collection plates. Part of the money went to us for the parish in an account overseen by the diocese in Morelia. Another, the one that came from my son and his comrades, went to Mexico City. We never saw any of that again."

"The school? The hospital?"

"Done directly by Victor. He hired the architect, the construction firm, and so on. That was from his guilt, not his superiors'."

"But is a widespread practice, yes?"

"Yes," Father Arturo said glumly.

Luis looked down. There was nothing left for him here. On one table was the evidence that his great-uncle had tried to do something right, however small, by the locals, only to be rejected. On the other was evidence that the church was at least partially complicit in one of the worst and longest-running bloodbaths Mexico had seen since the conquistadors.

"What does God say to you?" Luis asked.

"I haven't asked," Father Arturo admitted. "I haven't prayed, or at least I haven't listened, for an answer to prayer in some time. He must know I can't face him."

"Is that why you brought me here?" Luis asked. "As some sort of penance?"

Father Arturo was silent for a moment.

"They murdered my son," he said. "And by my actions I too . . ."

Luis nodded. He thought back to his conversation with Father Arturo after he had confronted the older priest in the confessional at San Elias Nieves.

Tell me, Father Chavez, what would you do in my place?

Luis didn't have a chance to contemplate this. The sight of movement in his peripheral vision snapped him back to reality. No, not movement. He looked to his phone. The information on the screen had frozen.

"Time to go."

Michael Story was on his deck in Silver Lake, staring out over the palm trees, when his cell phone began to buzz repeatedly, announcing the arrival of several e-mails. He'd been trying to recall the exact feeling of standing in that spot a couple of months back, arms wrapped around Naomi's waist, chin above her hair, her back pressed against his chest as a light, misty rain fell around them. The memory was secure, every aspect as fresh in his mind as if it had happened yesterday. What he was beginning to lose was the ability to recreate the sensations he'd felt, the loss he'd felt after, the warmth of being loved and loving someone else. The residual light in his life that Naomi had created was flickering, soon to be extinguished altogether.

He moved to his laptop, which was open on the picnic table. Swiping the mouse pad, he made the screen light up, showing no less than a hundred new e-mails delivered to the remote account he'd created for this purpose. They were all from Miguel.

Here we go.

He'd planned to take notes as he opened the files, but it was instantly overwhelming, the breadth of what Miguel had managed to extract from the Mexico City archdiocese so great, it would take a team of FBI investigators months to—

Wait.

FBI investigators? Sure, they were waiting across town for this, but with Deborah out and Michael interim district attorney, shouldn't he perhaps have his own office address this? Wasn't that his sworn duty? Besides, the FBI was sure to throw him over the moment they had what they needed from the cache, right?

Might as well make his case that "interim" should be dropped from his title as soon as possible, no? Particularly given the various skeletons in his own closet that might come out during a special election.

With a case like this he couldn't lose.

The only question—and it was a big one—was, could he afford to make an enemy out of the FBI?

Of course. I'm the goddamn district attorney of Los Angeles.

Luis hustled Father Arturo down the hallways of the Mexico City archdiocese as fast as he could without attracting attention. It was late at night now, so there were few others around, but the cameras were everywhere. Luis felt the eyes of the security guards watching from some monitor bank buried within the building boring into him with every turn.

He'd tried to communicate with Miguel, but the phone was frozen and soon shut down completely. Luis pocketed it and hurried on.

They took another turn, only to see two men in the white uniform of the archdiocese's internal security police at the end of the hall. Luis did a 180 and led Father Arturo away. Behind him he heard the voice of Father Manka call out to the guards. "That's them!"

Shit.

"Hurry," Luis whispered to Father Arturo, who tried in vain to pick up the pace.

The sound of the guards' quickening footsteps reached Luis's ears, and he sped up even more, practically dragging his fellow priest alongside him.

"Father Arturo! Father Chavez!"

Luis didn't turn. The footsteps broke into a run. It was only a matter of time before they caught up. But then Luis caught sight of a closing elevator door to their left and swung Father Arturo toward it. As the guards closed the distance between them, Luis pushed Father Arturo through the closing doors and slipped after. He turned in time to see the frustrated faces of the guards in the gap between the doors.

"That was close!" Father Arturo said.

It wasn't over yet.

The elevator doors opened near the reception area where they'd encountered the young priest. Still at the desk, the young man got to his feet and waved down the exiting priests.

"Father Chavez! Father Manka needs a word!"

Luis didn't respond, practically holding Father Arturo up as he walked. They were only a few yards from the glass doors that led out of the archdiocese when two more security guards appeared directly outside, the pair staring in at Luis and Father Arturo. Luis turned left and right, but the other exits seemed miles away.

"Father Arturo!" shouted Father Manka behind them.

Luis reluctantly turned as the formerly welcoming priest ran to him from the elevators, flanked by two guards, whose frustration had turned to anger. Father Arturo stepped in front of Luis and nodded grimly at Father Manka.

"What is it, Father?" he asked.

"There's a fire at your parish! It's consumed the building. It started on some construction site behind the chapel."

"The school!" Father Arturo cried. "It's gone?"

"Is that what it was?" said Father Manka. "I'm afraid so then."

Father Arturo's face fell. He sagged, until he was on his knees, head in his hands. "It's gone!" he bellowed.

One thought filled Luis's mind: *Sebastian.*

He was about to ask Father Manka if anyone had been hurt when his cell phone rang. When he saw his father's number on the caller ID, he said a silent prayer and answered. "Dad?"

There was silence, followed by a chuckle. "You are a very clever priest, Father Chavez. That I will give you."

The voice was instantly familiar. The pain in Luis's lower back, all but forgotten, returned at the sound of it.

"What do you want?"

"It's not what I want, but it seldom is," Munuera said. "Your father, however, wishes for you to join us. I would put him on the line, but he's screaming in pain right now. Perhaps you'd be so good as to come here. Bring this phone with you, of course, as I've been told the information your friends absconded with is copied there. So at least we can understand the breadth of the damage you've done. Then we can discuss how to put an end to your father's pain."

"I don't believe you," Luis said.

"Yes you do," Munuera replied. "But if it makes you feel better—"

The inhuman sounds that filled Luis's eardrums a second later related such pain, such agony, he could hardly bear it. Worse, the voice making the sounds, however strained and distorted, was unmistakably his father's.

When Munuera returned to the line, he sounded more amused than vicious. "Convinced?"

Luis was. He'd never felt so helpless before in all his life.

XIX

The return trip to Michoacán was so slow Luis felt as if they were driving to the edge of the world. There was little to mark their progress. The highway and surrounding landscape were completely dark, the only thing illuminated being the stretch of road immediately in front of the headlights. Somewhere at the end of it all, Luis hoped, was his father.

The address given to him by Munuera, the 10K man, was in the middle of nowhere.

"It might be an abandoned ranch or something," Father Arturo said. "But it's one of those roads with nothing down it. It doesn't make sense."

"Locating it won't be the problem," Luis said.

"He wants us to find them," Father Arturo agreed.

"He specified me alone," Luis said. "You've done enough for me and my family already."

"But I have nowhere to go," Father Arturo said. "They destroyed my church. They burned my school."

Your church? Your school?

"Then is this really the moment your parishioners can afford to lose their priest, too?" Luis asked. "They need you now more than ever. Yours would be an empty sacrifice."

"The cartel will come for me when they learn of my connection to my son," Father Arturo said.

"Die then," Luis said. "But until that last moment, be of use to your parish."

Father Arturo said nothing for the rest of the drive. Luis took this for penitence, until he realized that the priest had fallen asleep a few kilometers before the State of Mexico–Michoacán border.

Luis took the opportunity to empty his mind before saying what might be his final prayer. He asked God for guidance, but not for himself but for Father Arturo, for Oscar, for Miguel, for Michael Story, and for Sebastian, if he was alive.

God, if you are with him, please ease his pain. Amen.

Luis considered prolonging the prayer, then decided it was unnecessary. He stared out the window into the darkness, watching for the subtle differences in the silhouettes of the neighboring hills to differentiate earth from sky. If he was going to his death, he wanted the last things he saw to be earthly, not man-made. He focused on the sand creeping onto the shoulder of the road, the tall oyamel trees that rose abruptly against the dark backdrop, and the occasional star he could see over the halo of the pickup's headlights.

In a flight of fancy, he wondered if there was some way to communicate to Sebastian that he was coming as quickly as he could.

Either to rescue him or to die alongside him.

Oscar awoke in the middle of the night. His mouth was cotton dry, reminding him he'd been drinking the night before. He'd heard somewhere that the body began processing the sugars from alcohol a few hours after it was consumed, which was why so many casual drinkers popped awake at two or three in the morning.

As a committed alcoholic, Oscar was surprised to find it happening to him.

He looked down at the silhouette of Helen as she slept beside him. He loved her. Oh, how he loved her.

He climbed out of bed and wandered into the kitchen. He found his cell phone plugged in by the stove—he'd kept it in the bedroom for a while, until Helen decreed there were boundaries—and checked the messages. There were no voice mails, but there was a text from an international number. The area code was 664.

Tijuana.

It was a video file. He debated not playing it, unsure if it was some kind of virus that would capture his phone. Then he realized it could be much worse. Did he really want to see, say, Luis's head chainsawed off this early in the morning? There were things he didn't want to see.

He hit "Play" anyway. A house appeared on the screen, one shot from a distance out in the middle of nowhere. Oscar gathered from the terrain that it had been taken in Mexico, though the modern-enough-looking house could have been almost anywhere in the Southwestern United States. The cameraman walked around to the side and zoomed in on the backyard, where there was a short brick wall around an in-ground pool. After a moment a man and a woman exited the rear of the house, moving toward the water. Oscar was struck by a sense of dread as he recognized one half of the pair.

Dear God, what have you wrought now?

It was about an hour before dawn when Luis dropped Father Arturo off on the outskirts of El Tule. The older priest pointed off toward the east, where the sun rose.

"Down there. Take you half an hour."

"Thanks," Luis said. "I'll leave the keys in the truck when I drop it off later."

Father Arturo smiled at this. It was clear that neither thought Luis had much of a chance of returning alive.

"See that you do," Father Arturo said.

Luis was about to pull away when Father Arturo took his arm through the driver's-side window. Luis thought he meant to bless him, but Father Arturo bowed his head.

"Will you give me a blessing, Father Chavez?"

Luis put the truck in park and climbed out as Father Arturo knelt. They remained that way for several minutes while Luis spoke over the older priest, then finally put a hand on Father Arturo's shoulder. When he drove off a moment later, he saw in the rearview that Father Arturo remained on his knees in prayer.

Luis turned away and drove toward the sun. As Father Arturo had suggested, the road described by Munuera went off into the middle of nowhere. The pickup's suspension didn't do well on the unpaved, hard-packed dirt, launching Luis into the roof more than once. If it weren't for a recent set of tire tracks in the dust, he would've lost the trail long before.

He'd been hungry earlier, but it was worse now. He was also parched. He'd meant to stop for food and water at a gas station or *supermercado*, but everything he'd seen on the way back from Mexico City was closed.

After one particularly high bounce, the pickup came down hard on the right side, and Luis knew immediately he'd lost the tire. He glanced into the bed and saw a spare. If he made it back, he could change it then. He turned off the engine, placed the keys on the dashboard, left the door unlocked, and climbed out to begin the long walk.

As he crossed the desert scrub, Luis imagined what it must've been like for the Franciscan friars who came with the Spanish to convert the Aztecs with the same collar around their necks. It was hard to be in

Mexico and not think on the atrocities done in the name of Christian colonization. It was the greed for land and gold that motivated the Age of Exploration more than dogma. He wondered what the world would look like if the diseases that came west and wiped out the large Central and South American indigenous civilizations had instead originated here and gone to Europe with the colonists.

What would a world driven by the Aztecs look like, as opposed to Europeans? Would there even be a Catholic Church?

And yes, it meant that he wouldn't be alive, but he marveled at who might be walking across this patch of land in his place if that had come to pass.

He set these thoughts aside upon spotting a pickup truck up ahead with a couple of young men standing alongside. Munuera's men. They stared at him as he approached, and he saw that one held binoculars. They'd seen him long before he'd seen them. When he was within a few yards, one of the young men pointed an AR-15 at Luis's chest as the other hurried around to pat him down. Finding nothing, the young man indicated the bed of their truck, then got back behind the wheel.

As he climbed into the bed of the pickup, Luis quietly thanked God for giving his feet a rest.

About a mile down the road, an old, crumbling building appeared in the distance. A second pickup had pulled in line behind the first a few moments after they'd departed, and Luis realized they must've been in some kind of overwatch position, likely with a rifle aimed at his head if he had tried anything or brought backup. The caravan slowed as it pulled up to the rusted metal warehouse, where a couple of panel trucks were parked out front. Luis waited in the back of the truck until the driver parked and came around to lower the tailgate. A large sliding door was pushed aside on the warehouse, and two more young men emerged, carrying small machine guns. One nodded to Luis to follow them inside as the others waited by the trucks.

It was in that moment that Luis felt God return to him.

It wasn't words or a thought but a feeling. The absence of one. Luis knew he should be terrified at this moment, but he was not. He felt the eyes of God on him, moving with him. A tension he didn't even realize he'd been carrying throughout his body left it. A hot-blooded anger, the one he'd felt most acutely as he stood over the spot where his brother had died, eased out of his mind like a subsiding headache. The sense of loss for the late Pastor Whillans, for his mother and brother, and for the earlier, more confident version of himself ebbed.

He was whole again. He closed his eyes, said a prayer that somewhere within the building his father felt the same comfort, and entered the warehouse.

It turned out that the building had been some sort of factory or mill but now housed pallets, wrapped for transport, of brightly boxed disposable surgical equipment—dressings, plastic forceps, procedure packs, needle and sponge holders—all with "Made in America" on the side and "Finished in Mexico" hidden somewhere on a label. By the back wall was a dwindling stack of the equipment boxes, a group of men in a makeshift assembly line opening each, inserting waterproof packages of what Luis took for cocaine into various interior crevasses, before repacking them and placing them on a last pallet.

Luis figured if all of the boxes on the pallets contained as much cocaine as he was seeing being shoved into this equipment, it was literally tens of millions of dollars' worth of drugs.

A man who looked as if his facial features were sliding off of his face approached Luis, nodding to him matter-of-factly.

Munuera.

"Father Chavez," the man said, extending a hand. "Obregon Bortolo Munuera. Thank you for attempting no tricks and coming as you said you would. Follow me please."

Munuera moved to a steel staircase running up the back wall to a covey of second-floor offices. Luis followed, casting an eye back to the boxes of medical supplies.

"Ah yes," Munuera said. "Medical supplies this week. Next week it'll be peaches from Chile. In two weeks after that it'll be fenders for Mitsubishi. There's always someone on the north side willing to pay extra to CBP for expedited service. The trick is to know which, swim into that supply line, hijack enough for our purposes, then send them on their way. Our product is out before it even reaches their warehouse."

"Your doing?" Luis asked.

"I've learned that it's better to pay little notice to the other arms of the octopus," Munuera said, shaking his head. "I didn't want you laboring under the belief that every crime here doesn't have a complicit partner on your side of the border."

"Like Charles Sittenfeld."

"Who?" Munuera asked, seeming to be genuinely unsure. "That's the banker's name? No, he's just a man. His bank makes the lion's share of the money, not him. He enjoys taking the most risks. He has more to fear from his fellow bankers, who are afraid of being exposed, than us."

A train whistle blew outside. The workers below accelerated their progress as the back door of the warehouse was slid open. Pallet jacks were shoved under the completed pallets, which were then wheeled into line behind the newly opened door. The last two pallets were finished and were wrapped with plastic sheeting, customs forms slapped on each announcing the boxes as having been inspected already.

Luis looked out a nearby window and spied a decelerating train coming down virtually unseen tracks that ran alongside the factory. Freight car doors slid open as the train slowed to a crawl. The workers, about two dozen in all, rolled the pallets from the loading dock onto the moving train, then hopped off, pulling the pallet jacks with them.

It was like watching a carefully choreographed ballet. A freight car opened, the boxes slid on board, the door closed, the next freight car door opened behind it. In a matter of seconds almost half the pallets were loaded, all the freight car doors were shut again, and the train sped back up, to disappear into the desert.

"Come on," Munuera said from the steps above Luis. "Your father is finishing his shower."

The second-floor room turned out to be an empty employee locker room. Against the rear wall were the showers, though water was running out of only one. His arms held high as to chain him to the shower head, Sebastian was slumped under the stream, barely able to stand. His clothes were soaked through with water, blood, and sweat. His face was heavily bruised, as was, Luis imagined, the rest of his body.

"Be happy he lives," Munuera said, raising a long-barrel revolver. "But what happens next depends on you."

Luis didn't reply but instead went to his father's side. Munuera made no move to stop him. Luis placed a hand on the older man's chest and leaned down to his ear. "Dad, I'm here."

Sebastian's eyes rolled around without focus for a moment before finding Luis. When he saw his son, he reached for him, but his wrists merely clinked together on the shower pipe above.

"Why did you come?" Sebastian asked weakly, his voice ragged. "You should have run away or gone back to the States. I am all they can take away from you."

"That's too much," Luis said, putting his arms around Sebastian. "We're leaving here together."

Sebastian nodded, though it looked like he was about to pass out. Munuera's gun barrel tapped Luis's shoulder.

"You need to follow me," he said. "They're waiting for you."

"Who is?"

"The heads of the octopus."

Luis left his father's side and followed Munuera into a small office off the locker room. There was a desk inside with a single telephone on it. Munuera went to it, dialed a number, waited, then held the phone out to Luis. Luis took it.

"Who is this?" Luis asked into the phone.

"A planner," a man's voice said in an accent Luis took for Sinaloan. "You are clever."

This wasn't a compliment.

"But you choose your partners poorly," the planner continued. "Michael Story told you he'd be handing all of this information over to the FBI, correct?"

Luis didn't reply.

"We know he did, because we listened to the call. But right now he's colluding with Miguel Higuera and Gennady Archipenko to stage his first victory as newly appointed interim district attorney of Los Angeles."

This was news to Luis. He found the mention of Miguel particularly upsetting but knew he couldn't show it. "So?"

"You sacrifice for others even as they use you to realize their own ambition?"

"That has been my relationship to Michael Story since the beginning," Luis found himself saying.

"A deal with the devil?" the planner offered.

"He wishes he had such abilities," Luis replied.

The planner laughed. "Then maybe this will be easy. We don't like to kill priests or Americans but will do so if we have to. What's done is done. Since Sittenfeld's arrest, this outcome was inevitable, whether it came from his interrogation, an exploration of his contacts, or a rogue priest like you. Regardless, we have spent the preceding months preparing. What you found at the Mexico City archdiocese we allowed you to find."

"You mean there were real priests at some point?" Luis asked.

This time it was the planner who went silent. Then: "From you we want only one thing: information. Answer our question, and we will let you and your father go."

"And what's that?" Luis asked.

"You know something about Michael Story that no one else does. It weighs on you. We would like to share that burden."

"How do I know you'll free my father if I tell you?"

"There are no assurances I can give that would satisfy you."

Luis thought about this. He knew what they wanted to know. But they were wrong. It wasn't a burden. Luis knew Michael Story played both sides of many games and—

"What do you have on Michael Story?" the planner asked.

It was simple. Michael had taken money from a powerful entity who asked him to keep tabs on a young whistle-blower named Annie Whittaker. When she approached him about a case she was assembling, he reported back to them, took their money, and promised to keep them updated. Soon, however, he fell in love, or merely lust, with her and they embarked on an affair. At what point he stopped informing on her, Luis wasn't sure. But it was clear that eventually the young woman was murdered for what she knew.

Luis had pieced it together and had confronted Michael, but only Michael knew how directly or indirectly responsible he was for her death.

"If I tell you, will you answer a question of mine?" Luis asked.

"You can ask," the planner replied.

Luis told the planner everything he knew about Michael. It wasn't much, but it was what the man wanted to hear. He asked Luis to repeat a few details and elaborate on a couple of points, but the entire back and forth took only five minutes.

"Now," Luis said, "who arranged my brother's murder?"

The planner said nothing for a long moment. Luis thought he might be conferring with someone else. When he finally came back on the line, Luis expected a brush-off or a *no sé*. Instead he was given a name.

"Thank you for your time, Father Chavez. May our paths never cross again."

The phone call ended. Luis rose in a daze. He focused on the fact that his father hung by his wrists in the next room and pushed everything else from his mind. Munuera greeted him in the doorway, a set of keys, including one for handcuffs, in his palm.

"You can take the pickup you arrived in," Munuera said. "I won't make you walk."

Luis took the keys without a word and went to unlock his father's wrists. Sebastian fell forward, but Luis caught him and lowered him the rest of the way to the floor.

"We're getting out of here, Father," Luis said.

Sebastian nodded and fought his way to his feet. Arm around Luis's shoulder, the older man slowly made his way to the stairs, where Munuera was waiting. As they descended, Luis glanced around the factory below and saw that all the workers were now gone. Even the guards had left.

"I've heard that priests believe the devil whispers to them," Munuera said as they neared the front door. "Is that true?"

"We believe that, yes," Luis said.

"But how do you tell the difference?" Munuera asked. "Between God and the devil, I mean. Are their voices so different?"

"That's just it," Luis admitted. "They sound exactly the same."

Munuera smiled as they moved to the pickup truck. "Clever. So you could be speaking directly to Satan and think it's God?"

Luis looked past Munuera and saw the two men who'd driven him to the mill building loading the dead bodies of the guards, the train loaders, and even the overwatch gunmen onto the two panel trucks. Their hands and wrists had been bound, their throats cut. Luis could hear one of the young men telling the other how easy it was to get one group to bind and kill the other when they didn't know they'd be next.

"Somehow the devil always reveals himself," Luis said. "He can't help it."

"A fatal flaw," Munuera said. "But plenty give in to him, don't they?"

"Every minute of every day," Luis agreed.

Munuera waved him away as Luis helped Sebastian into the pickup and drove off.

XX

"Is this a joke?" Agent Lampman asked, though her voice betrayed a knowing sense that it was anything but. "Be careful how you answer, Michael. You only get one shot."

"I was as surprised as you are, but it's legit," Michael said, tapping the stack of pages on the table between them with grim assurance. "I called the judge this morning. She said she signed the warrant for Naomi six weeks ago. I sent her a photo of the signature. She confirmed it was hers."

Agent Lampman scrutinized Michael as if preparing to devour him. "It only now came to your attention?"

"In my defense, I was fired," Michael said. "I haven't been able to access my own office, much less evidence pertinent to ongoing investigations, in weeks. That goes for Naomi's case, too. I knew she had a warrant for Sittenfeld's e-mail accounts and bank records relating to the murder-for-hire case. I didn't know she'd surreptitiously gotten a secondary search warrant relating to money laundering."

"Shouldn't this have come out in subsequent findings?" Lampman asked, seething. "The case was reassigned within days."

"Probably," Michael admitted. "But all of these documents—the warrant, Sittenfeld's records, and the ones she managed to pull from the Mexico City archdiocese—"

"Let me stop you there. How *did* she get them from the archdiocese?"

Michael shrugged. "They must've been among Sittenfeld's records. I don't know. He was likely stockpiling evidence in case they ever turned on him. Regardless, it was on her home laptop, which had been sitting in a box of personal items, waiting to be picked up from the courthouse, ever since her death. I guess her parents never went to claim it."

"Not at your shared residence, where you have constant access to it, though, right?" Lampman asked with a sneer.

"What're you implying?"

"First off, you forged the warrant," Lampman said, sinking back on her heels. "Next, you received these records through illegal methods. Finally, that you loaded it all into Okpewho's computer and somehow managed to convincingly backdate it, a near-impossible feat in this day and age, in order to take the case back to the district attorney's office now that you're interim DA."

Michael whistled. "You think I'm capable of all that?"

"I think I'm still learning what you're capable of, Mr. Story," Lampman shot back. "Is this about the girl? You'll finally get your revenge when this all comes to light?"

"It's not revenge when it's justice," Michael said. "Or have you forgotten that somewhere along the way?"

Lampman leaned over the table, until her teeth were inches from Michael's throat. "Is it justice if you have to break every law on the books to get it?"

Michael didn't have an answer for this.

"Look, we've proven over the past few weeks that we work exceptionally well together," Michael said. "I would like to suggest that, going forward, the FBI, Justice, and my own office collaborate on the indictment. Everyone's worked hard. I don't mind sharing some of the glory."

"You're serious?" Agent Lampman asked, barking out a laugh.

"I am," Michael said.

"This is going to backfire on you," Agent Lampman said. "A *lot*."

"Is that a no?" Michael asked. "When we line this up in front of the bank's lawyers, you're going to want to be there to see their faces."

He held up the copy of the records he'd made for Lampman. She stared at them like a fox sighting down on a hare. When Michael thought she was going to lay into him all over again, she snatched the pages from his hand and stormed out of the room without a word.

As soon as he was alone, Michael let himself celebrate the victory internally. It was true that he'd probably broken more laws and statutes than he'd even be able to recite, but so had the bad guys, hadn't they? What mattered now was that those who had killed Naomi would pay.

All that mattered.

Sebastian was conscious when Luis reached the construction worker's pickup but asleep by the time he finished changing the tire. He transferred his father with difficulty to the new vehicle, then started out again. Bypassing El Tule, he drove up to Uruapan and the university hospital, bringing Sebastian directly into the emergency room.

The admitting nurse took one look at Sebastian and shook her head. "What happened to him?"

"Car accident," Luis said.

"Lot of car accidents around here," she said knowingly. "Not a lot of survivors."

Half an hour later Sebastian was wheeled into surgery. In the waiting room, Luis stared idly at a television broadcasting telenovelas before falling asleep himself. When he was awoken a few hours later, the same nurse was kneeling beside him.

"Your father has three broken ribs, compound fractures in his right arm, a broken scapula, and a broken left foot. That's the good news."

Luis inhaled sharply as the nurse waited to see if he could handle the bad.

"He received several blows to the head, resulting in a swelling of his brain," the nurse continued. "They needed to remove a piece of his skull to reduce the swelling."

Luis closed his eyes, said a short prayer, and nodded. "Okay."

"I'd say he was lucky to be alive, but it's obvious his attacker knew what they were doing," the nurse continued. "He was struck in ways to maximize pain but keep him alive. He went through hell."

Luis thanked the woman, asked when he could see him, and was told that Sebastian was awake then, but that there was no telling how lucid he'd be. When Luis arrived in the post-op room, he didn't recognize his father at first, so swollen were his features. What was visible of his face was gray, almost white, as if he'd been drained of blood.

"We are a pair," Sebastian whispered in a throaty voice. "One gets out of a hospital bed, and the other goes right in."

"How do you feel?"

"Like a man yanked back from death's door," Sebastian said. "I was asleep when someone beat on the doors of the rectory, shouting about a fire at the church. I ran over with Fathers Feliz and Barriga. By the time we got there, it was beyond rescue. It was terrible. Some of the women were crying. *I* felt like crying. Somebody told me there was a second fire, and I foolishly went around the corner to see. That's when they got me."

"You couldn't have known they'd target you."

"Maybe, but I didn't have to make it so easy for them," Sebastian said, grimacing at a new ache in his skull. "How is Father Arturo?"

"I don't know. I dropped him off before I went to find you."

"If he is well, will you pass along a message to him?" Sebastian asked. Luis nodded. "Tell him that when he is ready to rebuild, I'll be right there with him, hammer and nail in my hand."

It was a statement full of bravado, but Luis knew he meant it.

"You can't stay in Mexico," Luis protested. "You'll wind up right back in this hospital, or worse, in a coffin."

"You were right to tell Father Arturo what you did about his responsibility to his congregation. I worry that he needs help to make that happen, you know?"

Luis was about to challenge his father again when Sebastian took his hand, gently tightening his grip around his fingers.

"I'll give him the message."

Luis drove back to El Tule. He was exhausted despite his nap in the waiting room. He parked at the apartment building that served as San Nieves's rectory and jogged up the steps to Sebastian's room. He didn't have a key, but Father Ponce was home and let him in.

"He was so quiet, half the time we didn't know he was home," Father Ponce said. "Some nights he'd make dinner for us, then disappear into his room. He only put his hammer down to sleep or attend Mass."

Luis nodded and stepped inside. The single room was so bare that he wondered if he'd happened into the wrong one. It could've passed for an empty store room if not for the bedroll on the floor and the three threadbare work shirts hanging in the closet. His father lived like an ascetic.

There was one last artifact in the room, a familiar one at that, in the form of a small metal box by the window. Unadorned, with a lid that never closed properly, the box was one Luis's mother had used to keep recipes in when he was a child. He didn't remember it ever going missing but seeing it now realized it must've fallen into his father's care at some point. He walked over and opened it, unsure what he'd find. He gasped when he saw the contents.

Inside were about fifty to sixty old photographs, all long-forgotten images of Luis and Nicolas as children. There they were at Echo Park Lake; with their mother at a Los Posados procession at Christmastime; at a birthday party for someone—a relative?—Luis couldn't place; at the zoo; at the Santa Monica pier. Memories Luis hadn't accessed in decades reappeared. He remembered his clothes, a different aspect of his mother's smile, the way his brother's face looked at a certain angle. He'd let go of so much over the years, but here they were, his family returned to him.

As he sifted through the photographs a second time, he came to a couple that had been attached to the refrigerator with magnets, favorites of his mother. He wondered if they'd ever sat down and divided them up. What was most striking to him was that Sebastian wasn't in a single one, most likely occupying the space behind the lens. If he chose these himself, perhaps it was not to remind him of the family of four that had been but of the trio that had been left behind.

Luis sank onto the bedroll, holding the photos in his hands. He was out a moment later.

Michael hadn't expected his return to his offices at the Foltz Criminal Justice Center to exactly be auspicious, but he didn't expect them to be as decidedly downbeat as they were either. Deputy district attorneys, assistants, and investigators he'd known for years offered him the limpest of congratulations at being made DA or simple, curt greetings that left him wondering what he'd done. He didn't think the office was particularly loyal to Deborah, so it was surprising to him that her former coworkers were acting that way. He wanted to stop in the middle of the office and point it out but decided it could only embarrass himself.

When he got to his old office, which had been boxed up when he was fired, he saw a single note on the door.

Meeting with AG, Chandler Founders Room. 10.

It took Michael a moment to realize that AG must mean the attorney general, but he had to take out his cell phone and do a web search to find the Chandler Founders Room. Turned out to mean a spot three blocks north of there at the Music Center in the Dorothy Chandler Pavilion.

What on earth does the AG want with me?

He turned to find someone to ask, but no one would look him in the eye.

Fine.

In a fit of pique, he carried his satchel and computer bag not into his old office but over to Deborah's, left it right in the middle of everything, exited, locking the door behind him, and went downstairs.

No one said a word.

After several days of sunshine, ominous clouds hung over the city, lending it a feeling of dark portent. But Michael had lived in LA long enough to know the difference between clouds that moved on and those laden with rain. He wouldn't need an umbrella for a quick walk to and from the Chandler.

When he jogged up the steps to the Music Center's courtyard a few minutes later, he found a young woman in professional dress waiting at the Chandler's front doors.

"Mr. Story?" she called. When he nodded, she indicated inside. "He's waiting upstairs. Thank you for coming."

He? But the AG is a woman.

That's when Michael realized that the note didn't refer to the California attorney general but the one in Washington, DC.

Ah.

The lobby of the Chandler was all marble and gilt-framed glass, its design wholly indicative of its birth in the late fifties. Michael followed the thickly carpeted center stairs up a flight, took a left, and wound his way to the heavy wooden doors of the Founders Room. He expected to find an attendant or assistant waiting to usher him in, but there was no such person. Not knowing whether or not to knock, he tried the door, and it swung right open.

"Michael, so nice to finally meet you in person."

Michael was surprised to find the US attorney general, a man he'd seen so often on television and in the newspaper, rising from a plush sofa and walking over to meet him. He was even taller in person than he'd imagined. He was also the only one in the room.

"How're you, Michael?" the AG asked, extending his hand. "Congratulations on the new position. I know it came to you in unusual fashion, but you seem to have the chops for it."

"Thank you, Mr. Attorney General," Michael replied, shaking the proffered hand, the pressure giving the mostly healed wound on his forearm a jolt.

Michael sized up the official, trying to figure out what had brought him here. It was inconceivable that it was the promotion. Then he realized: *Lampman.*

"I apologize for springing this meeting on you, but it's come to my attention that though we have a common interest and goal, we suddenly find ourselves in danger of tripping the other one up."

"Is that why you needed to fly out here so quickly?"

The AG looked confused. "What? Oh, I've been back and forth to LA for much of the past month and half. Been here since last Thursday. Just the players from your office have changed."

Michael froze. He'd met with Deborah?

"In the past several weeks you've been hard at work with elements within the FBI putting together a case that, you'll agree, does not measure up to even the loosest judicial standard. Because of this recklessness, you have endangered a deal my office and that of your predecessor were preparing to put in front of—"

As the attorney general said the name of Charles Sittenfeld's bank, Michael felt light-headed. This was not at all what he expected this meeting to be about.

"Wait, why is there a deal with Sittenfeld's bank?"

The AG looked at Michael like he'd missed the forest for the trees. Michael realized he had.

"We were onto Sittenfeld long before his murder-for-hire charge," the AG said. "When he got arrested, we came to him about turning state's evidence against his confederates within the bank. He decided to make a deal with CIA instead. We knew we'd never be able to bust the cartel, but we could at least show the banks what happens when you do business with drug lords."

"You mean a plea?" Michael asked, feeling the floor turn to ice beneath his feet.

"A plea resulting in the single largest fine in US history," the AG said proudly. "Nine hundred fifty million dollars."

Because a billion would be too much of a headline.

Michael took a seat on one of the nearest sofas. He glanced around at his lavish surroundings, the magnificent oil paintings, the chandeliers literally brought over from a Hollywood musical spectacular, the antique furniture, the mahogany bar, and realized what an ironically perfect location the AG had chosen for their meeting.

"When the government bailed out that bank a few years back, how big a chunk of the seven-hundred-billion-dollar pie did they receive?" Michael asked flatly.

The AG looked surprised. He shook his head. "I don't know."

"Seven percent," Michael said. "Or forty-nine billion dollars. So, you got a rebate of one point nine percent. Congratulations. Now, if you'll excuse me, I have to write up an indictment for Sittenfeld as accomplice to murder for Naomi Okpewho. This is all going to sound amazing in court, by the way, loose judicial standards or not."

Michael rose to leave, but the AG caught his arm. "I'm sorry, Michael, but he is immune from prosecution. This includes the murder-for-hire case. Part of the agreement stipulates that the details of the case become sealed."

Michael remembered hearing he'd made his reputation as an organized-crime-busting prosecutor in New York City. He wondered what the AG's younger, crusader version would think of the man now standing in the Chandler Pavilion's Founders Room, talking about making deals with banks and letting cartels off the hook.

"Sittenfeld is the only thing that connects this case to Naomi's murder."

"Again, you're going to need to set aside your personal feelings and see the big picture."

Jesus Christ.

"These monsters killed people in the streets here! How can you not care about that?"

"I do care," the AG seethed. "But those individuals have long since fled south of the border. Given the life expectancy of a cartel hit man, perhaps you can rest easy knowing they're likely long dead, or will be soon."

"Maybe I can accelerate that process," Michael sniped.

"Careful, Story," the AG said. "You're on the same thin ice that sank Deborah Rebenold."

"What're you talking about?" Michael asked.

"Oh, she wanted to do right by Miss Okpewho as well. When we told her the agreement stipulated that Sittenfeld had immunity, she tried to resign. When the mayor refused to accept, suddenly all the triad stuff showed up in the paper."

So the mayor's full of it. And Deborah's a saint for publicly immolating her career rather than allowing Naomi's death to be swept under the rug.

"What happens if I walk away and take all this stuff to the paper, too?" Michael asked.

The AG sat back down on the sofa, crossed his legs, and shrugged. "That'd make for a pretty heady couple of days. But you have to ask yourself, what're you going to do next week? Or the week after? Or next month? Or next year? You won't have an FBI task force to hang out with then."

Michael thought about this. As he did, the AG pulled a trifolded stack of papers from his jacket pocket, as well as a pen.

"What's that?" Michael asked.

"Your office's signature is the most important in all this, ironically enough. Legal immunity for Sittenfeld for a crime in your jurisdiction. You sign this, and I have it on good authority that within two weeks the mayor gives a press conference, hails your assistance in landing said largest fine in US history, and drops the interim part of your title. Which is ultimately what you want, right?"

Michael stared at the pen. He didn't know what he wanted in that moment.

"So what about Lampman's task force? Were they keeping an eye on me?"

"Don't flatter yourself," the AG said. "They were there to make a case against the church. But you've proved it's an issue for the Mexican government, not ours. There'll be no indictments against the Los Angeles archdiocese."

Michael shook his head as the AG held out the papers. "But there was that murdered kid, Nicolas Chavez. He was onto something early on, wasn't he? I outlined it for Lampman. Somebody put Sittenfeld together with the banks on the US side. It had to be."

"Of course," the AG agreed. "But you sure as hell can't prosecute him."

"Why not?"

The AG eyed him derisively. "Correct me if I'm wrong, but Osorio was already found with his throat cut by the cartel. Another loose end tied up. The only case against the church would involve those within the Mexico City archdiocese and the parish priests that passed cartel money up to the bank. They're middlemen at best. And you'd better believe no elected official in Mexico is going to go after both the cartels *and* the Catholic Church."

XXI

It was dark when Luis awoke. He gathered the photos, work shirts, and a pair of socks and underwear he found in the zippered pocket of the bedroll and headed out to the pickup. He knew this would be the last time he saw El Tule, knew it as much as he knew it was God telling him that was the case, and was at peace with that. He drove by the ruins of San Nieves, hoping to catch sight of Father Arturo, but saw Father Barriga instead.

"He's in Uruapan. Visiting your father I think."

Luis nodded, told Father Barriga he hoped he would stay on in El Tule (to which he received a dubious shrug), then drove on.

The drive to Uruapan was slower this time, as there were more cars on the road. Luis turned on the radio and was surprised to hear what his father had described so many days before in El Tule, a Cumbia version of a Morrissey song. He listened all the way to the end, amazed by how well the music translated, then turned it off when the station went to the next song to preserve the moment.

It was almost midnight when he arrived at the hospital. He parked, was ushered right back by a nurse—the same kind that would've scolded him about visitor's hours if this had been the States—and found Father Arturo kneeling in prayer beside his sleeping father's bedside.

"How is he?" Luis asked when the priest rose.

"Fine, fine," Father Arturo said wearily. "It is so hard to see him like this."

Luis nodded and pulled up two chairs. Father Arturo sat down and looked Luis over as if there was more to say. Turned out there was.

"You saved a pregnant woman and her mother during the gunfight at the hospital, yes?" Father Arturo said.

"I led them out," Luis said.

"When they arrived here, they were both in distress," Father Arturo said. "The pregnant woman gave birth prematurely, and it looked like the baby might die."

"After all they'd suffered? That's downright cruel."

"That's what I thought, too," Father Arturo said. "One of the nurses asked me to pray with the women, but I couldn't bear it. I didn't want to give them false hope if there was no chance. The baby got worse and worse, and soon I was called to give last rites."

"Did you go?" Luis asked.

"I did," Father Arturo admitted. "But when I saw the baby, I couldn't do it. Instead I began to beg for the child's life. To ask God to take me, not him. I prayed for over two hours, until I'd just about collapsed from exhaustion."

"And? The baby made a miraculous recovery?"

"No, but he is still alive," Father Arturo said. "He should've died hours ago, but yet—"

"But yet."

Father Arturo nodded. "So, I return to my vigil now. Maybe as I try to reignite my own faith, its glow will be enough to sustain a single child. If that faith grows, maybe one day it'll be enough to elevate a congregation again."

Luis nodded and embraced Father Arturo. The older priest held on tight, then finally excused himself. Luis thought he might say more, but he was gone a moment later. Luis turned back to Sebastian, glad for a few moments alone. He didn't think his dad would wake, but that didn't matter. He took his father's hand, prayed with him for the better part of the next hour, then left the hospital for the airport in Morelia.

Oscar had already been good and drunk when he turned on the TV looking for a ball game and finding the local late news. He was about to switch the television off when a number caught his eye: $950 million.

He paused and let the story play. As the broadcaster read quotes from a press release out of the US attorney general's office, images of a bank's logo were intercut with pixelated crime scene video from cartel killings in Mexico.

"Hey, that's Juarez!" Oscar said to no one in particular. "There's a movie theater right around there. And a shrimp joint. Great spot."

What was clear from the news report was that despite the trumpeting of the largest fine in American history, the bank itself had not been made to apologize and cited poor oversight, with a promise to improve training and tighten regulation.

There was no mention of any tie to recent criminal violence in Los Angeles. Nothing relating to the Catholic Church acting as middlemen. And no suggestion whatsoever that the bank would not go right on laundering money until it was caught a second time, though this time with a better understanding of what the fine would be.

What surprised Oscar was that the investigation was described as a multiagency collaboration that had taken over a year to assemble. He wondered if this was true.

"Back to rolling cash through T-shirt wholesalers in the Garment District," Oscar said.

He turned off the television, grabbed another beer, and went out to the balcony. Helen wasn't home yet, but Michael had the kids tonight. Given what Oscar had to get done that night, he was glad they were away. This wouldn't be easy.

As he stared out over the city, he grew angrier and angrier.

These pinche *cartel shooters ruining my life.*

But he knew if it hadn't been this, it would've been something else. The injustice of it all pissed him off. A man tries to off his wife, gets caught, buys his freedom by selling out all his secrets to the CIA, and the drug lords, being perfectly evolved to do one thing—survive—mop up the loose ends and start again elsewhere.

The Feds want their share. Much ado about nothing.

Too bad Nicolas Chavez had to be the first victim.

He heard the front door open and tensed, then recognized Helen's gait as she moved through the living room to the balcony. He glanced back in time to see her take in the sheer number of empty beer bottles on the coffee table before sending him a reproachful look.

"You've been enjoying yourself," she said, eyebrow raised.

"Yep," he said, wishing he could apologize in advance for what was coming next.

"I tried to call you about ten times," Helen said, taking a swig from his beer. "You've got fifteen messages on your phone. What if one of those was business?"

Oscar shrugged. Helen moved in front of him, tone turning serious.

"I got a couple of calls today from one of the new restaurants on the list," she said cautiously.

"They called you?" Oscar asked with mock surprise.

"They couldn't get through to you," Helen continued. "They missed their delivery from our partners. When I called over to the warehouse, they said that their own shipments were delayed and rang to tell you, but you never got back to them."

"Since when did chasing down triad lettuce suppliers become my job?"

"Since you agreed to partner with them and take large commissions when expanding their businesses," Helen shot back, a hint of aggravation in her tone. "Since you decided going quasi-legit might be worth it. Since we decided to build a life together."

No such thing as quasi-legit, Helen. Once you're in, you're in. Or did you miss the recent lesson?

"Build a life together? This is your life, not mine. I'm the dog you got to do a few tricks. Doesn't make me your poodle no matter how much you like it when I treat you like my bitch."

Helen reacted as if slapped. Oscar mocked her surprise with a cruel imitation, then headed back inside. "I need a beer."

"You what?" Helen snapped. "We're in the middle of a conversation here."

"Don't talk to me like I'm one of your kids," Oscar said, pulling away. She grabbed his hand in a gesture he realized a second too late was meant to pull him back to her, maybe yank him back to sanity. But he jerked away with such force that her hand slapped into the patio door. She yelped in pain and looked to Oscar for comfort, maybe even an apology, but he kept walking.

When he got to the fridge, he discovered he'd drank it dry. He grabbed a room temperature bottle from the liquor cabinet, popped the cap, and shot the entire thing in one long draught. When he finished, he tossed the bottle into the sink, where it made a satisfying crash.

"Is this an ego thing?" Helen asked, leaning against the dining room table. "Shatter whatever illusions I might've allowed myself, because you realized you'd rather steal a car than work for a living?"

"If you think this is honest work, then yeah, maybe you could do with a reality check," Oscar replied. "Steal a man's car and there's a chance you could get caught. Be made to pay for what you've done. This is just as criminal, but despite ruining someone's life by a lot more than the price of a car, you'll always get away with it. It's downright"—he searched for the word—"unsportsmanlike."

Helen glowered at him with disgust. "Oh, if there's no danger involved, it just doesn't give you enough of a thrill to be worthwhile? Am I supposed to be impressed?"

"You mean you're not? Wasn't this what you were looking for when you went trolling for some thug dick revenge back in the day?"

Helen slapped him. Hard. Oscar grinned. "There she is," he cooed. "Do it again and maybe, if you're lucky, I'll give you one back. That's what you're really craving, right?"

"Wait a minute," Helen said, altering her tone. "What is this? This is a smoke screen. What's really going on? What're you not telling me?"

You know me too well.

"Not a thing, babe," Oscar said, approaching her with all kinds of menace. "Realizing if I don't push back now, I'm going to lose the parts of myself I like."

There seemed to be enough truth in the statement to give Helen pause. She straightened.

"I've spent the last year figuring out who I am and how much I'm willing to take after so many years of letting that be decided by someone else," Helen said evenly. "I will not, repeat *not*, go down that road again. Because unlike you and whatever this nonsense is you've decided to conjure tonight, I do know what it's like to lose myself in a role. That will never be me again."

Helen waited for a reply. Oscar said nothing as he leaned against the table and stared the love of his life in the eyes.

"Are you going to keep pretending this doesn't turn you on, or do I have to carry you in that bedroom myself?" he asked coldly.

Picking up her purse, Helen moved wordlessly to the front door. Oscar was drawn to her as if being sucked into a black hole. He had to fight every fiber of his being demanding he go after her to tell her that he loved her, that she'd changed everything about him for the better right down to his DNA in such a short amount of time. That she was the only person on the planet that mattered, really mattered, to him. That she made him feel alive and he loved being in love with her.

But his old instinct for cruelty kept him rooted in place. This had to be a 100 percent, no leeway.

As Helen opened the door, she looked back one last time, staring straight into Oscar's soul. "How can you attack what we've made simply because it's less than what you might've dreamed of?"

Before Oscar could reply, she was out the door, the sound of it slamming behind her that of two hearts breaking.

Helen's eyes were filled with tears before she made it to the street, but she held them back in case Oscar could see her from the window. How could she have been so wrong about him? She got behind the wheel of her car, keyed the ignition, and was halfway down the block before she had to pull over.

She had sworn she'd never cry over a man after the way Michael had treated her, but here she was. During her most forgiving moments, she silently thanked her ex-husband for making her feel so expendable and unwanted that it forced her to change things in her life. If he hadn't been so awful, maybe she would've died a slow death, along with the marriage.

But he'd cheated on her, the woman had been murdered, and the killers had tried to blackmail him about it using her. She'd found out inadvertently, as he'd never said a word, never let on what was going on, and acted as if it didn't matter to him.

Maybe it didn't.

Oscar was right about one thing. She'd initially gone to bed with him, at least mentally, to get back at her husband. That it became so much more had surprised her. But just when she got comfortable, here he pulled the rug out from under her. He might try to apologize down the line, but what was said couldn't be unsaid.

As she wiped her tears, she realized that she didn't know where she was going. She didn't have a home anymore. Everything was in their house on Outpost. There was still the Bel Air house, but it was being renovated. It was a mess. At least the kids were with Michael for the next three days while she figured out her next move.

She angled her car back onto the road and drove in the direction of West Hollywood. There was a hotel there, L'Ermitage, that had one of the best spas and in-room masseurs in the city. She rang the front desk, made a reservation, then texted her assistant at the dealership and explained that a family emergency had arisen and she wouldn't be in for a couple of days, though she would be available by phone.

She then turned off her phone, tossed it in the cup holder, and began the mental process to reinvent herself yet again.

Given the late hour, Luis didn't expect to find anyone waiting for him when he disembarked from his plane at LAX. So it was a welcome surprise when he spotted the diminutive silhouette of St. Augustine's seventy-one-year-old administrative assistant/laywoman, Erna Dahlstrang, seated near the baggage carousel with a copy of *The Hidden Face* open in her lap.

"How's the book?" he asked.

"The introduction is so peevish, so male, that I almost wanted to throw it away," she admitted. "I'm glad I didn't, though."

She rose and put her arms around Luis, who returned the embrace. "Welcome back, Father Chavez. You seem intact."

"That's one word for it," Luis said. "How are you?"

"Never better now that you're here. We've heard so many rumors about you that it's a blessing to see you in the flesh."

"I figured you kept things in order, no?" Luis asked.

"I do what I can, but it's a man's ecclesiastical order. A woman, even a well-intentioned one, can only make you fellows get out of your own way for so long."

"I've missed you, Erna."

"And I you, Father Chavez," Erna said as she walked Luis away from baggage claim and out to the parking garage across the street. "I have had two phone calls while sitting here. One a reminder that the archbishop wishes you to stop by his offices this week at your convenience. He would like to speak to you."

"And I to him," Luis agreed. "As soon as humanly possible."

"The other was from an Oscar de Icaza. He asked you to call him the moment you arrived. He has something to show you. He said it couldn't wait."

Luis nodded. Oscar was going to be his first phone call, too.

"Thank you for the messages. I'll call him from the car."

Oscar waited half an hour to make certain Helen wouldn't return before going to his SUV, pulling up the backseats, and taking out the parts of his AR-15 to give them the once-over. Deep down he kept hoping to be illuminated by the headlights of Helen's car, though he'd known the moment she exited the door she wouldn't be back.

He ran his hand along the side of the cushion until he found the hidden seam, slipped a couple of fingers into it, and pulled out four magazines. He jammed one into the well, chambered a round, checked the action, then popped the round out of the breech and returned it to its clip. He then disassembled the weapon and returned it to its hiding spot.

Where they were going, no one would pay it any mind.

Luis arrived at St. Augustine's as Father Pargeter prepared to celebrate a late Mass. There were few congregants in attendance, but Luis took the single bag of possessions he'd brought from Michoacán to the rectory, changed into his cassock and surplice, then happily hurried to the chapel.

A few heads turned as Luis entered through the vestibule rather than from behind the sacristy. Father Pargeter, who hadn't yet begun, hurried over from the altar and handed Luis the Book of Gospels.

"Will you process with us?" Father Pargeter asked.

Luis enthusiastically agreed. He took the book, elevated it over his chest, and, as the organist began to play, stepped forward behind the acting thurifer as they moved up the aisle to lead the procession to the altar. Luis then served as lector, reading the first prayer, then sat as Father Pargeter moved to the pulpit.

It was reinvigorating. Hearing the voice of God meant Luis didn't only feel human again, he felt like a vessel, a priest. A man with a vocation. When the Mass was over, he went to the parish office, grabbed the keys to the '84 Caprice, and headed out. He knew the congregants had questions, but there'd be another time and place.

He hadn't been to a place Oscar called home since they were kids. If he'd had to meet with his old friend in recent years, it was always on neutral ground, like Oscar's place of business or the church. Oscar made no effort to include Luis in his personal life, but it wasn't as if Luis wanted to come over for Sunday afternoon barbecue and beer anyway.

He'd texted Oscar to say he was back, only to have Oscar text back an address. The implication was clear. *Come now.*

As he drove up into Hollywood, he was surprised to find Oscar living in that part of the city. Though geographically near to East LA, it was still perched high and away in the hills. The distance between it and their childhood neighborhood, though only a few miles, might as well have been an ocean.

After he parked, he heard music wafting in from somewhere close by.

"Hollywood Bowl," said Oscar from somewhere in the darkness. "A jazz singer and her band. Figure it's almost over, but pretty nice, huh?"

Luis's eyes adjusted, and he saw Oscar sitting on the curb nearby, drinking a beer.

"Still, it's considered noise pollution, so people who live up here get free tickets to a bunch of shows," Oscar continued.

"You going?" Luis asked.

Oscar scoffed. "Can you see me at the Bowl with Helen, her kids, and a picnic basket, like some fat postal worker and his schoolteacher wife?"

Luis was taken aback. Not by Oscar's words but the actual longing he heard behind them. That was exactly what Oscar wanted.

"What am I doing here?" Luis asked. "Where is Helen?"

"I faked a fight to get her to walk out on me forever. We were each other's biggest liability whether she'd want to admit that or not. Next question?"

Luis realized that Oscar was very, very drunk. This would not go well. He then saw that the doors to Oscar's SUV were open, the lights in the house all off.

"Are you going somewhere?" Luis asked.

"Yeah, same place as you." Oscar got to his feet and nodded back to the house. "Easier to see this on the big screen," Oscar said. "Follow me."

Luis hesitated, then dutifully followed his old friend up the sidewalk and into the house hanging from the cliff. As he glanced around the kitchen, living room, and to the balcony beyond, Luis marveled at how a young man who'd seemed so at home in a grease-stained garage could live in such a house.

"Over here," Oscar said, indicating a smart television mounted on the wall.

Luis waited while Oscar fumbled with a remote control. When he brought up the screen of his iPhone, he typed in a long series of numbers into the search box. A video popped up, the timer in the lower right indicating it was four minutes long.

"What is this?" Luis asked.

"Just watch," Oscar said as he hit "Play."

The screen filled with the image of a two-story house in the middle of a desert. There was a small wall around the backyard, but a pool was visible, as the camera was on a rise. From the style of the house, Luis figured it either down in Imperial Valley, California, or somewhere in Northern Mexico.

"Somebody sent this to me," Oscar said. "Interesting, no?"

"Not yet," Luis replied.

"Watch."

An elderly man and woman emerged from the back of the house. The man wore a robe, the woman a sort of gray nurse's uniform. She walked him to the edge of the pool, helped him out of his robe, then took his elbow as he moved down the pool's steps into the water.

But Luis didn't need to see any more. The moment the old man appeared, Luis had recognized him.

It was Bishop Emeritus Eduardo Osorio.

XXII

"When was this taken?" Luis asked, incredulous. "It's got to be old, right?"

Oscar fast-forwarded the video. Osorio's dog paddled from one end of the pool to the other, looking like a petulant child forced into chores. The angle then panned to the house's driveway, where a Range Rover stood.

"That's a new model," Oscar said. "I ran the plates. They were issued six weeks ago. When I checked the video's time stamp, it matched. It's recent."

"But I don't understand," Luis exclaimed. "I saw him dead. They buried him."

"And this would be the first time in the history of the LAPD where a couple of rogue cops helped out on a staged crime scene, right? And I looked it up. It was a cremation, not a burial. It looks like you were meant to see what you saw."

One of the missing pieces suddenly fell into place for Luis. Why Munuera stabbed him but missed killing him. He was meant to be a witness, not a corpse.

"Who have you shown this to?" Luis asked.

"You're the first," Oscar said. "I was tempted to show it to Michael Story, but he's back to being a pliable servant to his masters."

"Meaning?"

Oscar told Luis what he'd seen on the news earlier. Luis was stunned. He didn't imagine the banks would suffer any more than the cartels from this investigation, but after all of Michael's bluster a fine felt like a joke. People had died. *Many* people. But Luis wasn't in the business of what could be proven in a court of law. What he cared about was the truth, and this he now knew.

"Who sent you the video?"

"I don't know. And I mean that. I have absolutely no idea. But given that Apple videos not only give a time stamp when created, they log GPS coordinates of where they were made, the location won't be hard to find."

A single witness to tell the tale. If they could get to Osorio, force him to come back and confess his role, it probably wouldn't change a thing with the bank fine, but it could be the first step in bringing the church's role to light.

"When do we leave?" Luis asked.

"Right now. Got too many questions for the man, you know? Like if this Sittenfeld guy didn't have anything to do with Munuera and his men, then who sent them up to my house?"

And why did Father Belbenoit have to die? Luis thought.

"You want a gun?" Oscar asked. "Might not be pretty down there, and I've got a 9mm in the house if you want to borrow."

"I'm good, thanks."

"Then let's get going."

The house from the video turned out to be just on the other side of the US-Mexico border a few dozen miles east of Tijuana. It was some of the roughest territory in Northern Mexico to get to, not only due to the poor roads and desert conditions. It was also a prime area for traffickers of both humans and drugs, who might not want witnesses to their activities.

In the heart of that wilderness was Bishop Osorio, though Luis still found this hard to believe. A part of him still thought the footage must be some kind of trick meant to lure him and Oscar back under the border into some elaborate trap. But as the cartels had proven as adept at killing people on the streets of Los Angeles as on those of Huetamo, it didn't make sense.

Though he'd been drinking, Oscar insisted on driving.

"If there's anyone out there waiting for us, I trust myself behind this wheel, not you. No offense."

Luis could see Oscar murdering Bishop Osorio without so much as a second thought.

Depending on the outcome of his own conversation with the bishop, Luis wondered if he'd hesitate before trying to stop him.

At some point Luis fell asleep, only to be nudged awake by Oscar when they reached the border.

"Let's get that collar front and center," Oscar said, pointing to Luis's throat.

Luis straightened. They hit the inspection lane and crossed to the RFID Ready Lane. Oscar extracted a pair of passport cards from his pocket.

"Who thinks of everything?" Oscar asked.

The Mexican customs official barely glanced at the cards, told Oscar to make sure he got a tourist permit for the ride back across, then sent them on their way.

"A ride like this, California plates and licenses, and a priest," Oscar gibed. "If I was working that job, I'd know something was up!"

"What happens if they run your card on the way back?" Luis joked. "Got any late court fines or warrants?"

"Maybe Oscar de Icaza does, but Oscar Fuentes?" Oscar said, holding up the license. "A single moving violation three years back. Paid it the second the ticket hit the mailbox."

Luis chuckled. When Oscar covered his bases, he covered all of them. It was almost funny enough to make him forget they were on a mission of revenge.

They took Highway 2D out of Tijuana and followed the signs east in the direction of Tecate. Unlike the endless sprawl of Mexico City, Tijuana seemed to end abruptly, turning into rocky desert scrub and mountains. The highway had been blasted through the rocks, revealing rainbows of sediment rising on either side of the road.

But they'd only entered the mountains when Oscar tapped on his phone's GPS. "It's off a spur to the north up here. There's a wide valley between mountains. The house is out on the rocks there. Bad news is there's only one road in. If they've got eyes on us out here, we're going to have to hoof it the rest of the way."

Luis nodded. Oscar took the next left on what looked more like a path cut by water coming down from a nearby peak. They wound up the road higher and higher, until they came to the promised high plateau. Oscar killed the headlights after about a hundred yards and drove off the main road a quarter mile before slowing to a stop.

"Probably nine hundred rattlesnakes between us and that house," Oscar admonished as he climbed out of the truck.

"Good thing they don't bite their own," Luis shot back.

Oscar laughed, then opened the back doors, taking apart the seats to remove the parts of the AR-15, which he quickly assembled. Luis looked out into the distance to where the GPS said Osorio's house was located. There wasn't so much as a dot on the horizon.

"We sure it's out there?" Luis asked.

"Only one way to find out," Oscar said, placing the shoulder stock of the machine gun against his shoulder and aiming the barrel toward the ground. "Lead on, Padre."

The sand was hard packed, like there hadn't been any rain for several seasons. This lulled Luis into a false feeling of safety, as if he were crossing concrete in the dark. But every several yards or so his feet sank into a loose pile, likely the byproduct of a burrowing animal, and he almost fell. As his eyes adjusted, he was able to make out the larger silhouettes of cacti and scrub, but the smaller ones eluded him.

"You'd make an awful coyote, Padre," Oscar said.

A faint green-blue glow appeared on the horizon. As they neared, Luis saw that it was the light from the backyard swimming pool shining like a beacon in the otherwise-empty desert. He wondered how many mornings Osorio woke to find that all manner of desert animal had visited his oasis in the night. He also imagined that without the wall, a light wind coming off the surrounding cliffs would fill it so full of sand on a daily basis it would be unusable within hours.

Something skittered past to the right. Oscar raised the assault and peered down the sight.

"Jackrabbit," he announced.

It took another few minutes to reach the house's back wall. Luis was surprised to see it wasn't topped with barbed wire and there was no visible security system. Didn't mean there wasn't one, of course. The house was dark save for a single light in a kitchen window. There were several bay windows overlooking the pool on the back of the house.

"Around front," Oscar whispered.

Keeping low, they circled the house, only to find the driveway empty. Oscar moved to the garage and looked inside. "Range Rover's gone. Maybe it belonged to the nurse."

"No way he's in there alone," Luis said.

Oscar nodded, then pointed to a gate between the garage and house. There was a side door leading into the main house on the other side. Luis nodded in agreement.

The gate was locked. Oscar checked the safety on the machine gun and was about to use it to crack off the knob when Luis boosted himself over the five-foot wall and unlocked the gate from the other side.

"Thought you were some kind of tactical expert," Luis said.

"Nah, watched *Delta Force* on cable too much," Oscar replied, shrugging as they made their way to the house.

The side door was locked both with a door lock and a dead bolt.

"Guess we're going in loud," Oscar suggested.

Luis was about to ask what he meant by this when Oscar set the AR-15 to semiautomatic, fired a deafening three-round burst into the doorjamb, raised his booted foot, and kicked the door through. An alarm sounded inside the house as Oscar raced in, Luis close behind.

"Stay here!" Oscar told Luis, disappearing into the living room.

Luis complied, realizing he was in some kind of laundry room. He didn't have any kind of weapon and found only a mop. He unscrewed the head and held the handle like a staff. His makeshift weapon wouldn't protect him from gunfire, but it was better than nothing.

Luis heard screaming and stepped into the kitchen in time to see Oscar shoving the nurse, clad in a long nightgown, ahead of him, gun pointed at the base of her skull.

"Turn off the alarm," he bellowed before switching to Spanish. *"¡Inmediatamente!"*

Clearly terrified, she stumbled past Luis, found the alarm box in the laundry room, and typed in the code. The alarm went silent, but she shook her head.

"They'll come anyway," she said in Spanish.

"If they really cared, they'd be here already," Oscar replied. "Where's Osorio?"

She shook her head. Luis moved into her sight line. "You think a priest would kill a priest?" he asked. "We need to ask him a question."

"He's very frail! You have to leave here. They'll kill you both when they arrive."

Luis shook his head. "We don't mean you any harm. Let us see him."

"No," the nurse said. "If I let you up, they'll kill me, too."

Oscar touched the back of her neck with the still-warm barrel of the AR-15. "Sounds like you're in a tough spot."

The nurse shrieked and began to cry. As Luis was wondering if the situation could get any more out of hand, a voice called down from upstairs.

"Father Chavez, the woman need not come to harm," said the unseen Osorio.

And then to the nurse: "Marisol, make some tea for my guests."

The familiar request seemed to calm the woman. Oscar and Luis exchanged glances. Oscar sighed heavily, then moved the gun away. The woman rose and walked with purpose to the stove.

She smoothed her hair and put the kettle on the burner. Oscar silently raised his gun, as if to shoot her in the back of the head. Luis tensed and Oscar lowered it, exiting the kitchen. Luis followed. From the living room he could see a light coming from a bedroom on the second floor.

Bishop Osorio, he presumed.

"You know I'm going to have to kill her on the way out, right?" Oscar said, nodding over his shoulder.

Luis said nothing, already climbing the stairs.

Though the first floor of the house was sparsely furnished, the second floor was as opulent as a hotel suite. There were the same types of rugs, antique tables, and couches, and gilt-framed wall hangings Osorio favored in Los Angeles in a sort of common room right off the stairs. There was one bedroom that Luis took for the nurse's room at the top of steps, with another room next to it that looked like a study. Osorio's bedroom was on the other side of the house.

"Come in, come in," Osorio's voice said, leading them through the living room. "I expected you hours ago."

Luis moved to the doorway of Osorio's bedroom. The bed was a large four-poster affair with silk sheets of scarlet and satin blankets. The room looked less like that of a clergyman and more like a Turkish pimp's. Notably, the many crucifixes that had decorated Osorio's rooms back in Los Angeles were decidedly absent. There were no religious icons here.

Osorio himself was seated in a wicker chair in the corner of the room. He was lighting a cigarette, the first Luis had ever seen him smoke. He wore red silk pajamas, a red robe, and red slippers with the crossed gold keys of the first pope, Saint Peter, on them. He saw Luis eyeing the shoes and shrugged.

"Would you believe I wanted to be pope?" Osorio mused. "I would've been a great one, too. But I was ahead of my time. It took almost my whole life for them to seriously consider an American one, and now they've done it. At least I lived long enough to witness it."

"Aren't you dead?" Oscar said, entering the room but keeping one eye back on the stairs as if worried the nurse still might come charging in, guns blazing.

"Something like that," Osorio said, taking a drag from his smoke. "The ecclesiastical side is at least."

"But Belbenoit is," Luis said. "No resurrection for him."

"No, but he was a priest who craved martyrdom," Osorio said, waving away Luis's concern. "But his death is not the one you came to discuss, so let's get on with it."

Luis stared at Osorio for any sign of fear through the hazy cloud of cigarette smoke. There was none.

"What'd my brother have on you?" he asked.

Osorio shrugged. "I really don't know." When Oscar leveled his gun at Osorio, the bishop shook his head. "I'm serious. I really don't know. There were a great many possibilities, I've determined. A phone call he shouldn't have overhead. A letter or e-mail he read. An errand I carelessly believed wouldn't arouse his suspicion. It was my fault, that much is true. He trusted me, and it was too much of a betrayal."

"He loved you," Luis corrected. "You showed him the way to God. Kids like us grow up believing we're irrelevant. You changed that for him. It never takes much."

"For that I am sorry," Osorio said. "It was so early in my relationship with Sittenfeld. We'd made all the arrangements, and everyone was so thankful. He and his bank were going to make money, the church, already so poor, was going to make money, and our partners in the south had finally found an avenue into the United States that made sense. It was my own version of revolution, mind you."

"What're you talking about?" Luis asked.

"Mexico has so long been under the boot of Western interests and governments," Osorio explained. "Being able to support these peasant farmers at the expense of their corrupt government felt like what the church should've been doing this whole time."

"Innocent people died for your revolution. Like Nicolas," Luis said.

The bishop emeritus grinned. "And so we get to the business at hand, eh, Luis? So one of my partners chose to give you a name, my name. But not the name you wanted. Isn't that right? Perhaps you should have been more careful about what you asked. *And whom.*"

Osorio's grin widened. "Oscar," he chided, "isn't it time the truth finally came out?"

Luis turned to Oscar, who suddenly looked like an animal who'd walked into a trap. "Luis, I didn't kill your brother . . ." Oscar said, lowering his gun.

"I know you didn't," Luis said. "A young man named Narcizo Rua did."

"How did you find out?" Oscar asked.

"I had some help," Luis admitted. "Why don't you tell me how it happened?"

"Yes, Oscar," Osorio chimed in. "Why don't you enlighten us?"

Oscar moved swiftly to Osorio, raised the rifle butt, and brought it down on the old man's forehead with a crack. The bishop gasped as blood seeped from a gash above his left eye. Oscar raised the gun to hit him again, but Luis grabbed the hand guard.

"Oscar?" Luis said.

Osorio's mouth opened in a grin even as blood dribbled past his nose and through yellowed teeth.

"I was fourteen, Luis," Oscar said, taking a step back. "The bishop came to my house. Asked me if I really was a gangbanger. I wanted to impress him, like Nicolas did. Even my dad respected the priests, and he didn't like anybody. So, yeah, I told him I was all hard. He asked me if I knew any really bad gangsters, like killers, he could talk to. Said Christ Jesus came into the world to save sinners and he wanted to start with the worst."

"Christ Jesus came into the world to save sinners, of whom I am the worst," Luis thought, recalling the actual scripture.

"Said he'd pay me fifty dollars and had money for my guy, too," Oscar continued.

"So what'd you do?"

"I went looking for the biggest, baddest hitter I could find," Oscar went on. "That was Narcizo Rua. He told me it would be the easiest money he ever made. Looking back, I'm pretty sure he knew what was going on. Like knows like."

"And you never told me?" Luis asked.

"It didn't mean anything to me," Oscar said, "but maybe it made me feel like a big shot. Like Nicolas wasn't the only kid in the neighborhood who got to see people as important as that. And I was getting in good with a bishop and an OG! But when Nicolas was killed a few nights later, I knew that cross-fire story was bull."

Luis thought back to that night. He'd been under the Fourth Street Bridge, getting initiated into his gang. Oscar was there, too, delivering some of the most savage blows of the jumping-in while the man he'd introduced the bishop to was gunning down Luis's older brother.

"You betrayed me," Luis said. "I was your closest friend. What, were you jealous I had a brother or something? Thought he meant something to me in a way you didn't?"

"I was a kid!" Oscar cried. "What was I going to say? I hated myself over that. By the time I was man enough to know how to handle it, you were gone, following in your brother's footsteps. I tried to see it as a good thing. It wouldn't have happened for you like that if it wasn't for Nicolas's death. But I knew what I'd done. I knew what it made me."

"You never thought once that since it was the church that killed him, maybe that was information I could've used? Maybe if I'd known what kind of outfit I was signing up with, I might've had second thoughts. There were hundreds of priests in those files. They knew what happened to priests who try to say something. They killed my brother for it. And you let me join their ranks just like that? But I guess you know something about selling me out, huh?"

"What?" Oscar asked.

"To Munuera. Somebody knew when I was going over to Osorio's and was lying in wait. Was that you, too?"

"I told him that was the one thing I couldn't do," Oscar admitted. "I gave him everything else he asked. Gave up every partner I work with today. But I wouldn't betray you. Not a second time."

Luis nodded, unsure if he should believe him. He heard a gurgling sound and turned to Osorio, whose mouth was contorted into a sickening grin as if he were enjoying all of this. But then Luis noticed his eyes clouding over.

"No, no," Luis said, going to his side. "You're not getting out of this so easy. You're coming back to Los Angeles. I've got all the files on all the priests. And you're going to tell the FBI, the district attorney,

LAPD, *everybody* exactly how you put this together. That'll be your last act on earth."

"No, it won't," Osorio said, voice barely a whisper. "God has other plans for me."

With that, Osorio's body began to tremble, his limbs becoming rigid. The nurse, who'd come up with tea, pushed past them to Osorio's side. She took out a phone and quickly wrote a text.

"He's having a stroke," she announced, moving the featherweight Osorio onto the bed.

As Luis watched helplessly, she checked his pulse, then wheeled over an oxygen tank and mask.

"If you're still here when everyone else arrives, they'll kill you," the nurse told Luis.

Luis didn't care. Osorio couldn't die. He was their last chance. He pushed the nurse aside and grabbed Osorio's hand. "You will die unabsolved," Luis said. "You will go straight to hell. You won't confess your sins."

As the light in Osorio's eyes began to fade, Luis still saw no sign of despair. It was as if Osorio was saying he had no fear in life, so why should he fear hell? Only, there was no triumphant smile now. Mere resignation.

"No!" Luis shouted, trying to keep Osorio awake. "God, please! *No!*"

Luis was panicked now. Without Osorio, the church's role in the money laundering would never really be known. Which actual cartels were involved, which banks, and which members of the church facilitated this interaction. Was it all Osorio's idea? Maybe some random Colombian foot soldier who'd passed the suggestion up the line until it became de rigueur for cartels looking to move money from country to country.

But most of all, it meant that there would never be justice for Nicolas Chavez.

Osorio's breathing stopped. His heartbeat, already faint, vanished a second later. The nurse turned to Oscar, who put a hand on Luis's shoulder.

"We have to go," Oscar said.

"Get away from me!" Luis shouted.

Oscar's hand retreated. Luis saw something coming down hard and fast on the side of his head but didn't have time to react. A second later he was drifting into unconsciousness.

Luis woke up in Tijuana behind the wheel of the SUV. He was on a side street in what looked like a bad part of town. Still, no one had touched the truck, much less him.

Oscar, Luis realized. *His name carries weight even here.*

He looked around for any sign of where his comrade might be, but there was no note, no sign of the AR-15 or any other weapon. Nothing but the keys hanging in the ignition and his passport card and tourist permit on the dash. He spied a disheveled man sitting on a crate at the end of the block looking everywhere except at him.

Climbing out of the SUV, Luis wandered up to the fellow, who stared back at the priest as if through a drunken haze. "Did you see where my friend went?"

"No," the man said with a shrug. "But he told me where he was going."

"Where's that?" Luis asked.

"*Sur,*" the man said, pointing down the street. "South. Far south."

XXIII

It was half past nine by the time Luis got back to St. Augustine's. Erna was waiting with a message from the archbishop's office.

"He can see you at noon," Erna said triumphantly.

"Today?" Luis asked wearily.

"Of course! His office said that he was as anxious to speak with you as you with him."

Luis nodded and headed to the rectory to get half an hour of sleep. On the way he called to quickly check up on his father and sent an e-mail from his phone. When he woke up twenty minutes later, there was a reply and a location, a Cuban pastry shop off South Reno in Rampart Village.

As he pulled into the shop's parking lot half an hour later, he spied Miguel sitting at a table out front, a pink box on the table before him. Luis parked and walked over, Miguel raising half a flaky puff pastry in his direction.

"You gotta try the guava ones, Padre," Miguel enthused. "People drive in from all over to sample them."

Realizing he was again half-starved, Luis took a bite from the prof-fered strudel-looking confection and immediately understood why someone might drive all the way into the city for such a thing.

"It's good," Luis admitted.

"There's more in the box," Miguel said. "Eat up."

"Thanks," Luis replied, then eyed the teenager.

The last time he'd seen Miguel in the flesh, the young man practi-cally wanted to kill him, his actions having inadvertently led to the mur-der of Miguel's mother. Now he was smiling and offering him pastries. He wasn't sure what to make of this.

"How have you been?" Luis asked.

"Getting by," Miguel said with an air of a man twice his age. "You?"

"Same," Luis said hoarsely.

"Good to know," Miguel replied. "I was sorry to hear about your pastor. Seemed like a good guy."

"I lost more of myself than I thought I would when he died."

"I know how you feel," Miguel said. "My mother was the person that kept me tethered to the planet. My uncle, too. Like, everything was okay as long as I had them to fall back on. They were a constant. When they died, it was like gravity got weak all of a sudden. Nothing mattered. No one was there to hold me accountable."

Luis looked down. He knew Miguel wasn't trying to make him feel bad, but he did anyway. Miguel sighed.

"Hey, you're not hearing me," Miguel said, leaning across the table. "I'm saying how I felt. Past tense. What I've learned since is that I have to hold myself accountable. That's all that matters. I know what I'm doing right now, criming and all, is untenable. I keep it up, and it'll catch up to me. So now I'm winding it down. I'm doing all the favors I need to do in the short term so that when I walk out it's all good. No one gets mad and no one gets hurt. Then I start over somewhere."

"Like where?"

"I've heard Buenos Aires is nice," Miguel said.

Luis laughed. Miguel tapped the table.

"So who's holding you accountable these days?" Miguel asked thoughtfully.

"I thought it was God," Luis said. "But then I had to do without for a few months and learned that it wasn't his job. So now I'm on point. Things are going better."

"Cool. You're a good priest. A semi-busted man sometimes, but a really good priest," Miguel said. He reached into a backpack that was slung over the back of his chair and pulled out a thick file folder. "This is what you asked for, right? I was sorry to hear about how things went down in Mexico, but that's Mexico, right? Different world."

"Yeah."

Miguel slid the file across the table. Luis flipped it open and glanced at the pages. For better or worse, it was all there in black and white. What good it would do, he didn't know.

"Thank you," Luis said.

"It's all right," Miguel replied. "By the way, I heard through the grapevine that the guy who carved you up washed up dead in Lake Chapala last night."

"Munuera?" Luis asked in surprise.

"Yeah, hasty-execution-style. The cartels haven't gone to war over it, so I'm thinking it was an outside contractor. If I had to put money on it, I'd say it was somebody who works with my new friend Archipenko. He's got all sorts of buddies out there who owe him favors. Cold bastards, too. Wouldn't be surprised if someone was trying to make him happy by taking out the guy that took out his voice box."

Luis was thinking Oscar, but the timing didn't work out.

"A guy like Munuera makes a lot of enemies," Miguel concluded.

"Yeah, but he just jumps to another body," Luis said. "There'll be another Munuera tomorrow if there isn't already one today."

Miguel eyed Luis querulously for a moment, then looked as if he might bust out laughing. "That's pretty hardcore, Father. Maybe you should be writing heavy metal songs or something. A track for Brujeria, maybe Sepultura. They'd listen to a priest."

Luis chuckled too now. He asked Miguel more about where he hoped things were heading, and the teen told him. He spoke of his hopes, fears, and problems. Luis listened, gave the best advice he could when pressed, then listened some more. By the end of it, Miguel was asking if they could meet up again sometime.

"Of course," Luis said. "Drop me a line anytime."

"Will do," Miguel replied, rising to shake Luis's hand. "Though it might come up from Argentina."

"Here's hoping."

They went their separate ways, Luis taking the file folder with him.

The seat of the Los Angeles archdiocese at the Cathedral of Our Lady of the Angels was a short distance away on Temple. It was an ultra-modern blocky building of marble that looked like unfinished wood. Our Lady of the Angels stood in striking contrast to the Metropolitan Cathedral, right down to the great Robert Graham–sculpted bronze doors that contained an image of the Virgin of Guadalupe, as well as several other representations of more mystical stories from the Bible.

When Luis entered, he made his way to the administrative wing, an equally modern area of high white marble walls, interrupted by stained-glass panels. There were as many secular visitors in the wing as there were clergy, only adding to the feel that it was more like a hallowed concert hall or university building than a cathedral.

When he reached the archbishop's office, he gave his name to the priest out front and took a seat in the plush chair opposite the doors leading into the archbishop's private chamber. He'd met His Excellency on a number of occasions, but only after he'd solved the murder of a Chinese-American priest in San Gabriel did the man begin to recognize him at diocesan functions. Luis didn't know what to think of the archbishop really, as he seemed like a good sort but ambitious in a way Pastor Whillans had conditioned him to be suspicious of.

It didn't mean he was a bad man, however, particularly when compared to LA's previous archbishop. His predecessor had gone into semi-exile, surrounded by a cloud of shame relating to the worldwide molestation scandal and its cover-up, which had threatened to permanently tarnish the image of the church.

"Father Chavez?" said the young priest behind the desk. "His Excellency is ready to see you."

"Thank you," Luis said as the priest touched a button and the doors behind him opened automatically.

As Luis entered the archbishop's chambers, the man himself was already in motion, moving toward him. "The inimitable Father Chavez! Welcome! Thank you for seeing me."

"Thank you, Your Excellency," Luis said, recalling that it was he who had asked for the appointment.

"Please, sit with me," the archbishop said, leading Luis to a pair of chairs near a grand portrait of Bishop Alphonse Gallegos, the late director of the office of Hispanic Affairs for the California Catholic Conference. "Now, what can I do for you?"

"I'm hoping quite a bit," Luis said, taking his phone from his pocket. "I am at something of a dead end."

"Oh? Is it a crisis of faith?"

"Far from it," Luis said. "More like a restoration. But in the process I came across something very troubling."

"Another of your investigations?" the archbishop said cautiously. "Does this relate to Bishop Osorio? I know you were close with him."

"While I knew him well, calling us close is something of an overstatement."

The archbishop didn't seem to know what to do with this information and simply nodded. "His death threw many of us here for a loop."

"Then I can only imagine what his resurrection will do," Luis replied.

He dug into his pocket and extracted his phone. He selected the video Oscar had shown him and played it for the archbishop. As the senior priest watched, his eyes grew wide in horror.

"What is this?" he asked, bewildered.

"Bishop Osorio faked his own death, allowing Father Belbenoit to die and me to be almost mortally wounded in the process. Until this morning he was living on that small estate east of Tijuana."

The archbishop sank back in his chair, putting a hand over his eyes. "My goodness. Are you certain he was alive?"

"Yes," Luis said. "I was there this morning when he died. For real this time."

The archbishop's head wagged back and forth a moment. When he stilled it, he looked Luis directly in the eyes. "Start at the beginning."

Luis did. He told the archbishop about Charles Sittenfeld and the murder of Naomi Okpewho. He explained how this had led a deputy DA to link the banks with the cartels but then identified the Catholic Church as the middleman between the two in a billion-dollar money-laundering arrangement. He laid out his trip to Mexico City and how many priests across Mexico were taking money from the cartels and sending it to the archdiocese or using it in their own parishes, as he saw in action in El Tule. He explained how it was his own brother who would have been the very first whistleblower if he hadn't been murdered so many years ago now.

He concluded by explaining how an arrangement between the Justice Department and Sittenfeld's bank, the so-called largest fine in US history, wiped it all off the books. There would be no arrests, no trials, no fingers pointed at the church, as, after all, it was the Mexico City archdiocese that was to blame, not the Los Angeles one.

Save Bishop Osorio, of course.

When Luis was done, the archbishop's face was drained of color. "Can this be true?" he asked.

Luis placed the folder Miguel had prepared for him in front of the archbishop. "It's all here. But yes, obtained illegally and thereby impossible to use in a court of law. But as I have told our DA, his job is to deal in what can be proven. We in the church deal in belief."

The archbishop looked over the contents of the file folder as if the very pages would leave poison on his fingertips. It took him five minutes to get to the end, but then he closed it and held it close to his chest.

"Are there other copies of these records?" he asked.

"This is the only one I have," Luis said. "And I've been led to believe even they might be scrubbed from the Mexico City archdiocese's database at some point in the near future. I'm pretty sure the district attorney has a copy, too, but there's nothing he can really do with it."

Luis couldn't tell what the man was thinking. Yes, without legal repercussions, this was a scandal that could easily go away. The archbishop rose to his feet, went to his intercom, and called in the young priest who was seated outside. He handed over the file folder, then turned to Luis.

"Then we need to make copies."

The archbishop sent the young priest away with instructions to make at least a hundred copies and bring him back the originals. As the priest exited, the archbishop sat back down in front of Luis.

"We cannot go back to the arrogance of the past," the archbishop said. "It's cost us too much already. If this cannot or will not be handled by the local legal authorities, it's incumbent upon the church to do its own policing, wouldn't you say?"

"Yes," Luis replied evenly.

"Are we sure Bishop Osorio was the only priest within our archdiocese involved?"

"No," Luis said. "We're not."

The archbishop nodded. "Then we'll start an internal investigation but ask the Holy See to begin one in parallel. Complete transparency. What was the office they created to investigate the Calvi scandal?"

"The IOR."

"We'll call them," the archbishop said. "And I believe that there is no one finer in our own archdiocese than you, Father Chavez, to lead the internal investigation."

Luis bowed his head for a moment but then rose to his feet and extended his hand. "I appreciate the gesture, Your Excellency, but I cannot accept."

"If you're worried about your commitments to your parishioners, we can make any accommodation that works for you."

"No, Your Excellency. It's not that. I came here today to resign my office and leave the church. Effective immediately."

It seemed as if this was an even larger shock to the archbishop than the contents of the file folder.

"But why?" the archbishop asked. "There's so much good work to be done. We need men like you. We're *desperate* for men like you who can lead the church forward. Is it a question of your relationship to God?"

"No, thankfully," Luis said. "I have consulted with the Almighty in prayer and believe this is precisely what he wishes me to do."

"I don't mean to speak hyperbolically, but your loss to this archdiocese is nothing short of catastrophic I fear."

Luis put his hand on the archbishop's shoulder. "Have faith, Your Eminence. I am but a vessel."

With that, Luis walked out of the archbishop's office.

As he passed through the Robert Graham doors, Luis was surprised to feel more himself than he had in some time. He had been a priest for little more than a year and learned so much, but it wasn't enough. Not for the responsibilities that had been placed in front of him and the challenges that followed.

He needed to learn more. He had to make himself *more*.

As he went to retrieve the parish car which he would be returning to St. Augustine's for the last time, he found himself staring at a building a number of blocks down Grand. It called to him like a Siren, and he began to walk toward it. With every step a sense of familiarity swelled within him. When he could finally read the sign up top, "California Hospital Medical Center," he felt tears come to his eyes and he found a bus bench to sit down on.

California Hospital, where his brother had been born thirty years before on this very date. Somewhere in that warren of examination rooms and surgical suites, Nicolas had breathed his first breath. Luis closed his eyes and for the first time was able to hear his brother's voice as plain as day. It was a miraculous feeling.

Will you pray with me, Luis?

The words were indistinguishable as memory or whispered that moment, but Luis heard them as clear as he heard his own thoughts. He closed his eyes, bowed his head, and prayed.

And he felt peace.

ACKNOWLEDGMENTS

The author would like to acknowledge the many talented people who contributed their time, intelligence, and ideas to this book, beginning with, as always, my indefatigable first reader and editor, Lisa French, who is the first to see anything I type and rewards my labors with sheets and sheets of red-stained pages in return. Also, Charlotte Herscher, my developmental editor, to whom I owe any positive word said about these books and whom I toast often and heartily. She is a marvel and often knows the story better than I ever will. In addition, I would like to thank my friend and editor Jacque BenZekry, whose continued faith in this series has allowed it to develop and evolve over the past two years. I can only hope that I and it have lived up to her exacting standards. My long-suffering agent, Laura Dail, deserves my thanks and gratitude, not only for her faith and enthusiasm for this series but also because she must endure endless e-mails pitching mad and crazy ideas for crime stories that she bats away with great aplomb and more courtesy than I'd ever manage. Thanks also to Sarah Shaw at Thomas & Mercer just for being awesome.

ABOUT THE AUTHOR

Photo © 2015 Morna Ciraki

Born in Texas, author Mark Wheaton now lives in Los Angeles with his wife and children. Before penning his Luis Chavez novels, he was a screenwriter, producer, and journalist, writing for the *Hollywood Reporter, Total Film,* and more.